D1524342

Halligan
to my Axe
my

USA Today and Wall Street Journal Bestselling Author

lani lynn vale

OTHER TITLES BY LANI LYNN VALE

The Freebirds

Boomtown

Highway Don't Care

Another One Bites the Dust

Last Day of My Life

Texas Tornado

I Don't Dance

The Heroes of The Dixie Wardens MC

Lights To My Siren

Halligan To My Axe

Kevlar To My Vest

Keys To My Cuffs

Life To My Flight

Charge To My Line

Counter To My Intelligence

Right To My Wrong

Code 11- KPD SWAT

Center Mass

Double Tap

Bang Switch

Execution Style

Charlie Foxtrot

Kill Shot

Coup De Grace

The Uncertain Saints

Whiskey Neat

Jack & Coke

Vodka On The Rocks

Bad Apple

Dirty Mother

Rusty Nail

The Kilgore Fire Series

Shock Advised

Flash Point

Oxygen Deprived

Controlled Burn

Put Out

I Like Big Dragons Series

I Like Big Dragons and I Cannot Lie

Dragons Need Love, Too

Oh, My Dragon

The Dixie Warden Rejects

Beard Mode

Fear the Beard

Son of a Beard

I'm Only Here for the Beard

The Beard Made Me Do It

Beard Up

For the Love of Beard

Law & Beard

There's No Crying in Baseball

Pitch Please

Quit Your Pitchin'

Listen, Pitch

The Hail Raisers

Hail No

Go to Hail

Burn in Hail

What the Hail

The Hail You Say

Hail Mary

The Simple Man Series

Kinda Don't Care

Maybe Don't Wanna

Get You Some

Ain't Doin' It

Too Bad So Sad

Bear Bottom Guardians MC

Mess Me Up

Talkin' Trash

How About No

My Bad

One Chance, Fancy

It Happens

Keep It Classy

Snitches Get Stitches

F-Bomb

The Southern Gentleman Series

Hissy Fit

Lord Have Mercy

Quit Being Ugly

KPD Motorcycle Patrol

Hide Your Crazy

It Wasn't Me

I'd Rather Not

Make Me

Sinners are Winners

If You Say So

SWAT 2.0
Just Kidding
Fries Before Guys
Maybe Swearing Will Help
Ask Me If I Care
May Contain Wine
Joke's on You
Join the Club
Any Day Now
Say it Ain't So
Officially Over It
Nobody Knows
Depends Who's Asking

Valentine Boys
Herd That
Crazy Heifer
Chute Yeah
Get Bucked

Souls Chapel Revenants
Repeat Offender
Conjugal Visits
Jailbait
Doin' a Dime
Kitty Kitty
Gen Pop
Inmate of the Month

Standalones
Something' About That Boy

Madd CrossFit
No Rep
Jerk It
Chalk Dirty to Me

For a complete updated list visit: www.lanilynnvale.com

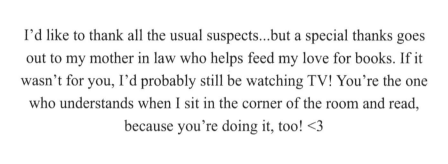

I'd like to thank all the usual suspects...but a special thanks goes out to my mother in law who helps feed my love for books. If it wasn't for you, I'd probably still be watching TV! You're the one who understands when I sit in the corner of the room and read, because you're doing it, too! <3

ONE

The only fire he can't put out is the one inside my heart.
-Adeline's future self

Adeline

"What is that smell?" I sniffed.

Getting up, I followed the smell with my nose until I wound up in my bathroom.

"What the hell is that?" I gasped as I saw smoke seeping through the floor of my bathroom.

"Oh, my God!" I wheezed.

Running to my room, I made a mad dash for my cell phone and started dialing 911 immediately.

"911, what's your emergency?" The thick Cajun sounding woman's voice asked.

"Um, yes. This is Adeline Sheffield. I live in the apartment complex of Hunter Hollows, apartment 1B. I can smell smoke, and something weird coming through the floor of my bathroom. I'm not really sure if anything is on fire, per say, but there is so much coming through my floor that it's leaving a hazy film in the air."

"Alright, we'll have the fire department and an officer alerted right now. Can you give me your physical address?" The woman asked.

I rattled off the address and hung up despite the woman's concern for me to stay connected.

I didn't have time for that.

If I had to evacuate, I needed to start collecting my pets. Pronto.

Running through my apartment, I started looking in Monty's usual haunts, but couldn't find him.

"Monty, you big bastard. Where are you?" I hissed when I didn't find him under the couch, above the mantle, or in the kitchen sink.

I knew he couldn't be in with the rest of my newly acquired friends, because I'd kept the door closed, and he was just too darn big to get in without me opening the door for him first.

After five minutes of no results, I started getting nervous.

Had he gotten out? Oh, shit. *Please be inside here somewhere, Monty*. I pleaded while going inside my spare bedroom and doing a quick inventory.

"BFD! Mrs. Sheffield?" A man's deep baritone voice echoed from the living room.

"Damn. Piss. Monty, you asshole." I growled before running back to the front door.

Disengaging the locks, I yanked the door open with barely concealed frustration and about fell on my ass when a fist the size of a phone book came inches away from slamming into my head.

"Jesus, I'm sorry. Are you okay?" Phone book hand asked.

I waved a dismissive hand. "I'm fine. You didn't touch me. Is the apartment downstairs on fire?"

The firefighter, who was taller than my door jam, shook his head as if he was confused. "I'm sorry. We don't know yet. You were the lady that called it in?"

At my nod, he continued. "Can I see the source of the smoke? We're trying to get management to let us in, but since there's no visible smoke from the outside, we're not allowed to enter without permission."

I turned and said, "Sure. Just close the door. I don't want Monty getting out."

That was if the slippery bastard wasn't already out. He was prone to do that from time to time. Not that anyone in my complex knew that. He always came back. He'd get hungry, and he was a really lazy boy.

"It's coming through the floor in my bathroom. There's a really weird smell to it." I said as I lead the large, intimidating man into my sanctuary.

"Nice bed." The man rumbled.

The man's voice was to die for, and somehow familiar.

I shivered as the low, deep tone of his voice slithered down my spine.

Smiling, I looked over my shoulder at him and my breath caught in my throat. The man was even more attractive inside where I could see his face. And I knew him. I'd seen him around town more than once. It's a small town, and really hard not to start recognizing people when you see them on your way to work every day.

The man ran. Daily. With his shirt off.

I sat on my porch every morning and watched as he ran from one side of the road I lived on, to the other.

Then I move to the front and watch him make a full circuit through the complex's parking lot before I have to leave for work.

Then I might possibly pass him on the way to work, depending on how far he ran that morning.

He was tan, and had the most piercing pale blue eyes I'd ever seen.

That wasn't even mentioning the rock hard abs, and the sexy grooves that ran down his stomach to form a V at the base of his abdomen.

Unfortunately, the helmet on his head kept me from seeing his hair color, and the jacket and pants kept me from seeing the rest of him, which was truly saddening, but I knew he was gorgeous.

What I came up with one morning, however, was that he was either taken or gay. 'Cause nobody that polished and good looking could be anything but. Life didn't work like that.

"Thanks," I said, trying to distract myself from asking if he wanted to join me on my nice bed.

Then his nose wrinkled as he took a sniff and grimaced. "Weed."

My stomach rumbled, and I closed my eyes in embarrassment.

"Huh?" I asked, taking a step further to the side to let him see my bathroom floor, or lack thereof, since there was now so much smoke in there that a blanket of it was making the floor nearly impossible to see.

Which was why when a large slithering body started to curl around my foot and then further up my leg I let out a startled shriek.

The shriek made the big man beside me react instantly, looking around as he tried to spy the threat that was looming over me. "What is it?" He asked urgently.

I placed my hand over my heart, willing it to slow.

"Nothing. It's just Monty." I said, leaning down and picking up my six foot long Burmese Python off the floor and settling him firmly around my neck and shoulders.

The man looked at me as if he couldn't believe I'd just picked up a snake the size of a pool noodle. "What?" I asked in confusion.

The man shook himself again. "Nothing. Can you come downstairs? I don't want to keep you up here just in case. Will your, ah... snake, run away...I mean slither away if you take him without his cage?"

I nearly laughed at the large man as his eyes kept dodging around the room looking for means of escape.

So he wasn't a snake person, was he? Maybe I shouldn't show him my other room. He might get a little freaked out.

"Of course," I replied. "I don't really know my neighbors all that well. I've only lived here for a month. My name's Adeline Sheffield."

I followed him out of the apartment and came to a stop on the landing. "Do I need to lock it?" I asked thoughtfully.

He stopped four steps down, and it put me right at eye level with him. Geez, how tall was this guy? Eight feet?

"Nah," he said. "We're just going to be right down there. It's probably nothing, anyway."

I nodded, and then followed him down until he came to a stop before another big man. Only this one wasn't as tall as him. And he was in just the bottom part of the bunker gear. His jacket was laying on the passenger seat of the big, red fire truck that was parked right outside my front door.

Wow. They sure did know how to grow 'em in the South, *didn't they?*

• • •

Kettle

Holy shit. The woman was hot.

And I'd nearly hit her over the head with my fist when I went to knock on her door.

That would've been fun to explain to my superiors. *'I accidentally whacked her in the face when I was knocking on the door. I didn't mean to knock her out. Promise.'*

On the bright side, I knew her name.

Adeline Sheffield.

It didn't fit her. Not with all those tattoos. She looked more like a Cat, or a Roxie.

The woman was hotter than fuck.

She had black hair that was slicked back into a funky ponytail at the tiptop of her head, and she was wearing a killer pair of jeans that made her ass look like a dream.

The shirt she was wearing was skimpy, and most likely was an undershirt of some sort. It showed off her small breasts perfectly, and I could make out every single bump of her hard nipples and areola.

It also showed off the multiple tattoos on her back, forearm, shoulder, and wrist.

"What's the situation?" Sebastian, my best friend, brother, and boss, interrupted my degenerating thoughts.

Sebastian and I had been best friends for over ten years now. We'd met while we were fighting fires overseas in the military.

Although that's where the similarities ended.

Sebastian had been a firefighter in the marines while I'd been a firefighter in the Army.

We'd been in different military branches, yet come together to fight a common enemy.

"Goliath thinks they're smoking weed in the apartment below

me and it's coming up through my floor." Adeline said, smoothing her dainty hands over the snake's lithe body.

Sebastian, who'd been watching the happenings going on at the bottom apartment, snapped his eyes to the woman. They promptly widened when he saw her.

Or maybe it was the six foot fucking snake wrapped around her neck and shoulders.

"Uhh, yeah. We've gotten calls to this place before. The man underneath you is dying of liver cancer and imbibes from time to time to control the pain. He lives with his teenage grandson, and the grandson isn't known for his restraint. They're probably lighting up together like they've done countless times before." Sebastian said, tilting his head slightly, trying to figure the woman out.

"Mr. Bonner? I thought he was just kind of crazy. I guess it makes sense though. How sad." Adeline replied morosely.

A commotion coming from the end of the parking lot had us all turning to see a frazzled woman in stilettos and the shortest skirt I'd ever seen running towards us.

Her tits were bouncing like the little bobble head dolls you see on dashboards, and looked perilously close to popping out of her skimpy little tube top all together if she didn't slow down.

"I'm so sorry," Bouncy Boobs apologized. "I was on a date. Which apartment do you need into?"

Adeline snorted. "Must have been some date."

I barely contained my laugh in time before BB was bouncing her way to us.

"1A, ma'am." Sebastian replied soberly.

He wasn't in a laughing mood, apparently.

"Yes, yes," she said hustling to the door.

The back looked even worse than the front. I could make out the red outline of her thong just above her slip of a skirt, and if I had to guess, a cell phone tucked into the back so-called pocket.

Nice.

"There you go; is there anything else I can help you with?" BB asked.

We waited patiently as the woman backed up and walked back to her car, not even giving the men entering into one of her properties another thought.

"Umm, is that your cat?" Sebastian asked worriedly, looking up at the window ledge of her apartment.

Adeline cursed soundly when she saw her cat leaning out the open window to her apartment. She disentangled herself from the snake, and thrust the beast into my hands before taking off at a sprint.

Now that was the type of ass you should be looking at and appreciating, I thought.

"The last time someone asked you to hold their snake it was that transvestite at the bar in Minneapolis." Sebastian observed lightly.

"Fuck off," I said as I held the large snake in my hands at arm's length.

"Give it to me and go check out the apartment. Be careful." He ordered.

Handing the thing off gladly, I walked slowly into the apartment.

It was cluttered.

Furniture lined the walls from one side of the doorjamb to the other, and in some places pieces stood two deep. In fact, there was a couch in front of a couch that had a coffee table in front of it.

This could almost qualify as hoarders, furniture style.

"Benton Fire Department!" I yelled once I cleared the first room.

After not hearing a reply, I cleared the kitchen, and then went to the back bedroom.

The smoke was thicker in the hallway, meaning whatever was done, was done in the bedroom area. Which explained why it was coming up through Adeline's floor.

"BFD!" I yelled again.

Then had to control a snicker. It got to me every single time.

BFD-Big Fucking Deal! Just kidding.

After getting my inner giggles under control, 'cause apparently it wasn't manly to giggle, I walked into the first bedroom and sighed.

We had a stiffy.

Reaching for my radio, I called over the airwaves. "Stiffy."

"Copy." Sebastian confirmed.

How did I know it was a stiffy? The man, who'd obviously been enjoying his weed based on the fifteen joints just in the *first* ashtray, was doing the thousand yard stare, and not from the high he'd gotten.

The thousand yard stare, in the medical field, was roughly based on a dead person having that 'look;' the one where there wasn't any life left there to give their eyes 'depth.'

This man was sporting that look, not to mention that his chest wasn't moving.

"What the fuck man, you said he was dead, not that he was murdered." Dallas whined.

"Stiffy means dead. And he's dead." I replied dryly.

"Well, shit." Dallas sighed. "Now we're going to be sitting here until the parish coroner gets here. Who knows when the fuck that's gonna be. It's Friday night, you know my poker nights are always on Fridays."

Dallas was a good kid. He was twenty-two and had passed the

firefighter certification just a few months ago.

He was also the Mayor of Benton's son. The mayor had also been a firefighter, himself, before he'd had a heart attack and his wife put her foot down, insisting that he leave the service before he died and left their young family alone.

Dallas was a quick learner, and didn't get pissed when you told him to do something he thought was below him like I'd seen some do.

He was also interested in prospecting for the Dixie Wardens.

The Dixie Wardens was my club.

I'd joined with Sebastian over ten years ago now, and I thought of them as family.

I'd been on the fence about them when Sebastian had mentioned the club to me the first time. Benton was a small town, and I knew that the town would know everything that went on with the club. I wasn't quite sure I wanted to be in the middle of town gossip for the rest of my life.

At the time, I was young and loved riding my Shovelhead wherever the hell I felt like it. I wasn't so sure belonging to a club was a way to stay free, to be what I wanted to be. There was no one and nothing stopping me from riding for two days straight like I'd been known to do now and then. Then Sebastian suggested patching in, having someone to share the road with if I ever wanted it, and my life had changed.

Suddenly, I had an enormous family.

A family that gave a shit about me and, by default, my sister when previously we'd had nobody.

"Alright, I'll be right outside. Make sure the body doesn't go anywhere." I tried to say as seriously as I could; which happened to be not that much.

Dallas rolled his eyes and backed out of the room until he was standing in the doorway between the hallway and the bedroom, taking up position.

I found Sebastian outside, snake still curling around his arms, and a worried Adeline standing beside him. "Do you think my other pets will be okay in that?"

I walked up on the latest comment, and Sebastian's expression clearly said, 'Fix this.'

"It's not the harmful smoke from a fire. It's just from the guy chain smoking his pot." I tried.

"So you don't consider pot smoke harmful at all, or is it only to animals you don't consider it harmful to?" She asked curiously.

Uh-oh. I knew a loaded question when I heard one. The question was, what exactly was she wanting me to say? That I didn't think weed was that bad, or that weed was the devil. Or was she only worried about her animals, and not herself?

Jesus. I hated women's minds. Why couldn't they just be straight forward?

"I think your pets will be fine. The smoke will clear out once we open a few windows, and you can do the same in your place." I sidestepped.

She smiled widely at me. "Nice save you just made there."

"How many animals do you have up there anyway?" I asked curiously.

She blushed. "Well, quite a few actually. But they're all in cages. And it's only temporary. I saved them."

Sebastian, who'd been doing his best to ignore the woman until she said she'd saved them, looked at me with widened eyes.

"From a facility that wasn't taking care of them." She hedged.

Then little facts started sinking in, mainly in the form of a huge news story that was sweeping over the South.

A week ago, a facility in Southern Louisiana that supposedly 'didn't test on animals' had some lab equipment go missing and they suspected an ex-employee. That ex-employee being about 5'5 with black hair and gray eyes, uncannily similar to the woman standing in front of me.

"Well, I think it's time for you to get Monty back into his cage. The police will be here any minute." Sebastian informed her, holding out his arms for Adeline to take the snake.

Adeline didn't waste any time hustling back up the stairs without a goodbye, and I couldn't help but be intrigued. A woman that looked like her didn't strike me as working in a testing facility at all.

"Cops are here." Sebastian noted a few minutes later.

My eyes turned in that direction and groaned.

Sebastian turned as well and barely stifled his laughter.

"Aw, shit." I sighed.

"Boys," the bane of my existence, and ex-girlfriend, Detective Annalise Hernandez, drawled.

Annalise wasn't a bad woman. I just liked my women a little less...brash and ballsy.

Annalise was a seasoned detective on the Benton Police Department, and she's beautiful. But beauty wasn't the only thing I was looking for. I liked my women soft and warm, not cold and hard.

I'd gone out with Annalise for nearly five months before I finally realized that no matter how much work I put into the relationship, I would never be able to make it work. Not to mention the fact that she didn't approve of the Dixie Wardens and went out of her way to make that known.

"Annalise," I nodded. "How are you?"

"What have we got?" She said briskly, ignoring the niceties that I tried to engage her in.

Annalise didn't know why our relationship didn't work, and I never had the desire to explain to her that she was too much like one of the guys, rather than a girlfriend. I didn't think she'd appreciate that too much. Instead, I'd just told her I wasn't interested in her anymore and left it at that.

Harsh, yes, but in the end it saved some hurt feelings on her part.

Sebastian answered her question when she raised her eyebrows at me in question. "Older male, late seventies. Dead. Sword through the chest."

"Witnesses?" She asked.

They both shrugged.

"Alright, back off and let me do my job." She ordered and left to speak with the officer that was first on the scene.

"You heard the man," Sebastian said.

At my glare, Sebastian laughed.

"Funny." I growled.

TWO

She asked me to say something sexy to her, so I whispered, "I'm a fireman."
- Kettle to Adeline

Adeline

"Can I help you?" I asked the woman on the front porch of my apartment the next morning.

I'd just come out to get my daily fix of the hot firefighter and found the woman on my doorstep about to knock.

That was the second time in two days that I nearly got smacked on the face.

"I'm Detective Annalise Hernandez," she said flipping her badge open and shut again. "I'm here to ask you a few questions. May I come in?"

"Actually, I was on my way to sit on the porch anyway. You may join me." I said politely, closing the door firmly behind me.

Wouldn't do to have Monty get out with her here.

She looked annoyed that I wouldn't let her inside, and I'd had to contain the urge to laugh. I wasn't a naïve little girl. I wasn't bringing some cop into my house. I knew better than that.

"I have some questions for you about last night." Detective Hernandez began.

"Shoot," I said just before my eyes locked on the heart-stopping, panty wetting man running down the middle of the parking lot.

Today he was in red Nike shorts, a pair of neon yellow running shoes, and nothing else.

Oh, boy.

And now he was looking at me. Should I wave? Yeah, I should wave.

He smiled at me and waved back before turning his attention back to the ground in front of him.

"You know Tiago?" Detective Hernandez asked sourly.

I didn't turn to face the woman until he rounded the corner and disappeared from my sight.

"Tiago?" I asked curiously.

I thought I'd heard his friend calling him Kettle, not that that name was any better, but still.

"Yeah," she indicated the direction the man had disappeared from just moments before with her head. "That's Tiago, AKA Kettle. Do you know him?"

If I wasn't wrong, I detected a hint of jealousy coming from the woman, but I couldn't be sure. Detective Hernandez was what you would call stoic. In the five minutes she'd been here, I hadn't seen the woman do anything but glare and look mildly annoyed.

"No, I met him last night, but that's it." I replied, taking a seat on the rocking chair and taking a sip of my coffee. I had things to do today, and sitting here being interrogated wasn't one of them.

"Can you tell me what happened last night?" Detective Hernandez finally asked.

I explained what happened from the time I smelled the smoke, until I went to bed later that night.

"Did you know the deceased?"

"No. I've never seen him before. Although I just moved in a little over a month and a half ago." I explained.

I'd heard them, but not actually made their acquaintance.

"And did you hear anything?" The detective persisted.

"No, I was watching a movie. I had the surround sound on."

"What movie?"

It was obvious to me that the detective was trying to catch me in a lie, but my explanation seemed to appease her some.

"I watched Black Dog. It started about an hour after I got home at six in the evening, and then went on until around nine. I smelled the smoke about twenty minutes after that."

The questions persisted, one after the other, until she made me start over again.

"What did you do between the hour you arrived home and when the movie started?"

"Jesus Christ, lady. I took a shower, masturbated on my bed to that tall, dark and handsome man who just ran past us, and then ate a frozen dinner. A kids' one that had a brownie in it. Anything else?" I snarled.

I was getting tired of the bullshit, and when I lost my patience, I seemed to lose the filter on my mouth. I probably shouldn't have told her I'd masturbated, but with a quick glance at my watch, it showed I was twenty minutes late for work, and she'd been sitting here for well over thirty minutes now.

A low masculine chuckle brought my face from the very pissed detective to the satisfied male eyes at the very bottom of the stairs.

Kettle was still dressed in his shorts and tennis shoes, except for the shorts were about twice as sweaty.

A dark red line went from the waistband of the pants to about mid-thigh, and up close, I could make out each individual drop of sweat that rolled down his chest and met the waistband of his underwear.

I hadn't realized I'd licked my lips until Kettle started laughing and Detective Hernandez snarled.

"Well, I'll leave you two alone. Stay in town." She directed towards me and stomped down the steps.

Kettle moved over slowly so the now extremely pissed off woman didn't run me over in her exuberance to get the hell out.

In the meantime, I was in the process of figuring out what the hell to say to him. I'd just admitted to masturbating to the man the previous night. *Before* I'd officially met him. He'd probably realize I was a perv and watched him run every morning. Then he'd get a restraining order

But before I could come up with something intelligent to say, the cocky son of a bitch decided to throw it in my face.

"So, you were thinking of me, huh?"

I didn't like to be teased. Just ask my sister.

Without another word to the rude man, I walked back into my apartment and slammed the door.

Smug bastard.

Luckily, I was already wearing my shirt and skirt, all I had to do was slip into my Converses and braid my hair.

I was a high school chemistry teacher for Benton High School.

On the weekends, I worked in a lab to help supplement my bills. Or I did until I found out they tested on living animals and stole them. Now I didn't have a job, but at least they couldn't report me or they'd be doing themselves more harm than good.

It'd be easier for them just to acquire new test subjects; however, I'd destroyed quite a bit of data when I'd left, so it'd take them some time.

"Purse, purse, purse," I chanted, as I made my way back to the living room.

I found it wedged in between the cushion and the back of the couch, which could very well have had to do with Monty sleeping behind the cushions.

Digging through my purse and looking for my keys, I walked to the door, then slammed it behind myself as I started stomping down the steps.

What I should've been doing was watching where I was going, instead of stuffing my head into my purse while I looked for my keys. If I had, I wouldn't have missed the last two steps and nearly fallen flat on my face.

Luckily, tall, dark and handsome was at the bottom to catch me.

Unluckily, he got sweat all over the front of my shirt.

"Ewww," I squealed as my linen shirt clung to his sweaty skin.

"Sorry," he said in his deep velvety voice.

I disentangled myself from him and then bent down to retrieve all of my belongings that were now littering the sidewalk.

He bent down as well and started picking up candy wrappers, a coke that was three days old, and my birth control pills.

"Here, I want those. These," I said as I shoved the trash into his hands. "You can throw away for me when you get a chance."

Kettle snorted. "Sure."

"Do you see my keys anywhere?"

Oh man, I was going to be really late. I was supposed to be there for driver's ED over thirty minutes ago. Now I was going to have to listen to Jesse Lawn's mother bitching about how she had to miss yoga class again.

I was habitually late, though. Mrs. Lawn missed her yoga appointments a lot. The school wasn't going to fire me, however. Nobody else wanted to deal with the little sixteen year olds that thought they knew more than their instructors.

I'd already gotten into four fender benders this year, and it was only four months into the school year.

"Here." He said standing up and leaving the trash where it was.

"You forgot that." I pointed to the offensive objects.

He looked down, then back up at me, and laughed. "Yeah, I'll get right on that."

Then I watched in flabbergasted silence as the man walked over one apartment down from my own, walked down the pathway, and entered his ground floor apartment.

The apartment I hadn't been aware he'd had.

The apartment that was supposed to be mine, but another person had stolen it out from under me.

That thieving *bastard*!

• • •

Kettle

Later that night

I watched as my new neighbor, the one I hadn't seen in my two months of living at this place, stepped out of her car in her fuck me skirt and stupid little tennis shoes.

She was wearing long sleeves, too.

In the middle of October when it was ninety degrees out.

Although, whatever job she had probably didn't like the fact that she had tattoos.

The tattoos I'd seen the night before, in all their glory.

Most jobs didn't.

"Evening," he called.

She stopped and turned, looking at me on my porch.

"What?" She snapped.

My brows rose at her tone, and I couldn't stop myself from standing to my full height before walking down the walkway and across the sidewalk to her. "Did I do something to piss you off?" I asked curiously.

She was so hot and cold. Last night she was nice, maybe a tad flighty, but mostly nice.

Same with this morning.

Then this.

Her arms crossed, and her breasts pushed together, drawing my eyes to her impressive cleavage.

"Yes, as a matter of fact you did. You were the one who stole my apartment." She said pointing to my apartment.

I leaned back on my heels and barely contained the need to smile.

"Uhh, I'm sorry?" I apologized. "I only called and asked for an apartment. When I got here, that's the one they showed me."

"It was mine. I'd even signed a lease for it. When I came to move in that day, the manager told me she'd double leased it out and offered me that one. Do you have any idea how hard it is to carry groceries up those freaking stairs?"

I didn't really know what to say. I'd already apologized. What more could I do?

"If I'm home, all you've got to do is knock and I'll carry them up for you." I offered.

Her eyes narrowed, and then her shoulders seemed to slump. "I'm sorry. It's just that my sister is disabled, and it scares me

21

when she comes to visit. Which she does a lot."

"It's okay. You know where I'm at if you need me." I said, before turning to go back to my own porch.

"Don't you ever wear a shirt?" She asked my back.

I turned back around with a smirk on my face.

"Yes," I said, shrugging. "I just don't like to wear them when I don't have to."

THREE

I love when you talk nerdy to me.
-Text from Kettle to Adeline

Kettle

Two weeks later

I set the weights down with a small clink and stood when I heard the knock on my door.

I wasn't expecting anybody until about an hour from now, but it wasn't unheard of for one of my brothers to stop by and shoot the shit with me on my days off.

I was completely thrown off guard when I opened the door to find my little neighbor, the one who'd been avoiding me at every turn for the past two weeks, standing there with her arms crossed against her chest.

Her eyes traveled down my body, taking in the workout shorts and my sweaty chest, before meeting my eyes.

"No shirt again, I see," she observed. "Do you ever eat at McDonald's?"

I shrugged. "Occasionally. What can I help you with?"

"I have some groceries," she said with a wide smile.

I couldn't help but let a grin tip up the corner of my mouth as I followed her out the door.

Today was much cooler, so when I saw the long sleeved, form fitted blue shirt tucked into another skirt that barely allowed her to walk correctly, I wasn't as surprised.

I *was* surprised when she brought me up to a rental car, though.

"What's with the rental car?" I asked as I went to her open trunk.

She usually drove around in a black Challenger with hot pink racing stripes.

The car fit her to a T. This one, on the other hand, did not. It was a non-descript white Ford Taurus.

"I had to take it into a body shop this morning. Someone hit me last night on the way home from school." She explained sadly.

My head turned, and I regarded her closely. "Are you okay?" I asked, strangely concerned about the woman's welfare.

Why I would be concerned, I didn't know. Maybe I just liked that she didn't just jump on my cock and start riding me. That was the main reason women came around me.

The first person to actually look at me, without eyeing my crotch, was my VP's woman, Baylee.

All women ever saw when they looked at me, was the body and the cut. And if they ever got past those two things, they saw that I was a firefighter, and they really had to have them some.

I hadn't had a meaningful conversation with a woman in well over ten years.

Even Annalise started dating me because I was a firefighter.

"Yeah, I'm okay. Little shaky. The guy didn't stop. He was in this big ass truck with a huge bumper. I'm just lucky he hit me on the passenger side, otherwise my face would've been introduced to his bumper." She sighed warily.

Something weird started to happen in my chest, and I had to physically restrain myself from going to her and holding her in my arms.

"I'm sorry to hear that. Which body shop did you take it to?" I asked.

I started to pick up all her bags, and then carried them all up in one go.

"Oh, my God! I need to borrow you every time I have groceries. Can we make a standing appointment for every Wednesday at seven in the evening?" She asked, as she raced up the stairs in front of me.

I had to chuckle. Women found the weirdest things amusing.

"Sure," I said. "Now, which shop did you take it to?"

"Uhh, I think Reed's Auto Body. Does that sound right?" She asked as she swung the door open wide and turned on the light.

The first thing I saw was that large snake curled up on the corner of the couch. The second was that the Adeline's house was trashed.

She didn't seem surprised about it, only resigned.

"You can put those in the kitchen. I'm sorry about the mess. It happens a lot." She said by way of explanation.

My eyebrows snapped together, and I looked closer at the woman who was trying her best to hide the fact that she was upset.

I probably wouldn't have even noticed if her hands hadn't been shaking, making the keys, still dangling from one finger, jingle together slightly as it happened.

Setting the bags down on the kitchen counter, I let my eyes roam over the destruction in the kitchen, before returning to the living room, where she was frantically shoving things back into drawers.

"You need some help?" I rumbled, causing her to jump.

She squeaked before turning around and shoving the drawer closed with her ass. "No, no. I'm okay. It doesn't take long."

My eyebrows raised. "This happen a lot?"

She shrugged. "Thank you for carrying my groceries, Tiago."

I hated being called Tiago.

It reminded me of my father, who hadn't spoken to me in over ten years.

But from her mouth, it sounded oddly...right. Coming from her full, beautiful lips didn't give me the instant hives it usually did when I heard it.

"Do you need to call the cops?" I asked.

At the vehement shake of her head, I knew I wouldn't be able to convince her.

I'd call Trance, a member of the BPD as well as The Dixie Wardens MC, when I got back to the house and report it to him. It wasn't much, but it was something.

"Okay," I nodded. "Just tell me this. Are you in danger?"

She sighed and her shoulders hung. "No," she said, with a shake of her head. "It's my brother. He likes to pawn my stuff when he needs a fix. I don't even have a clue how the hell he gets in. Past any lock in the world. He's always been good with locks."

It wasn't much, that admission, but it was enough to calm the raging beast in my brain telling me to drag her back to my place and wait until the cops arrived. Knowing that it was her brother wasn't really that much better than just a random act of violence; but, for some reason, knowing it was her brother allowed me to calm the beast to somewhat manageable levels.

At least levels that didn't require me to drag her by her hair to my cave.

"You should probably report it anyway. I don't really want

to tell you how handle your family situation, but stuff like this doesn't just go away. One day, it's not going to be just something small. He'll take something of yours that will be irreplaceable or, if you're lucky, just use you. Don't let it get that far." I advised.

When she didn't respond, or look at me, I knew it was time to leave.

"Alright, well let me know when you have need of strong hands to haul your groceries." I said before heading back to her door.

If I didn't leave, I'd try to convince her, and Lord knew I was one to talk about family.

My sister was one giant fucking mess, and I hadn't spoken to my parents in ten years. What did that say about me?

Her nearly silent, "Thank you," preceded me out the door.

Walking down the steps, I was surprised to see Annalise sitting on my front porch.

I'd spotted her when I was halfway down, and saw that her eyes flared at the sight of me coming out of Adeline's apartment sweaty and shirtless. I didn't say anything though. It wouldn't help.

She was jealous, and egging her on wouldn't help the situation.

"Annalise," I said as I made it to my front porch.

Her nose and lip lifted into a snarl. "Did I interrupt something?" She sneered.

"What can I help you with?" I asked, ignoring her snarl.

It wasn't like she had any claim on me anymore. Still, I could see how she would be upset by it. So I'd give her some slack.

For now.

"I came to see if you wanted to go grab something to eat, but I can see I'm too late. You already ate the girl next door." Annalise spat.

"I think it's time for you to leave if you don't have anything worthwhile to say. I've got somewhere to be."

"Do you really have somewhere to be, or are you just saying that because you want me to leave?"

Her question was answered moments later when Trance pulled up on his bike and pulled into one of my assigned spots.

He shut it off, put down the kickstand, swung his leg over the bike and stood.

Annalise's face turned down into a severe frown, which was another reason I'd ended it.

She didn't accept my family. And Trance was family as well as one of my best friends.

She especially hated Trance.

Trance was a K-9 officer with the Benton police department.

Although not in the same department as Annalise, they still passed each other on occasion, and she'd gone out of her way to let it be known that she didn't trust him.

I hadn't been aware of it until Trance had come to me one day, finally telling me his problem with Annalise. Not that he'd needed to, because I'd broken up with her the night before.

"Kettle," Trance said as he offered his hand.

Trance was named after his eyes. They were two different colors, one blue and one green; the girls loved them.

Something about the man's curly blonde hair and weird eyes did it for the women.

When you added the cut and the badge, he was nearly unstoppable.

"Trance," I shook his hand.

"Well, as nice as this is," Annalise said as she stood up. "I think I'll go home. Sorry I even bothered."

Trance and I watched her go, neither one concerned in the least that she left.

"Are you ready for a ride?" Trance asked.

I nodded. "Just need to go change. I'll be out in ten. My neighbor needed some help carrying in her groceries."

Trance nodded and took a seat on the couch as I went to the master bedroom to find a shirt and a pair of pants.

I chose the ones that were less holey than the rest, as I expected it to get a little colder out within the next few hours.

Just as I'd slipped the cut over my shoulders and swiped on some deodorant, pounding came from my front door.

"Kettle!" My neighbor screeched, pounding hard on the door.

I wasn't aware I was running until I got to the door just after Trance had yanked it open.

She poured inside and rushed towards me, completely bypassing a stupefied Trance.

"Oh, my God. I need your help. Can you help me?" She pleaded, grabbing me by the t-shirt and drawing me closer to her.

"She's blind and I don't know where she is. Oh Jesus. Please," she cried.

I grabbed the flailing Adeline's arms and held them firmly, looking into her eyes with a calm expression. "Adeline," I said gently but firmly. "You need to calm down and give me the whole story."

Trance met my eyes over the top of her head, both brows raised in question.

"Oh, God. Oh, God. Okay," she said nodding her head. "My sister called me to tell me our brother came to borrow some money from her, since he didn't find any at my place. When she said she didn't have any on her, my brother took her to an ATM, and then dropped her off somewhere. She can't hear any noises, and she doesn't have any way to move. She can't see. She's blind."

Adeline was frantic again by the time she was done.

I was worried myself. What kind of low life brother would drop his blind sister off knowing she couldn't fucking see to get herself home?

Trance was on the ball, pulling his phone out and calling the station to put a BOLO (Be on the lookout) out on her.

"Hey, what's the cell number?" Trance called out.

I looked down at a clearly distraught Adeline. "What's her number, Adeline?"

"Uhh," she said, turned around, and rattled off the number

Trance relayed the number, and hung up the phone.

"Okay, once she uses the phone again she'll be traced. Can you call her?" Trance asked calmly.

She seemed to understand that she needed to get her shit together, because she took a deep breath, and blew it out before explaining. "Her phone died. We were in the middle of speaking and she'd told me that it wouldn't be long until it would die. I came over here as soon as it did. She said he took her to her bank, and then dropped her off a couple of blocks past it, as far as she could tell."

Taking her hand, I led her to the door and down the stairs before she finished speaking.

I did glance down to make sure she was properly dressed, at least. If she hadn't been, I would've had to send her to her place to get something more suitable on. I wouldn't be able to help the sister if I was worrying about the one that was on the back of my bike. The road didn't really agree with bare skin, for some reason; I was always leery about what I wore when I was riding.

Trance followed me, closing and locking my door behind me as he went.

I fit my helmet over her head, and then strapped it on tight. "Feel okay?" I asked. At her nod, I patted the side of the helmet lightly and then straddled the bike.

"What's she look like?" I asked her before she sat.

"Black hair like mine. About my height as well. She looks exactly like me, in fact." She explained.

"Which bank?" Trance asked from his bike that was parked next my own.

I held up my hand for her to climb on, and she took it without a second glance.

"The one off Fourth. Benton Bank and Trust." She said, moving as close as she could without actually touching me.

I only had a small pad on the back fender that allowed for just part of an ass, not a total one, so for her to be that far away, she had to be nearly hanging off the pad.

"Scoot up," I instructed.

She scooted maybe a millimeter at most.

"More," I urged.

Another millimeter.

Sighing in exasperation, I rounded one of my arms around the obstinate woman's ass and yanked her forward.

After a startled squeak, I fired up the bike and started walking it out of my spot before giving it gas and heading out of my lot towards the bank.

She wrapped her arms tight around my torso, holding on way too tight for comfort.

I didn't stop her though. She was scared; if I had to deal with a little bit of discomfort, I'd deal.

Trance followed beside me, but split off once we got to Fourth, going in the opposite direction.

The search took well over twenty minutes of back alleys and

side streets with no luck.

Then my phone vibrated in my pocket, making me pull over hastily and rush to answer it. "You find her?" I asked quickly, not bothering with a hello.

"Yeah," he answered. "She's off of Old Miller Road. She's pretty scared, too. Won't let me come near her without freaking out."

"Alright," I said, giving Adeline's leg a pat. "We'll be there shortly."

The ride to Old Miller Road was a quick one. It was only five minutes away, and I dropped it down to only two and a half with no objection from the woman currently plastered to my back.

Adeline's sister looked so much like her that it made me do a double take. Adeline, however, didn't waste any time in going to her sister, who was hunkered down beside a building and a picnic table.

The sweater she was wearing was stained and dirty, as if she'd fallen down more than once to get to where she was.

Poor girl. She had to be scared to death.

"Viddy!" Adeline called as she ran towards the cowering woman.

Trance was standing about six feet away, watching the woman with an intense expression on his face.

"Addy?" Viddy called, standing up by bracing her hands on the building behind her.

"Right here," Adeline said, just before she dropped to her knees and wrapped her arms around the woman. "Are you okay? Did anything hurt you?"

The woman shook her head. "No, I'm okay. Trance here pulled up about five minutes ago and scared some guy off, but other than that, nothing. Stupid Jefferson just left me here. Didn't let me take my cane. God, if I could see him, I'd kick his ass."

I barely suppressed the urge to laugh; Trance, however, did not. He just let it all out.

So the woman had an attitude similar to Adeline.

Made sense, the two of them were so similar they had to be twins. Both of them had long brownish black hair that curled into waves down their backs. Both had the same body, with just the correct amount of padding that every man liked. And both had nearly the same tan.

The only thing different about the two was that Viddy wore dark glasses to hide her eyes.

"That's okay, I'll kick his ass for you. I just can't fathom why he's doing this. Stupid piece of shit got $1500 out of me that I was saving to put new tires and brakes on my car. Since when does he ever need that much? Asshole."

That was news to me.

She must've figured that out after I'd left. There was no way she would've been able to keep that news from affecting her extremely expressive face.

"He got $500 out of me, too. Luckily, I'd just transferred some money into my savings or he'd have gotten a lot more!"

Looking over at Trance, I saw the same emotion expressed in his eyes as I had in my own.

Outrage.

What kind of piece of shit would do something like that?

I didn't have to worry about justice, though. I could see with just one glance that Trance didn't plan on leaving this alone.

He was a police officer, as well as a Dixie Warden.

We didn't condone hurting women. Even if no physical violence was actually done.

"Are you ladies ready to get out of here?" I asked after another ten minutes of rocking and crying between the two women.

In answer, Adeline stood, and yanked her sister up behind her.

"Viddy, I'd like you to meet Kettle. He's my neighbor. You've already met Trance. He's Kettle's uhh, friend?" Adeline finished on a question.

"Yeah, we're friends. It's nice to meet you, Viddy." I said offering my hand.

To the blind woman that couldn't see the hand.

Jesus Christ.

"Uhh," I said, face flaming in humiliation.

Adeline whispered something in Viddy's ear and Viddy's arm raised, searching blindly for my hand. I reached for her hand, gave it a slight shake, trying my hardest not to crush her tiny hand, and dropped it.

"It's nice to meet you, too, Kettle. My name's Vidalia. I'm Addy's twin sister. I'm older by four minutes. It's nice to be treated like a normal person. Next time say you're holding your hand out for me to shake, and I'll proceed in kind." Viddy replied.

Trance's eyes were shining with mirth as he sidled closer to us and offered his own hand. "My name's Trance and I'm holding my hand out to you."

Adeline snorted, but a smile the size of Texas lit Viddy's face as she held out her hand for him to take. "It's nice to meet you, too. Thank you for saving me."

Trance didn't let go of Viddy's arms for a long while, as he watched the play of emotions run across the woman's face.

"So, I guess, that means you're riding with me, since none of us were really thinking ahead. Can you ride on a bike?" Trance asked Viddy.

I hadn't really thought about that part of the plan, either. But it worked out as long as she would ride on the back of Trance's bike.

It wasn't as if they were asking her to drive.

Adeline and Viddy snorted. "That's how we got into this mess." Adeline laughed, leading Viddy to Trance and then straddled my bike.

"You can't just throw that out there and not expect us to be curious." I observed dryly, as I followed in her wake.

"Feed us and we'll tell you." Adeline smiled widely from her perch on my bike.

Twenty minutes later, I found himself sitting at Longhorn Steakhouse with Adeline at my side, Trance, and Viddy across from me.

It wasn't how I'd planned to spend my night, but I sure as fuck wasn't going to complain.

Trance didn't look like he was complaining either.

"Okay, you've got your food on the way. Time to tell us." Trance said, eyeing the woman sitting next to him.

"It was my fault," Viddy began. "We were fifteen when I dared her to ride my father's motorcycle. We hadn't the first clue what it took to ride one. She was just going to ride it in the driveway, but she lost control and we wrecked."

"My dad had just gotten a new motorcycle." Continued Adeline. "It was the prettiest thing I'd ever seen, and he wouldn't let us anywhere near it. Said it was too much for the either one of us, and refused to take us riding on it. We'd heard him and my brother talking about it a few days after he'd gotten it, and it was supposed to be some beast of a Harley that could take a crotch rocket... whatever that is... and I really wanted to ride it. So, one day after my dad had gone to work on his daily rider, Viddy and I went for a little spin. Literally."

I hadn't realized how horrifying it would be to hear about a teenage girl wrecking a big, muscle bike like a Harley V-rod.

I'd seen quite a bit in my fifteen years of being in the emergency services, but just picturing what she was about to explain hurt to think about.

"Anyway, daddy had this old five speed motor under the front porch covered in a tarp. It was hoisted up off the ground by a cherry picker by about two or three inches, but the angle of the shifter was pointed out instead of up." She said swallowing a drink of her coke that the waiter had just set down. "Well, I spun out in the middle of the driveway. I wasn't really sure how to drive a bike, but I'd done pretty good until it kicked up and started shooting the both of us forward. Things get a little fuzzy after that, and I only remember what I've been told."

I winced, seeing where this was going before she'd even recounted the eye witness accounts.

"Yeah, I was thrown across the carport and my head struck the outside brick wall. I don't remember anything past that terrifying moment when the bike sped forward and we hit." Viddy explained.

"So Viddy hit the wall and got a concussion, while I was thrown into the old 5-speed motor under the carport." She grimaced.

Trance groaned, and I had to swallow the bile that was threatening the back of my throat. "You were impaled."

It wasn't a question, but a statement. I was waiting for confirmation.

"Right. I woke up in the hospital lying on my side with the arm of the shifter sticking out of my lower chest." Adeline confirmed.

"Fuck," Trance and I said at the same time.

"Yeah, daddy was frantic. He wanted to yell and scream at us, but we were both so hurt that he couldn't. The yelling didn't come till later when we were released from the hospital. He'd gotten rid of the bikes, the motor, and anything else hazardous in the house after that day. We didn't even drive until we were eighteen and moved out of the house because he refused to teach us."

"And what about you, Viddy?" Trance asked.

"Viddy was diagnosed with a severe form of Cortical Visual Impairment after our accident. The doctor's and specialists she saw had high hopes that Viddy would gain some of her vision back, like most do, and she did gain some back, but not enough to make anything easier on her. She can make out the difference between bright and dark. She can see a very narrow field through her peripheral vision, but only such a minimal amount that it only does her more harm than good." Adeline explained.

Viddy nodded her head with the explanation.

"So this was your first time riding on motorcycles since?" I asked Adeline.

She laughed. "Oh, we were little devils in high school. It was our father's fault though. He was so freaking strict after that that we barely got to go out of the house without him following us. Viddy in particular. He hated the fact that she was out there with a disability, but Viddy didn't let anything stop her. Hell, she even competed in track in high school."

Viddy snorted, drawing our eyes to her. "I competed in the high jump because it pissed my dad off. Nobody even knew I was blind until I completely missed the bag one time and fell flat on my back after jumping into the air."

Silence hung in thick waves before Adeline's tinkling laughter broke it.

"Oh, God. That was the funniest thing in the world to see." She giggled.

"That's kind of morbid that you find it funny that your blind sister fell," I said to her just before I took a drink of my water. "I kind of like it."

"It's either you laugh or cry, and we made a pact ten years

ago that neither one of us would cry about our disabilities." Viddy confirmed.

"Disabilities?" Trance asked with a raised brow.

"Yes, I'm blind and Adeline's stupid." Viddy said with a straight face.

"I am not stupid! I'm a science teacher; how much smarter do I have to be?" She laughed and threw a chip at her sister.

Trance caught it and popped it in my mouth, while Viddy smiled at him, knowing he'd done something to thwart her sister's attack.

"Do y'all have family?" Viddy asked Trance and me.

"No," Trance answered. "Kettle has a sister, though."

I was saved from having to talk about my eccentric sister when the food arrived, causing the table to lapse into silence.

"Damn," Viddy said as she felt her food. "They didn't cut it up like I asked."

I looked at her plate of parmesan chicken and realized how truly hard it would be to be blind.

I'd never thought that being blind meant you couldn't see to cut up your food. It'd never occurred to me.

Sure, the usual about not seeing where you walk and not being able to drive had occurred to me, but it'd never struck me how hard just simple everyday tasks, such as cutting your food up, could be.

"I got it. Here," Trance said as he started cutting up Viddy's chicken.

I didn't watch Trance or Viddy, though; I watched Adeline.

I'd learned a lot about her tonight, and each new thing I learned made me more and more curious as to what made her tick. What made Adeline, Adeline.

Dinner passed in relative swiftness after that, and we were

heading out to the parking lot less than an hour after arriving.

Trance offered to drive Viddy straight home, and Viddy accepted.

We'd said our goodbyes before Adeline came to a stop beside my Harley Soft Tail.

"This is really pretty. It reminds me of my dad's old one." Adeline said as she ran her hand along the shiny gray paint.

"He didn't ride ever again?" I asked as I handed her the helmet.

"Yes and no," she shook her head. "We were never around when he did."

I'd witnessed quite a few motorcyclists over the years that never rode again after a bad accident. It wasn't unheard of and didn't surprise me in the least. After an accident of any type, there comes that time where you get back on just to say you did; but for some, that courage just isn't there.

I nodded in understanding, and mounted the bike before offering her my hand.

She took it and settled herself against my back, pressing her soft breasts against me, igniting a fire in me that I'd not felt in a *very* long time.

I hadn't been aware that a certain something was missing until I saw my best friend get it, making me realize that I needed to get my head on straight or life would pass me right by.

I was thirty-four, and not getting any younger.

I wanted kids. A wife. And a place to call home, not just a house.

I wanted what Sebastian had.

What I'd almost had once.

And with Adeline wrapped around me on the ride home, I felt that, maybe, I could find that with her.

Pulling into the apartment's lot, I parked the bike in my assigned spot, and shut off the bike before dismounting.

"Jesus, but that seat sucks," Adeline said as she swung her leg over the bike.

I laughed. "Sorry, girl. It's only a small pad. You keep riding with me and I'll see about getting something different."

"Thanks. I don't know what the point in having a pad there is. I felt like I was riding on the back wheel. Didn't notice it so much before when we were looking for my sister, but now I'm feeling it."

I smirked. "It ain't called a p-pad for nothing, girl. Seriously, all it's meant to do is keep your pussy off the fender and not much more. Hence why it's called the pussy pad."

Her face flamed when I said pussy, and didn't stop flaming as she gave me a quick kiss on my cheek and hightailed it up her stairs.

"Night, Kettle!" She called from the top and then entered her apartment, closing it quietly behind her.

It wasn't until I was in my room shedding my clothes, and hanging up my vest that I realized that she hadn't asked about my cut.

I knew she had to have noticed that I was wearing it. Hell, her tits had been plastered up against my back the entire time, right up against my colors. It wasn't as if I was hiding it.

I was proud to be a member of the Dixie Wardens MC. I'd have told her everything I could have if she'd asked, but she hadn't. She hadn't given the cut a second glance. She hadn't stared at it in disgust, as Annalise had. She acted like it was just a part of who I was.

Which made me wonder...was this an okay thing in her book, or was she just that unobservant?

FOUR

If you don't understand how a woman could love her sister but
also want to kill her, you probably were an only child.
-Adeline to a coworker

Adeline

"Oh, fuck." I breathed as I entered The Tug and Chug, one of the only bars in Benton, and stopped abruptly.

Viddy, who'd been following closely behind me, came to a stop abruptly as well. By way of her face hitting my shoulder.

"Owww," Viddy whined. "That hurt. Why'd you stop?"

Viddy's cane that she normally used started flailing wildly between my legs, making me yelp and jump to escape it.

Oh, and drawing the attention of my neighbor who currently had his arms wrapped around a blonde woman from behind.

A very beautiful woman.

I grabbed Viddy's cane that was thrashing between my legs like a snake with its head cut off, and firmly yanked it from my sister's hands.

"Stop," I hissed. "It's my neighbor, and he has his hands

around a woman."

I hadn't realized he was seeing anyone.

Every time I'd seen the man in the last week since he'd help rescue my sister, he'd never had anyone but the other men in his club with him.

I'd also seen his bike.

I was no newbie to the biker way of life.

My father had been in a motorcycle club until the day he'd died, when I was twenty-three.

Of a motorcycle wreck, at that.

After Viddy and I had left the house, my father had finally felt comfortable enough to bring his bike back home.

He'd kept it at the club when we were still living at home, and had driven his truck home from there.

Inconvenient, yes, but whatever helped him sleep at night and all.

He'd died doing what he loved, and that was all that mattered to me.

Sure, it sucked horribly to not have him there to harp on my lifestyle choices, but I knew he'd died happy, and was finally with my mother, blissful in their afterlife.

Therefore, that was how I knew that a man that had women riding on his bike often didn't have p-pads on their bikes because it was incredibly uncomfortable for the women. Instead, they invested in a seat, allowing the woman to have a more comfortable ride.

"What's the big deal? Y'all aren't going steady." Viddy whimper-yelled back and started feeling me up so she could get her cane.

I thrust it back into her hand before she could check my boobs, and started to walk forward to the hostess stand.

"How many?" The young girl asked, eyeing Viddy as if she had leprosy.

"Blindness isn't contagious," I growled.

I *hated* it when they stared at my sister as if she was infectious. Hated it with a passion.

"Uh," the young woman stuttered. "Will it be two?"

At my nod, she asked, "Smoking or non?"

I rolled my eyes. "Non," I said impatiently.

"Are you sure?" The hostess asked.

Viddy, who'd been quiet up until now, started snickering behind me, burying her face into my hair. "D-do you p-plan on taking up s-smoking in the next few minutes, Addy?" She laughed.

"Shut up or you'll draw their attention. You're embarrassing me." I hissed.

"Ladies," a deep voice said from behind us.

Directly behind us.

We both shrieked and whirled.

The cane in Viddy's hand spun with her movement, striking the older man that was behind us across his right calf, making him jump back in surprise.

Both of us stared in shock as the man winced and rubbed his bruised leg.

"Jesus, you just hit their leader." I moaned to my sister.

"Like the alien leader or their president leader?" Viddy asked worriedly.

"President leader," an amused voice said from behind us.

We whirled again, but this time, the intimidating man standing behind us caught the cane with his hand, preventing it from smacking him as it had done his president.

"Kettle," I said breathily. "Hi."

He grinned. "Not many people can get away with taking a pot

shot at our president. He's usually a little quicker than that. He must be getting slow to get taken out by a blind woman."

My eyes widened in humor, but I didn't dare laugh. I knew better.

"Funny," the man said, as he walked past us towards the tables that the lot of them were occupying in the back.

Kettle was dressed in his fire department uniform of navy blue pants, navy blue shirt with the fire department logo on it, and black boots.

The outfit itself wasn't that great, but the man filling it out made it look orgasmic.

His large arms made the sleeves of the shirt strain. It fit tightly across his chest, shoulders and abdomen, leaving very little underneath it to the imagination.

It also made my frumpy sweat pants and old cut-off t-shirt I was wearing look hideous.

What was I thinking when I wore this? Oh, yeah. My face hurt like a mother.

"Y'all want to come join us?" Kettle asked.

My eyes left the man's straining biceps and landed on the five men that were gathered around three tables that had been pushed hastily together at the back of The Tug and Chug.

"Uhh," I hesitated. "It doesn't look like you have that much room."

"Come on, it'll be enough." He said extending both arms. "I'm holding out my arm for you, darlin'." He said to Viddy, making her laugh.

Viddy and I curled our hands around his massive bulging biceps, and walked cautiously towards the group.

"Ladies, I'd like you to meet Loki, Silas, Sebastian, Dixie, and you already know Trance." He introduced them from left to right.

Loki looked like a golden God. That is if you didn't take the scar that ran across his throat into consideration.

A thin, raised line went from one side of his jaw to the other.

His eyes were a pale blue, and trained on our every move. Dissecting us as if we were insects.

He nodded, but said nothing else at the introduction.

Silas was the President, and the person that Viddy had hit with her cane. He was older with silverish, brown hair shaved short, and a wicked looking beard that came to a point about two inches under his chin.

His eyes were sharp and focused, as if he'd seen it all and lived to tell about it.

Sebastian was the man I'd met at the fire, and the VP, according to the patch on his vest. He was wearing a black ball cap over his brown hair, and severe eyes peeked out underneath the bill of the hat. He took in our surroundings as if waiting for something unseen to pop out around the corner and bludgeon us all to death.

Dixie was the oldest of them all; he also had a pudge that rivaled Santa Claus.

Viddy kicked me under the cover of the table, and I became aware that I was drawing attention with my less than flattering description of Dixie.

I liked to make Viddy feel like she was included. So I spoke about where everything was, what everyone was doing, where she was sitting. Who was behind her. I told her everything. It was so much of a habit that I hadn't even realized I'd been doing it. Describing nuances of what each one of them looked like.

"Sorry," I flushed.

They all laughed, and then Trance spoke. "Have a seat."

Then there was Trance. I hadn't seen him well the other night, due to the dark of the night, and then the dimness of the restaurant, but with the bright fluorescent lights of The Tug and Chug shining down and illuminating him visibly, I clearly saw the different colors of the man's eyes.

"Holy shit!" I exclaimed. "You have the same color eyes as Viddy!"

I reached across Kettle, pressing myself flush against him, and ripped the glasses off of Viddy's face, allowing her eyes to become visible to all those that were in front of us.

"Viddy!" I said. "His eyes are the exact same as yours. One blue and one green!"

Trance had sat forward when I ripped the glasses off her face, and was smiling now. "Sweet. Never seen another person with two different colored eyes like my own. They're gorgeous."

Viddy blinked a few times, processing that fact, and then smiled. "Awesome."

"Take a seat, ladies." Silas ordered.

We sat.

It was just a simple fact. The man ordered it and we did it.

We'd just sat down when the woman Kettle had had his arms wrapped around earlier came up and sat down drinks for everyone.

She was really pretty with blonde perky hair, big, bouncy boobs, and a small, trim waist; exactly what I'd picture any man with. She was what every woman secretly strived to be.

"Shannon," Kettle stood wrapping his hand around my waist. "I'd like you to meet my neighbor, Adeline and her sister, Viddy. Ladies, this is my sister, Shannon."

I didn't really know what to think of the fact that I was relieved. I wasn't ready for a relationship with a man like Kettle.

I was tired of being understanding. I wanted a man that put me first for once, not someone that would always put his club before me, or his job.

The last man I'd been in a relationship with had done that to me, and I hadn't realized it until he'd proposed to me.

Jaxton was a great man. He was honest, caring, and committed.

To his job.

He was an OB/GYN in Henderson, TX where I used to live with him.

He was a great doctor but a lousy boyfriend, and I realized that now, and knew that I had to have someone that would be willing to put me and our relationship first.

Which was why it was scary that I actually felt relieved that the beauty was his sister, and not his woman.

"Jesus, Shannon." Silas spat. "I said a beer, not a Bud Light."

Whatever internal battle I was struggling with dissipated at that comment, and conversation began to flow.

"What brings y'all to The Tug and Chug, Adeline?" Kettle asked me after telling Shannon their drink orders.

Viddy, who'd been busy speaking quietly with Trance at the end of the table perked up at Kettle's question, and just had to tell everyone about my awful day.

"Addy got punched in the face by one of her students. He was a football player." Viddy crowed. "So I brought her here for a sundae and a cheeseburger to cheer her up."

Six pairs of eyes locked to my face, and only then did they realize that my face and right eye was swollen. I'd done a good job at hiding it with makeup, and then wearing my hair down to add to the camouflage, but Viddy didn't know how to keep her trap shut.

"What happened?" Kettle barked, turning my head so he could examine my eye.

I shivered at the touch of his rough fingers on my chin, and looked into his piercing blue eyes, becoming lost.

"Addy?" He asked, worry evident in his deep baritone voice.

I blinked, and then told him what happened earlier that day.

"I'm a high school science teacher, Kettle. Most of the kids use my class to blow off steam since there's a mandatory lab, but today was a little worse than normal since it was a pep rally day. One of the boys on the football team was picking on a young girl, calling her names, and another boy, one of the ones that has a crush on the girl, intervened. I'd just walked around the corner when the football player threw a punch at the kid, who incidentally moved out of the way just in time, causing the player to punch me in the face instead."

Kettle's teeth ground together, making an audible noise as he listened.

"What did they do to the kid?" Silas' voice broke the connection causing me to turn and look at him.

I shrugged. "Suspension. Benton High has a zero tolerance policy for fighting. He'll be gone for well over two weeks."

"That's it?" Trance asked from further down the table.

I shrugged again. "I don't know. It was an accident. Or at least the hitting the teacher part. So I can't really get too mad at him."

"Fuck that," Kettle growled. "You sure as fuck can get mad at him. Nobody should be throwing punches with people that close around them. They should be aware of their surroundings. That shouldn't happen at all in a school. What did the school resource officer have to say about it all?"

I would've replied if a commotion coming from the opposite corner we were in didn't capture everyone's attention, including my own.

"Let me go!" Kettle's sister shrieked at a young man that was wrapped around her from behind, groping her boobs.

Kettle's chair scooted back loudly as he took in the altercation, and then he exploded.

Literally.

One second he was in his chair and scooting back, and the next second he was across the room, punching the guy across the mouth with his fist with the force of a sledge hammer.

"Oh, shit." Sebastian groaned.

The sentiment was echoed by the other four men as they, too, got up and started heading over towards the altercation.

I didn't know if it was to help Kettle, or restrain him.

I'd seen many fights in my tenure as a high school teacher.

I'd broken up many of them, too.

The sounds that always surround a fight are unique.

There is the jeering from the crowd, the scuffling sound from the two people grappling, and then the actual sound of flesh meeting flesh.

Kettle's fight resembled none of those.

The bar became so silent that the only sound that was heard was the ice machine dropping ice into the dispenser. No talking, laughing, cheering, no nothing. It was as if everyone was anticipating the upcoming events about to go down. Like watching a tiny car stuck on a railroad track and a freight train barreling down the tracks toward it.

Then the sound of Kettle's fist meeting the guy's face tore through the silence like a clap of thunder.

That's all it took. One single punch.

The sound of the impact was difficult to describe.

It resembled the sound of a large thick textbook dropping down on a table top from a foot above the table.

There was a low, dull thwack, and the guy holding his sister's boobs went down like a tree falling; blood poured from his mouth and nose, and three of the man's teeth laid on the floor beside him in a small puddle of blood.

Kettle stood over the man, chest billowing air before he bent down to grab the man again. Only his club was there to intercept him before he got too far.

Sebastian's brawny arms went around Kettle's chest, anchoring him to his upper body. Once Sebastian had his arms locked around, Trance and Loki each took an arm, while Silas stood in front of Kettle talking to him calmly.

Dixie used the opening to drag the trash out the back door and slam it closed before rushing back to the table and taking a sip of beer.

"Fuck, but that boy can throw a punch. We haven't seen Kettle blow in a long time. It makes me damn thirsty!" Dixie jabbered giddily.

"What happened? Did Kettle hit someone?" Viddy asked into the silence.

"Kettle's got a bit of a temper. We're just lucky that he's slowed down a bit in his old age or he'd have gotten quite a few more punches in before anybody could've stopped him." Dixie replied.

My face moved from Santa to the place Kettle had been standing moments before, only to find him gone. The group had disappeared outside, leaving Shannon there shaking her head, cleaning up the spilled glasses on the table she'd been delivering a drink to.

"Where'd they go?" I asked Dixie.

His eyes flicked to the back door that he'd thrown the man out of, and the back to me. "To have a discussion, I'm sure."

I rolled my eyes.

"Daddy used to have a lot of discussions, too. That really meant he was beating the shit out of someone. He used to be the enforcer before his hands got too arthritic, and then he just supervised the prospects and told them how to do the most damage. Is Kettle the enforcer of your club?" Viddy asked casually as she reached out carefully for her drink.

Dixie, who'd been taking a drink of beer, choked, and turned his eyes to mine.

I wasn't sure what the big deal was. Although, I'd never been around another club besides my father's club before, I was fairly sure Viddy didn't just commit a huge social faux pas. I also wasn't privy to very much information about the club, either, so I didn't know if there was some sort of protocol we were supposed to abide by and didn't.

"What's wrong?" I asked Dixie worriedly. "Were we supposed to not say that?"

My mind was whirling. Was it a secret? Was there some sort of club code that Viddy had inadvertently trampled over? Was I going to have to take Viddy and make a run for it?

Before my mind came up with an answer, Kettle pulled the chair out from beside me and took a seat, looking no worse for wear.

"What's wrong, Dixie?" Kettle asked. "I didn't kill him."

Kettle's tone had been light, but when Dixie's eyes turned to him, and then flicked back to me, he became tense. "What?"

"Viddy just asked me if you were the enforcer for our club like her pop was for theirs."

The statement, although sounding innocuous, dropped like a bomb among the men surrounding our table, and all of their eyes turned to the two of us, pinning us like specimens under a microscope.

"What?" I asked nervously.

"Your pops belonged to a club?" Kettle asked me in neutral tone.

Unaware of the raptor-like attention we were receiving, Viddy continued to talk about our father's club. "Yeah, daddy was a member of The Lone Star MC for thirty years. He joined after he got out of the Marines. He was their enforcer. Although that's about all we really know. We weren't allowed at the clubhouse; nor did we go to many parties. The only ones we went to were the ones that were had for the families."

Viddy finished her announcement with a long sip of her iced tea, and set the empty glass down carefully.

At the mention of my father's MC, every single one of the men took a breath, shoulders slumping.

Something in my stomach released at the sight, allowing me to breathe again.

"Your pop was Tenor? He was a good man." Silas said; there was no tension to this question, as if the threat that was on their threshold vanished, no longer needing him to be on guard.

I smiled wistfully. "Yeah, Daddy died, gosh, seven years ago now."

Viddy's arm went around my shoulders and pulled me in tight.

We loved our Dad like crazy, and still thought about him every day; if Dad were still there, we wouldn't have had to worry about what our crazy brother would do next, because he'd have had his shit straightened out at the first sign of a misstep.

"We had a pretty good relationship with them when Tenor was still there. Then the old President died, followed by your Dad that next month, and the new leadership came on and we haven't spoken much to them since." Silas explained.

I was nodding my head in agreement and trying my hardest not to shutter. "Yeah, we moved away after my father died. It was really hard for us to be there after both of our parents were gone. When Viddy found a school to work for here that taught the blind, and I found a high school job with Benton High, we figured that was a really good opportunity to spread our wings. It's been six years now, and we haven't been back to Lone Star since."

"Here you go, gentlemen; ladies, yours will be another few minutes." Shannon said airily as she set down the food.

I eyed Kettle's steak that had onions and mushrooms smothered over the top and wondered why I'd ordered chicken when I could've gotten that.

The corn on his plate wasn't as appealing, but when he lifted the cob to his mouth and took a bite, I could see the merit of the butter. Especially melted butter when he licked his lips, and then his fingers free of the melted goodness.

"Here y'all go. I took the liberty of giving you the low-fat cheese and sour cream since you didn't specify what you wanted. For you, I got the low fat ranch dressing." Shannon said as she placed Viddy's baked potato, and my hot wings down in front of us.

That dig was directed towards Viddy more than me, since Viddy was busy carrying on a conversation with Trance, whom it was more than obvious Shannon had a thing for with the lingering touches and the shy glances, but I still took offense.

"Uhh, in fact, I would like it if you brought us both out the real kind. The other stuff doesn't taste as good." I all but growled, causing the table to chuckle.

I was pretty particular about food.

I liked it to taste good, and I liked to eat a lot of it.

Silas handed over his ranch that he wasn't using. I thanked him readily.

"Are you hungry?" Trance asked me while eyeing my plate of chicken wings.

"A little," I said picking up a hot wing and devouring the meat from the bone.

At one point, I'd had to stop due to no more ranch, and had to resort to the low fat shit that Shannon had brought earlier.

"Ick," I said after my first taste. "I need some more real stuff."

Deciding to risk it, I started to scarf down my wings like a man. Only after I'd finished nearly half of the hot wings did I realize that I really should've waited for the ranch. My mouth was on fire, and I started panting. It wasn't surprising that I had no drink, either.

I wasn't sure who gave it to me, but a cup of half-eaten ranch was sat on the table beside the shitty ranch, allowing me to finish my meal without having to wait twenty minutes for Shannon to get back.

After finishing the very last wing, I fell back into my seat with a groan, brought my fingers up to my mouth, and was in the process of licking them clean when I realized the entire table was staring at me as if I'd grown horns.

"What?" I asked as I finally settled on Kettle to look at.

He only shook his head and went back to his half eaten steak.

"Did I eat too fast or something?" I asked warily.

Viddy, the cruel bitch, chimed in at that point. "No, you just did your Hoover Vacuum impression in front of a bunch of hot guys that make a living being bad ass. You also ate the hottest wing on the menu without even batting an eyelash. They're just impressed."

"I didn't eat that fast." I grumbled, tearing open my wipe package and cleaning my fingers of the stickiness.

"Actually, you did. You've got sucking the meat off a hot wing down to a fine art." Dixie said, waving his hand in front of my face wildly.

Then I saw Kettle shift, move his hand down to his crotch, and adjust himself before he cut into his steak again, causing my face to flame.

Thirty minutes, a slice of cheesecake, and another glass of sweet tea later, Kettle was standing beside my rental car as I leaned against it.

"How much longer are they going to be on your car?" Kettle asked, eyeing the car with disgust.

I felt the same way. I hated the rental car. Especially after I was used to driving my own car. This car was too bland for my tastes, and didn't have the get-up-and-go my own car had.

I missed my baby.

I sighed. "I don't even think they've looked at it yet. They said they had some paying customers come in that they had to do first, and then they'd get to mine since mine was an insurance job."

Although I could understand the reasoning, I hated that they weren't even looking at it until they felt like it.

It wasn't my fault that jackass had hit me.

A clunk, thunk, and then a curse came from the side of the car, and we both looked up to see Viddy holding her forehead. "Oww."

"Your sister just hit her head on the door," Kettle observed, slightly concerned.

"Yeah," I agreed. "She does that quite a bit. She doesn't like to draw attention to it though, so just act like you didn't notice."

"Alright," he agreed reluctantly.

I guessed it went against the grain of my personality not to help those in need, but I knew my twin sister like the back of my hand. I knew that Viddy wouldn't like help, and she hated calling attention to her weakness.

I'd learned long ago not to even bother with helping her if she had her mind set against help. Which was why I had a scar that ran along the underside of my chin from where my sister threw a vase at my head because I had the nerve to offer to assist Viddy outside for prom our senior year.

"Well, thank you again for dinner. You didn't have to buy ours, but I appreciate it anyway." I smiled at Kettle.

Then I noticed how close we were standing. How very, *very* close.

"Kettle?" I breathed.

Kettle's eyes, those beautiful blue eyes went from my mouth, where they'd been staring, to my eyes, and the sexual awareness that flashed in them fairly electrified my nerve endings.

He leaned in, pressing me slightly against the door of my car, and leaned in until he was only a hairsbreadth away before he said, "Yeah?"

I could feel the hard ridges of his body where he leaned against me, and then the very hard part of him that I was dying to rub against.

Then my fucking asshole sister honked the horn, making us jump apart like we'd had a vat of boiling oil poured over our heads.

"Jesus Christ," I breathed, pressing my hand against my heart.

Kettle was three feet away from me, his hands linked on the top of his head as he glared daggers at my sister. "Your sister's a...a..."

"Bitch?" I supplied.

Kettle shook my head and smiled. "I was going to say-"

"Asshole?" I cut him off.

"Shit head. I was going to say shit head." Kettle chuckled as he moved closer to me.

Then the asshole honked the horn again, making both Kettle and I look at each other helplessly.

"Alright, well the queen asshole has spoken," I shook my head and then opened my car door. "I'll see you tomorrow. I plan to have groceries."

"I'm working tomorrow." Kettle told me.

Was that a hint of sadness in his voice, or was it only me wanting it to be there?

"When are you off next?" I questioned.

"Friday." He answered.

"I'll get them then. Maybe you can stay for dinner." I offered hopefully before dropping down in my seat and slamming the door without listening to his response.

"You just asked your hot firefighter neighbor that belongs to a motorcycle club to dinner. Does this mean you want to bang him? Shine his fire pole? Work his throttle? Ride him like a Harley?" My sister jeered.

I let my hand fly and smacked her across the boobs. "You're such an ass. I was totally going to get a kiss from him before you had to pull out the asshole and honk the horn."

"A little bit of mystery goes a long way, sister dearest."

Indeed it does, I thought.

What I hadn't planned on was letting the two months following my bar experience turn me into a raving lunatic that would do just about anything to have the man.

One thing after another came up, and the sexual tension was building so high, I couldn't handle it. I was willing to do just about anything to have that man. Even if I had to shine his pole while he was on-shift at the station during my conference period.

FIVE

*What is a hero? Someone who does something that has to be
done, regardless of the consequences.
-Plaque on the wall at the Benton Fire Station*

Kettle

One week later

I fairly stomped up my front walk.

I'd had a bad day at work, Sebastian had been a royal dick
all day, and my father had called.

For the first time in years.

Then I read the note on my door and wanted to curse.

*Sorry I missed you. :(Maybe you can come for dinner this week.
I even bought extra for tonight. You owe me 17 bags, Mister!*

She'd had to carry seventeen bags up her stairs and all because my boss and VP, Sebastian, had needed 'a day to himself.'
Normally, I had no problem pulling a shift if he needed me to, but
today, of all days, had been a total clusterfuck.

The next morning, I'd gone to knock on her door after my morning workout to find her gone. She'd mentioned some sort of school testing to me in passing, and needing to go in early for them, but that also meant I couldn't see her until next week since I worked this weekend.

Thinking she needed to have my cell phone number so we could get in touch, I ran back to my house, found an old receipt, and scribbled my number down with a Sharpie before finding a tack and pinning it to her door.

Text me. Sorry I missed carrying your bags. 665-0021 –K.

Two weeks later

Texts between Adeline and Kettle

Addy- I had a good time last night. Even if that kid did puke on me.

Kettle- Sorry about that. Probably shouldn't have given him so much ice cream.

Addy- That's okay. I live next door to you. It was an easy fix.

Kettle- Still gross as hell. Dinner Friday?

Addy- Absolutely.

Two days later

Addy- I can't make it. I was volunteered to chap-
erone the homecoming dance. Rain check?

Kettle- :P

Addy- Very mature.

Two hours later

Kettle- How's the dance?

Addy- I broke up a drug deal in the boy's bathroom. Then they threatened to 'fuck me up'
and they were arrested. Fun stuff.

Kettle-Are you okay?

Three hours later

Kettle- You never answered me.

Addy- Fine. Pissed. I don't like talking to the
cops. Saw Trance though. :)

Kettle- He told me. Said they had to bring Radar up there to sniff some lockers.

Addy- The Dog? He was the shit. He also ate my
cake.

Kettle- Yeah, Trance told me that, too. I'll buy
you some more next time I see you.

A week and a half later

Addy- I could really use that cake today.

Kettle- Why? What's wrong?

Addy- They had some layoffs today. Luckily, I'm the one with the highest education here. Otherwise, it would've been sayonara Adeline. The seniority bitches are giving me the evil eye.

Kettle- Tell them you have a boyfriend that'll kick their ass.

Addy- Do I?

Kettle- Do you want to?

Three weeks later

Addy- I've been thinking, and the answer is yes.

Kettle- To what?

Addy- To that question you asked me a few weeks ago.

Kettle- If you were a virgin?

Addy- No.

Kettle- No, you're not, or no, that's not the question you had in mind?

Addy- Yes and no.

Kettle- I'm confused.

Addy- You should be.

Finally getting frustrated, I picked up my phone and hit Adeline's number.

It rang all of two times before she answered in a flurry.

"Hello?" She said breathily.

"Hey," I said. "What are you doing?"

Why was she panting?

"Hey!" She said excitedly. "I was just about to go on a walk. Do you want to go with me?"

Looking over at the clock to gauge how much time I had left before work, I decided to take her up on her offer. I had nearly an hour and a half, and if I put my uniform on, all I would have to do was get on my bike and leave within fifteen minutes to the start of my shift.

"Yeah, I'd love to." I rumbled. "Just give me ten minutes to get my shit together, and I'll meet you downstairs. Or you can come over to me. That okay?"

"Yes, I'll be there in just a few minutes. Just have to put Monty up." She said before hanging up.

I was just putting my uniform in my duffel bag and zipping it up when a knock sounded on my front door.

"Hey," I said brightly when I found her on my front porch.

She smiled exuberantly at me before coming inside and closing the door behind her. "You want a water?" I asked, trying not to notice the shortness of her shorts.

She was wearing really short, and by really short, I mean, I could see her ass cheeks short, gray knit shorts. Her top resembled what used to be a t-shirt that had the sleeves cut off with what resembled a butcher knife. The shirt said "Lone Star Saturday Night" on it with a bear smoking a cigar underneath it. The arm-holes of the shirt weren't actually armholes, but more like large... slits. I could see the black sports bra she was wearing, as well as the tattoo's that ran down both of her sides.

She nodded. "Yes please."

A couple of minutes later we were walking up the sidewalk that ran along the road beside our apartment. We lived in what amounted to a large circular subdivision of apartments. It was a large loop about a mile and a half all the way around.

We took a left once we reached the end of the parking lot, and I finally scrounged up the nerve to ask about something I'd wanted to know for a while now.

"So, tell me about your...pets." I said hesitantly.

She looked at me sharply and smiled a little hesitantly.

"I thought you guessed. I wasn't really trying to keep it se-cret." She said dryly.

I shrugged. "I can guess for the most part, but I would love some confirmation. My imagination runs away from me some-times."

She giggled. Fucking giggled, bringing my attention from the road in front of us to her mouth.

"There's not really much to say. It's exactly like what you heard on the news I'm sure. I worked at Evan's Pharmaceuticals for a little over seven months. There were quite a few things that were bothering me while I worked there, but the 'testing on ani-mals' thing really took the cake. I broke them out, loaded them into a rented UHAUL trailer and then came back home. That's why I had to move from my old place in the Hills." She explained.

I nodded. "You didn't want them to know where you lived."

She nodded enthusiastically. "Exactly. I just couldn't live with myself if I allowed that. But I'd been having problems with them before that. It was weird. One time I'd stayed a little late, and I ran into a man coming into my lab that I'd never seen before. We were assigned small labs of our own where we tested the products to make sure we abided by the state regulations. He'd been surprised to see me there so late, and I never saw him again, but I knew instantly he wasn't supposed to be there. The next day was when I started keeping count on all my supplies. The weird thing was, was that I started losing my tools, not the drugs. Beakers here. Large glass vials there. I'd started getting suspicious right along the time I left."

I looked over at her face before returning my attention to the bike rider who was headed our way before replying. "That's weird. But a lot of people that make their own drugs steal things like that so they don't draw attention from the feds. Did you ever do a full inventory?"

"No," she shook her head. "I was going to, but then when I wandered out of my area of the building and found the animals; well, let's just say I didn't take it very well."

I rolled my eyes. "No, I probably wouldn't have either."

We walked in silence, watching the neighborhood kids play a bout of kick the can, laughing at their antics as they pushed and shoved to get the runner out.

"I used to play that when I was little. Gosh, I didn't think kids got out to play like that anymore." Adeline observed.

"I never got to do anything like that. I would've killed for a neighborhood like this when I was growing up. Well, when I wasn't sick, that is." I said.

"You were sick when you were a kid?" She asked sharply, startling me out of my observation of the kids.

That's when I realized what I'd just said. Fuck. Would she look at me differently when she knew how sick I once was? I didn't really want to ruin what was left of our walk on things that neither she, nor I, could change.

"When did you get your first tattoo?" I asked, changing the subject, and hoping that she went along with that subject change.

I saw her eye me speculatively out my peripheral vision for long moments before deciding to answer me. "When I was sixteen. My sister bet me thirty dollars to do it, banking on me chickening out. Thirty dollars was a lot of money to a teenager whose father refused to give them money because he thought they'd spend it on frivolous stuff. So I got this one." She said, pointing at her wrist. "Walked up the tattoo parlor and asked for a sugar skull on my wrist, and the woman gave it to me that day, not even asking me if I was eighteen. Little did I know that the woman was an apprentice and was super excited to get anyone to work on besides fake skin. Should have found out how much it was beforehand, though, because otherwise I would've never done it. Cost me two hundred bucks, and I had to call my dad down to the shop to pay for it."

I burst out laughing. I could just see her dad storming down to that tattoo parlor in his colors, ripping the apprentice a new one for tattooing a minor. "And what did he have to say about that?"

She smiled wistfully. "He didn't, really. At first, he was kind of miffed, but eventually he got over it. He was the one that took me for the next couple of them. This one," she said, indicating a line of script I'd read a million times before. "I got the day he died."

The writing was simple and said, '*Squeeze you to pieces.*'

"What does that mean?" I asked, realizing that it meant a lot to her.

"My mom and dad always said it to each other when they hugged and said goodbye. She'd say, '*Squeeze you to pieces*' and he'd reply with, *'Squeeze you back together.'* They said it to us every chance they got. And when he died, Viddy and I got it tattooed on us. Mine on my wrist, and hers on her ribs. Her tattoo says 'Squeeze you back together.' It was her first and only tattoo." She said wistfully.

"My mom used to have a saying similar to that. 'I love you, you who.'" I said just as we arrived at the entrance to our complex.

She smiled widely at me, grabbed my arm, and walked with me hand in hand until we arrived at my bike.

"Do you want to do this again tomorrow night when you get home?" She asked hopefully.

My hand came up involuntarily until it rested just under the line of her jaw. I could feel the fluttering of her pulse, as it beat wildly against my palm, and I barely squashed the urge to jeer in acceptance.

"Sure." I replied as flippantly as I could manage.

Leaning forward, she went up to her tippy toes before giving me a quick kiss on the cheek. "I'll see you tomorrow, then. Be careful at work, do you hear?"

"Yes, ma'am." I acknowledged as I watched her climb the steps to her apartment.

"Good boy," she teased as she disappeared inside her apartment.

Oh, if only she knew the thoughts that were pouring through my mind right now, then she wouldn't be thinking of me as a 'good' anything.

• • •

Kettle

One month later

"What's up with you today?" Sebastian asked from the station's kitchen table.

I shut the refrigerator and turned with a bottle of water in my hand. "Nothing."

It wasn't nothing, and he and I both fuckin' knew it.

I was sexually frustrated.

I hadn't fucked anyone in well over two and a half months now, and everyone kept telling me that I needed to get laid.

Well my fucking dick didn't want to get laid by just *anyone.*

It wanted to get laid by the hot as hell chemistry teacher next door.

Except one thing after another kept coming up whether it be my job, or her job, or my club, or her sister.

It was as if the universe was conspiring against us.

We hung out, but it was never alone.

Her sister was there. Or my sister. Or someone in the club.

In fact, the last person to interrupt us was the asshole staring at me right that very moment.

"You're acting like a rabid porcupine. Your temper is legendary and all, but this is an all-new high. Dad wanted me to make sure you got your shit straightened before this weekend when we went on the Toys for Tots ride."

My jaw clenched. Yet another weekend off I couldn't spend fucking Adeline.

Not that the charity wasn't a good reason, but my dick needed some relief, and my hand was getting tired; that was if it even did the job that day. There were times I'd work myself to the brink of coming, and then nothing. Nothing at all happened. It was as if my dick knew what it wanted, and my rough palm just wasn't getting it done.

The last two months was the definition of deprivation.

My phone buzzed, drawing me out of my wallowing thoughts.

The message flashing on the screen had me seeing red.

Addy- A kid just grabbed my ass.

"I gotta go somewhere real quick. I'll be back in twenty." I gritted through clenched teeth as I headed to my room to grab my keys.

"Where're you going?" Dallas asked from the recliner in the living room.

"The high school," I replied as I stopped by the back door for my jacket.

"Mind if I tag along? I need to run by the grocery store for some dinner tonight and pick up a prescription for Baylee." Sebastian asked from the doorway.

I shrugged. "Sure."

"We'll take the engine. Anyone else want to come?" Sebastian asked as I shrugged on my jacket.

"Sure," Dillon said, as he stood from the recliner and walked with us out the door.

"Where we going first?" Sebastian asked, as he hopped into the passenger seat of the engine.

I hauled myself into the driver's seat of the engine and started the big beast up.

Our newest acquisition was a 24 foot long by 12-foot wide mammoth monster that was powered by a 600 horsepower 2013 Cummins Diesel engine. The lovely brute was paid for by the citizens of Benton for a cool six hundred thousand dollars. It purred like a kitten and made my heart sing.

And it was worth every fucking penny.

"High school." I said simply.

They didn't ask questions, which was the norm for them. They didn't need to know why, and they trusted me implicitly.

Which had to be done if you were going to put your life on the line with them day in and day out.

The ride to the high school was short.

I parked the engine at the curb along the fire lane of the school, hopped out, and locked the doors behind us.

I didn't bother to ask if Sebastian and Dillon were going with me. I knew they were. They didn't miss an opportunity for gossip if they could help it.

Walking into the school made me frown.

I'd gone to Benton High sixteen years ago; it hadn't changed one single bit.

The doors were still shitty, and a stiff wind could probably blow them down.

The office was beyond the large foyer, being blocked by just one wooden door and surrounded by glass.

"Jesus, it hasn't changed a bit." Dillon said, eyeing the colorful green and black banners hanging from the ceiling.

"Go Benton Bengals." I said dryly and raised my fist.

"Bengals, fight, fight, fight," Dillon sang loudly, becoming even louder as the sound of his voice echoed off the stone walls.

I rolled my eyes at the imbecile and walked through the office door, closing it firmly behind me.

"Can I help you?"

The woman asking it was the same woman who'd been there all those years ago when I'd attended.

The evil Mrs.Threadgill.

Mrs. Threadgill was the foul biddy who used to write me tardies, and send me home if my shirts had anything 'provocative' on them, regardless if they did or not. Hell, I'd been sent home my senior year for a Coke shirt because she'd thought it was promoting drugs.

I'd hated her guts, and I damn well knew she remembered me as soon as she saw me. It was kind of hard to forget a kid that was 6'4 and 200 pounds with the face of an Italian Stallion in my freshman year of high school.

Now I was two forty, but who was counting.

"Mr. Spada, what can I help you with?" Mrs. Threadgill asked coldly after I'd taken too long to answer.

"We're here for Ms. Sheffield's chemistry class. Can you tell us where to go?" I asked nicely.

Mrs. Threadgill looked at me as if he'd grown a second head. "You're," she sneered. "With the fire department now?"

I smiled widely at her. "For ten years now." I informed her brightly.

She sniffed and then stood stiffly before walking to the door and opening it.

"I'll take you. I have to escort Mr. Fairway back to Ms. Sheffield's class anyway." She said gesturing to a young boy that was sitting outside the principal's office.

Of course, the first thing the woman heard was Dillon singing the Benton fight song at the top of his lungs to a crowd of young girls.

"Dallas Berry, that is quite enough." Mrs. Threadgill reprimanded. "Mr. Fairway, please follow me."

Dallas, not one to stop when he was told, finished the song despite the old woman's glare, drawing chuckles from his underage fan club.

"This way," Mrs. Threadgill snapped before shuffling down the back hall towards the science labs.

The young boy who looked like a little punk dressed in designer clothing seemed like a real winner.

His clothes were about three sizes too big, and he was holding his pants up by the buckle of the belt.

I wanted to pants him.

"Michelle, please tie your hair back or get out of my lab. You probably wouldn't look so good bald." Adeline's voice scolded from behind the chemistry lab's door.

"But Ms. Sheffield, if I tie it back it gets creases and looks like shit..."

Mrs. Threadgill opened the door so quick I barely saw her move. "Ms. Cox, I suggest you follow Ms. Sheffield's direction or you won't get to see the fireman do their demonstration, and if I hear you curse on the school grounds again, I'll be speaking with your parents."

Yep, the old goat still had it. She used to use the same line on me sixteen years ago. Worked every time.

"Firemen?" Michelle and Adeline asked in unison.

I smiled widely as I followed Mrs. Threadgill into the room that also hadn't changed in sixteen years. Jesus, it was like being in a time warp.

"Ahh, our guest speakers are here early. Michelle, please allow Shane his seat back so we can discuss some fire safety. Mr. Spada, please introduce yourself." Adeline said gleefully.

I rolled my eyes. This wasn't my first rodeo.

Therefore, I had no problem spewing out the usual spiel I gave to the five to eight year olds, bringing Dillon and Sebastian in while I was at it.

After about fifteen minutes of speaking, I finally stopped and waited. "Any questions?"

Of course, Adeline had one. "How do you put out a chemical fire?"

Her eyes were practically dancing with happiness, which made me want to gather her up into my arms and hug the shit out of her.

We hadn't seen each other in well over a week, although my phone bill would definitely be hurting from all the text messages we've been sending over the last two months. I'd been called into work twice on the days we'd planned to hang out due to the flu going around.

"It depends. What kind of chemical is it?"

After going on to explain what we did during certain situations, Sebastian finally broke up our verbal foreplay by asking if there were any other questions.

We of course got the usual questions.

Do you have a Dalmatian at the station?-No.

How much water does it take to put out a fire? –A lot.

Do we have a fire pole? –Yes.

Do you slide down the fire pole? –Duh. Yes.

Whose hose is the biggest. –Mine.

That last one was whimpered by Adeline into my ear, which I promptly answered with nothing but the truth.

"You had me ready to beat some teenage ass. Was it that Fairway kid?" I asked her, scrutinizing the boy who was trying to look anywhere but at me while Sebastian and Dallas answered more questions.

"Yes," she agreed. "He was sent to the principal's office, which in my opinion is more than enough of a punishment right there." She shuddered, eyeing Mrs. Threadgill who hadn't left yet.

"Doubt it. That woman used to be like a junkyard dog in my days. She's gone soft in her old age." I laughed quietly.

"I didn't know you went here." She asked confused.

"Yeah, I was home schooled until I was in junior high, and then my mom decided I needed to get out and experience high school and meet new people, so she enrolled me in my freshman year." I hedged.

The reason I was home schooled was because I had zero immune system. I'd had Leukemia when I was a young child, and battled it for a year when I was nine years old. After that, I was a very sickly child who could barely walk out of the house without catching a cold.

Then, when I was twelve, I suddenly kicked all the colds and sicknesses, and was able to actually be a child.

I begged my father over and over again to let me go to school, and when I was fourteen, he'd relented. Mostly because he was tired of hiring tutors to come to the house to teach me the stuff. He had better things for me to do than sit on my ass all day. He didn't want my mother to be teaching me either. Her role was mainly to play his perfect little house wife and attend brunches, and show her face in the community.

But Adeline didn't need to know all that.

When people realized that I'd had cancer as a child, they looked at me differently. With pity and something else I could never identify, and I hated the way it changed the way they treated me. I didn't want to see that change in Adeline, although she'd probably understand more than most where I was coming from.

"Well that's good that you got to go to public school so you didn't miss everything. Were you a basketball player?" She asked eyeing my large frame.

I hadn't realized that the class was done with their questions until one of the kids that sat in the back piped in. "Nah, Ms. S, I bet he was a defensive lineman. Look at the size of the man's arms."

Little did they know that I was the size of a beanpole in school. "Actually, I was on the debate team and played the violin in band."

You know those moments when something crashes to the ground in the middle of a crowd, and there's silence for a few heart stopping moments as the people process that sound? *Yeah.*

Of course, it had to come from my own boss and best friend. "You were on the debate team?" He laughed.

My eyes narrowed on my friend. "What's so wrong with that?" I blasted as I crossed my arms over my chest.

He held his hands up in surrender before backing up a few steps. "Nothing man. It just makes so much more sense now."

I wasn't sure if I should take that as a compliment or an insult, but I chose to take it as a compliment and let it go.

"Do you play violin anymore?" A skinny boy asked hesitantly from the middle of the room.

My eyes moved to find a tall and skinny boy with large hands that he'd soon grow into. I resembled him sixteen years ago; down to the preppy clothes that didn't help my popularity in the least.

"I can and do, yes, but that was never really my instrument. The fiddle is; I just settled for the violin since they didn't have those in band."

The boy looked confused, and I knew the exact question that was about to come out of his mouth.

"But aren't the fiddle and the violin the same thing?"

Sebastian laughed beside me, drawing my cyes for a split second before they returned to the young boy.

"You can't spill beer on a violin."

I had to explain that a lot.

There was really no difference, instrument wise, between the two. The only real difference was the type of music one played on the fiddle. It wasn't the classical shit that I was forced to play during band. My fiddle plays the song of my heart.

"Mr. Spada, we do not discuss beer at school." Mrs. Threadgill reprimanded.

Oops.

Just as I was about to apologize to the old woman, the tones on our radios dropped.

"Engine one respond to a house fire at 122 South Fuller."

I took one more look at Adeline and responded, pressing my finger against the radio clipped to my shirt. "Unit one responding."

With a tiny tug on her ponytail, I walked out the door.

"Be careful!" She yelled at my back.

"Always." I responded.

● ● ●

I took the stairs to Adeline's apartment, two steps at a time, before coming to a halt just before her new mat.

" 'Home is where the Harley is. Bikers welcome.' " I read aloud.

Without stepping on the new mat, I stretched my arm out and knocked on her door.

"Come in!" Adeline yelled from the door beyond.

Twisting the knob, I found Adeline with her blue jean short covered ass shaking in the air with her shoulders and head to the ground. She was looking underneath the couch muttering something about a 'big bastard.'

My dick, which had been under control for nearly ten whole minutes after my hand action in the shower, roared to life; I had to shift and settle my dick down the right leg of my jeans to make it more manageable.

"You talking about me?" I asked stopping just behind her.

The t-shirt she was wearing had ridden up so the expanse of

her back was exposed from her lower hips to shoulder level; that was when I realized she wasn't wearing a bra.

My breath hissed in through clenched teeth, and I took a step back just in case my dick decided to leap out of my pants and find its way inside of her.

"Monty is missing again." She said as she crawled to the other couch.

She was wearing purple panties under her shorts.

Closing my eyes, I said, "Monty's on the top of your book shelf."

I'd seen the snake as soon as I'd walked in, but then Adeline's shaking ass had captured my attention.

I heard her shuffling, and when I opened my eyes, I saw her reaching on top of the bookshelf for the snake.

"Why are you looking for him?" I asked.

"I called the police a few minutes ago about some more weird smells coming from my bathroom, only these don't smell like weed. My chemistry brain started coming up with all sorts of scenarios. Anyway, I went to knock on their door earlier to ask about the smell and they slammed the door in my face. I called the police only after the smell kept getting worse and worse. I normally keep Monty in his cage when I expect people over, just in case. He's a slippery devil." She explained as she walked to the large cage in the corner of the room and placed the snake back in his home.

"What kind of smells?" I asked as she turned and started towards me.

She walked slowly, as if she was waiting for something to interrupt them, and unsure of her welcome.

When she was just a hairsbreadth away, my hand reached up slowly to wrap around her neck, and I'd started to lean down when a loud boom shattered our moment.

Instinctively, my arm went around Adeline's waist, pulling her close.

My erection, that was insistent seconds before, deflated, sending the blood that was localized in my lower body straight to my heart as my flight or fight mechanisms started firing in my blood.

The apartment underneath my feet shook, and the floor rippled.

"What the fuck was that?" She gasped, clawing at my shoulders to get closer to me.

My brain started filtering through all the possibilities, and only one thing kept coming back to me, and that was to get the hell out.

Lifting Adeline off her feet and swinging her around to my back, I waited for her to hang on tight before I started towards the cage that Monty was slithering back and forth across.

With my free hand, I grabbed the snake and ran for the door.

"Did you find a home for the cat?" I asked quickly as I opened the front door.

Why I was worried at this point I didn't know, other than Adeline would, and that's all that mattered.

"Yes," she said nodding her head against my back. "My sister took her to one of her friends."

With one look, I realized that the stairs were a no go. They were broken and mangled, making me wish I'd said something about them months ago.

And the heat was astounding.

I knew the apartment underneath of us was on fire. I just hoped the back looked a little better than the front.

Turning around, I pounded through her living room, into the kitchen, and yanked the back balcony door open.

She didn't have a fire escape, which I'd expected. What I didn't expect to see was a wall of fire so high that it reached the tip of the balcony and started curling over.

"Goddammit." I growled, slamming the door closed.

"You got a window in your spare bedroom?" I growled, heading to the room.

I hadn't actually seen that room. She'd kept it closed because of all the mice and shit she'd stolen from the lab she used to work at.

Thank fuck she'd gotten rid of the animals over the past few weeks, donating them to the schools as class pets.

I knew my own room had one, but hers was a two bedroom compared to my three bedroom, and I didn't know if that would change the layout any.

"Yes, it's covered by a bookshelf though." She squeaked.

My jaw clenched.

I hated when people covered their windows with furniture. That was a fire hazard, and it made it incredibly hard to get into places in times of emergency.

Or, in this case, get out of.

"We'll have to have a talk about this later." I grunted as I pushed through her spare bedroom.

Dropping her down on her feet, I took in the room in a glance, saw there wasn't anything other than books on the shelf, gestured for Adeline to move aside, and threw the bookshelf over onto its face, spilling books everywhere.

The shelf hit with a small slam, revealing the window that Adeline had covered.

The window faced the apartment above my own, and I said a silent prayer that there was no fire consuming the back bedrooms of the one underneath yet, otherwise we'd be stuck.

Thank God she'd gotten rid of the slew of animals she'd stolen from the lab she used to work at. Those animals would've burned. There was no way I'd have been able to get them, her, and me out in time.

When I lifted the window and looked down, I was relieved to find nothing there, except smooth grass and the chilling breeze outside.

"Come here," I snapped and held out my hand.

Adeline grabbed my hand firmly with hers, and stepped up on the bookshelf before dropping down to the carpet in the little space where the shelf used to be.

"I'm going to lower you down. You'll still have a three foot drop. Bend your knees, and hold on to Monty. Okay?" I said looking into her wide brown eyes.

At her nod, I hoisted her up onto the window's ledge; taking a firm grip of her forearms, I lowered her down carefully.

My muscles strained instantly, bunching in exertion.

She squeaked in startled surprise when she didn't have anything but my arms to support her anymore, but she adjusted quickly and tried to keep the squirming to a minimum.

Once I had her where her body was fully extended, I said, "Okay, going to drop you now. Ready?"

At her nod, I let her drop.

• • •

Adeline

Heart pounding, I felt Kettle's iron grip around my forearms loosen, and then let go all together, then I was airborne for a few heartstopping instants.

I landed with my knees bent slightly, just as Kettle had suggested.

My feet held true, and I scrambled forward and out of the way before turning and looking up at the window I'd just been dropped out of.

Kettle was sitting on the windowsill and ready to jump out just as a cop and a K-9 officer rounded the edge of the apartment from the front.

I didn't realize I was nearly face to face with Trance until the wind shifted some of the smoke up, allowing me to see his face.

Trance and Radar.

It was getting thick and heavy, and starting to pour out of the open window of my own apartment now, too.

Kettle jumped, landing easily.

"Let's go!" He yelled, grabbing my arm and moving quickly, following Trance.

At a particularly strong bank of smoke, I started to cough, and didn't stop again until we'd reached the sidewalk on the opposite side of the parking lot.

"Oh, my God. She has a snake!" A young girl shrieked.

I ignored her, and threw my arms around Kettle, burying my face into his chest.

His shirt smelled like smoke, but I didn't care. Especially not when Kettle wrapped his large arms around me, snake and all.

Monty slithered from around my left hand to Kettle's neck and arm causing him to shiver.

"Your snake kind of creeps me out, you know." He said as Monty settled onto his shoulders.

"Yeah, he does me, too." I shivered.

We were interrupted by Trance, and he was pissed. "I need you two to come with me. Now."

Kettle wasn't surprised that Trance was angry, and gave me a 'be good' glance as we walked behind the man and dog.

Radar's ears were straight up, and his big body was shaking with pent up energy.

Radar wasn't your normal German Shepherd. He was pure black with longer, shaggy fur, but had the normal brown eyes, pointed ears, and sharp wit.

As I watched, Radar froze, and then sat before giving a loud woof.

Trance, who was slightly in front of Radar, halted immediately, moving his eyes from the front of him towards the car that he'd just passed.

Then he pulled a white towel off his belt loop that I hadn't noticed before, and shook it in front of Radar, who immediately latched on to it and started tugging.

"Good boy," Trance encouraged, tugging on the white torn cloth until he said a word in another language, causing Radar to stop tugging and drop back down on his hindquarters.

"What the hell?" I whispered to Kettle as I watched Trance circle the vehicle.

He reached for the radio at his shoulder and said something, but with all the commotion from the crowd, the police sirens that were coming into the parking lot, and the crackling of the fire now destroying my home, I couldn't make it out.

"The dog found something," Kettle explained, moving closer to Trance.

I reached out to touch Radar, as I'd done quite a few times before, but Kettle stopped me with a hand around my wrist.

"He's working, don't touch him." Kettle said, receiving a thankful nod from Trance who'd heard the command.

At my wounded look, Kettle softened. "When he's working, he needs to be focused on the task at hand, not on you. He won't do anything to you, it's just that Trance likes to keep Radar's attention on work, and he's in work mode right now."

SIX

Save a fire truck. Ride a fireman.
-Text from Adeline to Baylee

Kettle

"What'd he find?" I asked Trance, as we got closer.

Trance shrugged. "I don't know yet. I called in the car's plates to headquarters, and now we're going to wait until we get permission, although, technically, we don't need it since Radar found something."

Two younger boys standing off to the side by the office were eyeing their group warily, drawing my gaze.

"Those boys over there are looking quite alarmed that you're standing by this car." I observed.

The car was a Volkswagen hatchback with spinning rims that probably cost a mint to buy.

Trance turned fully and faced the boys who, of course, took off running as soon as Trance saw them.

"Retrieve!" Trance barked as he ran after the boys.

Radar, who'd been sitting alertly on the ground at the back of the car, reacted instantly, taking off after the two young teens.

I stayed where I was. If I was needed, I'd be called, but for now, I only watched.

"Holy shit," Adeline breathed as she watched Radar take down the first teen, followed closely by the second.

Radar was a fast dog.

He could run twice the speed of a person, without being winded.

"Yeah," I agreed as Trance caught up to the two teens and Radar, calling the dog off instantly.

Trance cuffed them, leaving them on their stomachs.

Radar sat and watched as Trance was once again on the radio.

Two hours later found Trance, Sebastian, Silas and me standing outside my place discussing today's events.

"What the fuck happened?" Silas asked as I watched Adeline go into my apartment and shut the door.

My eyes went from the door, to the charred remains of Adeline's apartment.

"Meth lab. The two I arrested were cooking it when I showed up. From what I can figure out, I interrupted them in the process. From what they told me, they bailed out the back deciding it would be best to torch the place instead of leaving evidence behind. I'd just walked back to the cruiser to call it in when it exploded." Trance explained.

I nodded. "Matches up to what Adeline had to say earlier. She said she went down there and knocked on the door because she kept smelling chemicals coming up from her bathroom. When the smells got worse, after she confronted them, she called the police."

Trance looked down at his boots as if contemplating whether to say anything, but he finally worked through whatever it was and spoke, making me feel a rage I'd never experienced before course through me

"Those two boys weren't the only ones there. The other boy was the grandkid to the old guy that died in the apartment. That kid's nowhere to be seen. Either he was in there when they blew it up, or was somewhere else while the other two kids waited for a chance to get to their car. Anyway, the two kids were spouting their mouths off about 'some bitch paying,' while I was questioning them. How she'd 'get her due.' I'd guess that was Adeline."

"Fuck," Sebastian growled.

"Do we know whether they were selling it all this time from the apartment, or whether this is a new thing?" Silas asked Trance.

Trance shook his head. "I don't know. They clammed up about the time the other cops got there and I had to call Radar off. They weren't very helpful after that."

"It was new. I've never seen that car before today. It's right behind where Adeline normally parks, and I've kept an eye open after the old guy died. Plus, Adeline's never noticed the smell before today. She would've said something, or done something like she did today."

My mind was whirling. Was Adeline in danger?

"Alright, well I need to get Radar back home and fed. My head is fucking pounding and I have to be at the school tomorrow with Radar for a drug search." Trance said as he walked to his police issued SUV and let Radar inside.

He started the vehicle before coming back and offering a bag. "I called Viddy earlier and had a patrolman stop by her house for these. You might want to have Adeline call her so she doesn't do anything stupid like come over here at midnight."

I took the bag and gripped Trance's forearm before giving him a half hug and a smack on the back. "Thanks man. I'll catch you tomorrow."

After Trance left, Sebastian and Silas waited until the tail lights of Trance's vehicle disappeared before offering their own goodbyes.

"Alright, man. We're gonna head out. Let us know if you need anything. We'll have church tomorrow evening and discuss this problem. We'll figure this out." Silas said solemnly.

I nodded in thanks. "See y'all tomorrow."

The sound of their engines followed me into my house as I closed the door quietly.

After a quick search of the living room and kitchen, I was all the way to the hallway before I realized I heard the shower running. That meant that Adeline was naked, and slippery, and wet. There was just one single flimsy door between us.

Forgetting all about the bag of her clothes in my hand, I all but ran into my bathroom and slammed the door closed.

I was yanking at my clothes the next moment all the while trying to convince myself that bombarding her in the shower, after she nearly died in an explosion, probably wouldn't work out so great for me.

Instead, I stepped into a shower that was just this side of too hot, and scrubbed myself vigorously with my washrag, scraping hard to get the ingrained smoke smell out of my skin.

Scrubbing my skin after a fire was nothing new to me, but having someone in the shower just a few dozen feet away, *was*. Running those silky hands all over her body led me to scrubbing harder than normal to get my mind out of the other shower and into my own.

I felt it when the water pressure changed signaling the end of Adeline's shower, and I sent a thankful prayer up to the heavens that I didn't have to think about the water droplets running down her chest, curving around her nipples, down to her navel, and disappearing between her legs.

Somehow, I found myself stroking my dick without conscious thought, and only became aware of it when there was a soft, hesitant knock on my door.

So soft that I wasn't sure I actually heard it.

Moving the curtain to the side, I kept my hand on my dick, moving it slowly and kept my eyes on the door while listening intently.

The knock came again.

"Need somethin'?" I called out.

I hadn't expected her to open the door. Hadn't expected her to walk right in. In a towel no less.

Even so, she did, and caught a load of my hand stroking my raging erection.

I didn't know who was more surprised, her or me, but I kept slowly stroking, and she kept staring.

"I...I needed some clothes." She stuttered.

I let my dick go and pointed to the bag I'd brought into the bathroom with me.

She reluctantly pulled her eyes away from my cock, and looked over to find the bag that was sitting on the ground beside the hamper behind the door.

Which meant she had to come in further, close the door, and bend over.

Which she did.

Forgetting that she was wearing a towel the size of a dishrag, meant when she bent down to retrieve the bag, I got a good look at her pretty pussy.

Pretty, bare pussy.

And I was lost.

Fuck it. I never claimed to be a good man anyway.

In a bound and a leap, I was out of the shower pressing Adeline up against the wall with my big, wet body.

She squealed in surprise, but didn't fight one bit when I plastered her body up against the wall with my own, and plucked at her now exposed nipples.

"Kettle," she breathed. "We shouldn't be doing this right here. I want to see you the first time."

Not, we shouldn't be doing this at all, but we shouldn't be doing this here.

"How about the bed?" I rasped, rubbing my stubbled jaw down her shoulder and back up again.

Then I worked my cock over the crack of her ass, rubbing gently as my fingers started to roam.

"That's perfect," she growled. "Just do it now. I'm dying."

Wasting no time, I gathered her up, carrying her with her back against my chest, out of the bathroom and onto my bedroom.

Unceremoniously, I tossed her onto the bed and watched her bounce twice before I followed her.

The position she happened to be in was on her back, which worked out since she wanted to see. But I would've started on the back first if that was how she landed.

"Jesus, you've got the greatest nipples I've ever seen." I groaned, before I pulled one turgid nub into my mouth and sucked. Hard.

Her body arched off the bed, leaning forward as if to feed me more, or to follow my mouth as I leaned back some, allowing the nipple to slip free of my mouth with a soft, wet pop.

She cried out at the loss of sensation, but I wasn't done.

I quickly seized the other, sucking voraciously until she was moaning for more.

After a few more languid sucks, I released her nipple with another pop, and looked at my handy work.

Her nipples, already darker in color than most I'd seen, were now flushed a darker shade due to the blood rushing to the surface, and the tips that had been pebbled before were now hard enough to be painful.

"Jesus, you are so fucking hot. I can't wait to feel you around my cock." I groaned as I descended her body, letting my tongue out to play at her belly button, and then moved down further to her bare pussy, with not a single hair in sight.

"I think I might be jealous of whoever does this for you," I observed, as I ran my tongue languidly down the crease of her outer lips.

"Me," she breathed out shakily. "It's me who does it."

"So how do you reach all the way back here?" I asked reaching my tongue back as far as I could, just barely brushing past her perineum and into the forbidden area.

She didn't flinch from the intrusion, only shivered. "Mirror."

Her entrance was wet, and when I finally parted her outer lips to my hungry eyes, I couldn't resist sinking my stiffened tongue into her weeping entrance.

The flavor that met my tongue wasn't like anything I'd ever tasted before.

Sure, I'd given plenty of attention to women's pussies over time, but none of them had tasted sweet like this. So creamy. Like honey on my tongue.

"Oh, God," she groaned. "You haven't even touched my-"

I leaned forward so my face was buried. The tip of my nose hit her clit while I fucked her with my tongue, alternating the speed with slow short thrusts at first, and then burying my tongue as far as it could go, making her detonate.

If my hair weren't so short, her desperate fingers would've

latched on and ripped it out by the roots. Instead, she just grabbed onto my ears, and pulled me closer until I couldn't breathe without inhaling her.

Not that I'd have it any other way.

Death by Adeline's pussy sounded nice.

Once her orgasm was over, she collapsed on the bed, arms and legs going limp allowing me to stand up fully and head back to the bathroom for a condom.

My thick dick bobbed with each languid movement, and she watched the entire show with hooded, lazy eyes, licking her lips as if what she saw made her want more.

Her eyes lowered down to the foiled wrapper in my hands, and then back up to my face.

"What's that?" She asked breathily.

My eyes tipped down to the condom and back up again.

"Condom," I said ripping into the foil. "I'm allergic to latex though, which is why I have to buy the ones in the shiny package."

"Oh," she said. "I thought it meant that your penis was so ginormous that you had to buy the king sized packaging."

I didn't tell her that they were the large size, finding that it freaked women out at first when presented with my dick.

When I'd lost my virginity in high school, I hadn't been aware it was even big until the girl I'd tried to have sex with left crying because I'd 'ripped her a new one,' according to her, making my dick size a hard subject to broach.

I was 6'4 though; it was to be expected.

Rolling the condom with little effort, I brought Adeline's hips to the side of the bed, allowing her legs to hang over both of my arms as I pressed my hard cock up against her entrance.

"You ready?" I asked, pressing in slightly.

She bit her lip and moaned, tilting her hips up in answer, taking more of me than I'd intended to give just yet.

"Yes," she growled, wiggling her hips as she tried to get more. "Now, fuck me already. I won't break."

I stayed her hips with my hands, and started pressing forward before withdrawing.

She hissed when she felt me withdraw, but I didn't want to hurt her.

Working myself in slowly, and withdrawing to smooth the way, I sank inside of her, balls deep, and stilled, evaluating her eyes and body language to make sure I wasn't hurting her in any way.

When all I read in her body was need, I withdrew all the way, until the tip of my condom-covered dick kissed the rim of her entrance, and drove in hard.

Her tits bounced with my first thrust, drawing my attention from her face, and I leaned down to capture one stiff tip into my mouth and sucking with each thrust of my hips.

Her body arched off the bed; the new position allowed me to go deeper than I had been only moments before.

"God, I knew you'd feel good around me. Your hot pussy feels so right," I ground through my teeth, pumping hard.

With each subsequent thrust, my balls slapped against her ass, and her tits bounced.

One breast was shining from my earlier attention, so I bent down and gave the other one the same consideration.

Adeline's sharp nails dug into the side of my neck, causing me to growl and pull roughly away from her nipple.

"I'm so close," she whimpered.

Her face was the perfect picture of pleasure as I ramped up my thrusts, only withdrawing part way before drilling myself forward, burying my dick so deep that it pressed against the entrance to her womb.

She cried out louder and louder with each thrust until it became one long scream as she came hard, clamping down like a fist on my cock.

"Oh, fuck!" I roared as the orgasm that was just playing at the base of my dick shot forward, propelling me into a new reality where I saw stars. "Jesus," I said, grinding my dick into her as the walls of her pussy contracted and released around me, coaxing my orgasm into new and untried lengths.

Long minutes, or maybe only seconds, later, I peeled my eyes open to find myself collapsed on top of Adeline.

Her legs dangled off the side of the bed near mine; my head was resting on the comforter just to the side of her own.

"I think you killed me with pleasure," she wheezed.

I propped myself up on my elbows before looking into her eyes and responding. "That's okay, I think you might have killed me too. Those pussy walls of yours nearly clamped my dick off."

She grimaced. "Pussy is such a naughty word."

I laughed and disengaged my softening cock from her body before walking to the bathroom and disposing of the condom.

When I got back, she was still in the same position I'd left her in, and I laughed. "You weren't joking about that killing you thing, were you? Do you need a little help?"

"I need one of those life alert buttons. Do you think they get a lot of calls from people that have had sex and can't get up?"

I laughed. "Actually, I haven't had one of those yet. It'll have to be put on my EMS bucket list."

"Glad I could be of service," she said tiredly.

I moved Adeline until her head was resting on a pillow, and rolled her upwards until I could yank the comforter out from under her.

Once she was where I desired her to be, I set the alarm on my phone to six a.m. and settled my tired body in the bed beside her.

"I'm beat," I said as I gathered her limp body up and curled my own around hers.

"Mmmm," she agreed.

Or at least I thought she agreed.

"Night, Addy." I said, kissing her on the neck behind her ear.

"Night, Tiago."

I was going to regret her knowing my real name. I just knew it.

SEVEN

That moment when your woman asks you if her butt looks big.
-Kettle explaining one of his worst fears.

Kettle

I watched from the doorway as Adeline fell backwards on the bed, shimmied her hips, thrust upwards, jumped up and down, and finally got the pants she was trying to pull up over her hips.

Then she stood, squatted low to the ground while holding on to the waist of the jeans and bent forward, before she gathered a deep breath, sucked in, and then buttoned the jeans.

"That thing's not going to pop off and nail someone in the eye, is it?" I asked dryly.

Adeline collapsed backward on the bed, panting slightly before answering. "It would serve that bitch right. I can't believe she gave me these jeans. I haven't fit into these since I graduated from college. We used to fight over them constantly."

She stood and walked carefully towards me before collapsing into my arms.

I caught her easily enough, supporting her weight with my

arms as I walked her backward to the bed and let us both fall.

She bounced with me, landing in a heap with the corner of the comforter covering her face.

She didn't remove it, and I waited for a good ten seconds as I ground my hips into hers before realizing that she didn't plan on moving it.

Sighing, I reached up and flipped the blanket off her face to find a smile on her lips with her eyes closed.

"I'm not into paper-bagging my women." I quipped.

"Paper bagging?" She asked, looping her arms around my neck.

"Yeah, covering their faces as I fuck them." I teased.

She scowled, leaned forward, and bit me on the neck.

Her pointy little teeth sank slightly in without breaking the skin, causing me to jerk in reaction.

"Hey," I said, tickling her.

She started laughing. "Uncle! Uncle! Stop!" She squealed.

I stopped reluctantly and started to move off her when she wrapped her legs around my hips, causing me to still. "Yes?"

"I need to make a stop somewhere before you take me to school." She said, running her fingers along my bearded jaw.

I raised my arm and glanced at the watch on my wrist before looking back at her. "You don't have time to stop anywhere and get there before eight."

She shrugged. "I'm always late. They wouldn't know what to do with me if I wasn't late."

I laughed and stood up, taking her with me.

"Get your shoes on," I said, enforcing the demand with a quick slap to her ass.

She dropped her legs from around my waist and laughed before turning and heading to the bathroom.

Her ass looked great in the jeans, which was no surprise since they were so tight she had to wiggle and squirm to get into them. I just hoped she didn't rip them in the middle of class or something. I couldn't even make out a panty line.

"Keep your pants on."

"If you're lucky!" I yelled as I made my way out to my living room.

I would be taking Adeline to school today, due to her rental car being damaged in the fire. Or, at least, that was what she thought. In reality, I wanted to keep an eye on her, otherwise I'd have let her use my truck.

Sure, the rental had seen a bit of damage, but not enough to make it unusable. She didn't need to know that, however. I'd had it towed by Dixie last night, so she wouldn't even see it to know that I'd lied.

Although 'lied' was such a harsh word. I liked 'omitting the truth' better.

Once I dropped her off, I'd be stopping by her mechanic and having a word, because two months was just an insane amount of time to have someone's car, warranty job or not.

It was also something I'd been meaning to do for going on two weeks, but hadn't found the time to accomplish it yet.

"You're going to need a coat today! It's colder than hell!" I yelled to her.

"Do you have a sweatshirt I can borrow?" Adeline yelled back from my bedroom.

I laughed as I flicked on the coffee pot and started it before going back into the bedroom.

"Why is it I always find you on your knees?" I asked when I found her down on her knees looking under the bed. She wiggled her ass, taunting me. "How hard do you think it would be to get those pants back on?"

"Too long. I'd be really late for work. Ewwww!" She yelled as she backed out from under the bed, flicking a pair of black lace panties at me.

"All I wanted was my socks!" She yelled shrilly giving me a nasty glare.

I shrugged. "I never promised to be a princess when you met me. But I also haven't slept with another person in well over two months now. Although, I haven't cleaned out from under my bed since I moved in."

Her face lost a little bit of its disdain, and then it soon filled again with horror. "Please tell me you've at least washed the sheets since then." She pleaded.

I thought back to the last time the sheets had been washed, taking a few moments too long in coming up with the answer. Which led to Adeline fake gagging, dropping down on the floor to her knees, and then further to her back where she proceeded to pretend to convulse.

I watched her antics with a smile on my face, and let it go on for a good three minutes before she finally tired herself out.

Panting, she said, "I'm gonna need another shower."

I eyed her. "Yeah, you probably will. There's sweat on your forehead. You probably worked up a good sweat everywhere else, too."

"That's okay, I used your deodorant. I probably smell all sexy like you always do. I'm more talking about the sex cooties I caught from your sheets."

I rolled my eyes, leaned down, captured her waist, and hoisted her onto my shoulder.

Then I leaned down, grasped her shoes, stopped by my own dresser for a pair of socks, walked into the living room, and then tossed her down on the couch where I proceeded to pull my socks up past her knees, where I started putting her tennis shoes on.

"Wow, I don't think I've ever had this happen to me before." Adeline giggled.

"I can see how you're late every morning with the way you jack around. We'd have been there by now two times over if you hadn't seized." I quipped.

The un-socked foot slithered up my leg, and came to a rest between the juncture of my thighs.

The toes of her foot scrunched and released, massaging my balls, and making me really contemplate the daily activities I had planned.

"I can't be too late. I have a teacher conference with the kid who hit me, and his parents." She said, moving her foot up and down my growing shaft.

My eyes went from her shoes to her face and tilted to the side in question.

She shrugged. "Apparently, they didn't like the fact that he was suspended for two weeks. Personally, I think that was pretty fair on my part since I was the one who got punched, but who am I to say anything?" She asked as she dropped her foot and shoved it into the shoe without even untying the strings.

I glared at her. "If you could've done that, why'd you let me tie the first one?"

She smiled and stood, which put her crotch perilously close to my face.

My hands went from my knees to her knees, and then traveled up her legs to come to a stop where her ass met her thighs, and I squeezed.

Then I stood, sliding up until our bodies were touching from chest to thigh.

She looked up at me, smiled, and then patted my chest before she went to the kitchen and drank my cup of coffee.

"Hey!" I said indignantly.

She shrugged. "You snooze you lose."

Thirty minutes later, I pulled up to the front of the school, and dropped my feet to the ground as I waited for Adeline to dismount from behind me.

"Thanks for the ride!" She yelled over the sound of the engine.

Before she could get too far, I yanked her hand and pulled her down low so I could plant a long, wet kiss on her mouth, delving my tongue only slightly in before I let her go and rumbled out of the parking lot.

Then I set out to Reed's Auto Body to ask about a car.

• • •

"What's this I hear about you knocking Reed's head against the glass window of his shop?" Silas asked.

I ground my teeth, annoyed that I'd let that little fucker get to me.

I'd never intended to do anything but inquire about Adeline's car, but when I'd walked in and found her car in the very corner of the shop covered in dust and in pristine condition, I'd gotten a little pissed.

"Reed had Adeline's car fixed for nearly a month now and hadn't given it back to her because of some miscommunication between Reed, Adeline and Adeline's insurance agency. He'd gotten a mechanic's lien on the fucking car because the insurance was refusing to pay any added cost. Instead of taking it up with Adeline, he waited the required thirty days it took for him to get the mechanic's lien, and now he owns her car. I was able to get the title back... with a little persuasion."

I was still pissed about it. Reed was a little weasel dick of epic proportions, and today I'd gotten very close to beating the shit out of a man nearly half my size in front of, at least, four other people.

Luckily, Trance was the one to show up since he was closest to the call, and refused to take Reed's statement.

"What?" Silas barked in astonishment. "You've got to be shitting me!"

I shook my head, pelting back the last swig of my beer before I slammed it down on the counter.

"You're only staying for one beer?" Loki questioned, as I made my way to the door.

I nodded. "Yeah, I just had to come in here and drop some paperwork off in the safe. Adeline gets off in," I said glancing at my watch. "Fifteen minutes, and I have to take her by her sister's house to help move a couch and some chairs. Trance is meeting me there."

Loki nodded, taking a sip of his own beer before tossing the empty in the metal barrel at the end of the bar, and asked, "Need any help?"

I looked at Loki and saw that he wasn't looking so good. "Absolutely. We're going to go out to dinner later. Want to come to that, too?"

Loki only nodded. "Yeah, that would be good. Thanks."

Loki was an undercover cop for the Benton Police Department.

Right now, he was in the middle of an undercover operation that made him grow his hair out, as well as look and act like an addict. He even used sterilized needles to break his skin at certain popular body parts that most junkies used to shoot up for authenticity.

He also looked shittier than I'd ever seen him look in my ten years of knowing the man.

Silas only waved as he went about working on his laptop, which he'd been doing for the entire time I'd been there, and would probably continue to do for the rest of the night.

I never asked what he did for a living, but I assumed it had something to do with the US Government. Maybe one of the ABC agencies.

Not that it mattered what he did.

Silas was a good man, and I'd follow him into the pits of hell.

"Where's she live?" Loki asked as he mounted his bike.

I noticed that he no longer wore a helmet like he'd done before this job, and had to wonder why he'd made such a drastic change in something that was so ingrained that it became second nature; but I wasn't sure I wanted to pry right now.

"The Eastland's. She has a town house in the first complex." I explained as I moved to my own bike.

The helmet that I normally wore slid on my head, and I got a faint whiff of Adeline, making me sad that I wouldn't be smelling that anymore. I'd purchased Adeline her own helmet that morning.

Loki followed me to Adeline's school where we both pulled up to the red fire lane before turning our bikes off.

School had let out over an hour ago, so we were alone in the parking lot, which was why Loki said what he said next.

"After this next assignment, I'm thinking about going nomad for a while. I can't breathe here." Loki said, surprising the shit out of me.

I looked over at him sharply, taking in his appearance, the bruises on his arms, scrapes on his fists, and finally, the way his clothes were starting to get loose. They weren't fitting anywhere near how they used to.

Therefore, I said the only thing I could, knowing Loki was going to do what he wanted to do, no matter the consequences. "Do it."

His head hung, as if having the support of another brother took some hidden weight off his shoulders and made him limp with relief.

"I met someone. She hates cops." Loki admitted a few silent minutes later.

I leaned forward, resting on the gas tank and asked, "Why?"

Loki studied the brick facing on the schools outer walls and shrugged. "I should've never taken this job. I knew going into it that it'd be my last. I was tired of playing somebody else. The girl, Channing, lives next to my 'house' and looks at me as if I'm the scum of the earth. Scared shitless of me. Anyway, I have all the evidence on Varian Strong that I'm going to need and this case will be wrapped up by the weekend. I'm going to talk to Silas once it's all done and probably take off after the run this weekend; they're going to need me to stay gone until the trial. Might go visit my momma in Florida for a while."

"You love her, don't you?" Adeline's sweet voice said from in front of us.

My eyes snapped forward, surprised to see Adeline standing in front of us. She had a bag over her shoulder, and the sweatshirt I'd let her borrow was tied around her waist, allowing the tattoos on her arms to be seen clearly.

And her face looked stricken.

For my brother.

Something about her being concerned for one of my brothers, my family, made a piece of my jaded heart start to burn. I didn't know with what, yet, but I knew it was something important.

My brothers meant the world to me.

When my father kicked me out of the house, I'd joined the Army since I had no other options. I didn't have anybody I could turn to; no close friends or family that might be able to help me. Over time, though, I'd made good friends and gained a family. Consequently, it was important to me that Adeline liked my family and that my family liked Adeline.

Loki shrugged. "Doesn't matter. I'm not pursuing anything with her. She's already made up her mind about me, and I have a feeling that finding out I'm a cop might make it even worse."

"I think you'd do better giving her the benefit of the doubt. You don't know what she'd do until you ask her." Adeline said softly before handing her bag to me.

I stowed her bag and smiled when I saw her place a soothing hand on Loki's shoulder before she came to me, gave me a soft kiss on the lips, and mounted the bike behind me.

"Ready to go to your sister's?" I asked as she wrapped herself around me.

At her nod, I handed over the helmet that was resting on my lap, causing her to squeal in excitement. "Woo hoo! It even has my initials on it!"

I rolled my eyes, winked at Loki's amused expression, and started my bike.

The road to Adeline's sister's place was one of the less traveled ones, and when I got onto the grounds that the complex was located on, I was surprised.

The complex was one of the newer ones in between Benton and Shreveport, and I'd only seen it from afar.

It was new, and had live in staff to help those that needed it, but allowed the residents to have some sense of self-reliance.

Adeline had told me that this complex was booked full for nearly a year in advance by those that were blind, deaf or both.

There were a few people here that would've never been able to make it on their own otherwise.

I didn't need directions to which house was Viddy's, because I could see her lying on her couch. The couch that was outside the apartment building sitting on the front lawn of the closest condo.

I could see Adeline out of the corner of my eye shaking her head, and had to suppress the thought that I knew Adeline wouldn't appreciate.

But the facts were glaringly obvious; they were exactly alike. I could see Adeline doing the very same thing at her own place when she moved in.

We pulled up to the parking spot that was directly in front of Viddy's couch and shut the bikes off.

Viddy didn't even stir.

If I didn't know better, I would've assumed she was deaf because she never even flinched when two huge Harleys came within three feet of her face.

Adeline jumped off the bike as soon as I set the kickstand down, going from one fantasy to another in a split second.

"Oh, my God." Loki said. "I've never had twins before."

I punched Loki in the shoulder hard enough to make him fall back a few steps. Hell, the same thoughts had flashed through my own head the first time, too.

Loki laughed at my reaction, taking a step backward so he was out of punching range, just in case.

Adeline had flipped over the back of the couch to where she was smashed up between the back of the couch and Viddy. Their bodies were plastered together and, for some odd reason, my dick thought that it was just the best idea in the world to have two hot sisters on the same couch together, entwined around each other.

Three hours later, we'd moved in Viddy's couch, bookshelf,

dresser, and wrought iron bed that weighed nine hundred pounds.

Trance had shown up just in time to help move the bed from hell, thankfully, or we might not have been able to do it.

The good thing was that Viddy was on the first floor, and we didn't have to maneuver the beast up the steps. That would've been something to watch.

"Viddy, I'm going to go find some clothes. Do you still have some of my spares in your closet?" Adeline asked Viddy.

She nodded, too absorbed in her conversation with Trance to notice her all that much, and I was working with Loki to get a bookshelf anchored to the wall to notice Adeline stop by Viddy's purse and put something in there.

• • •

Twenty minutes later, I found myself eyeing the lipstick Viddy was using with surprise.

Was that shaped like a dick?

Upon closer examination I found that it was, indeed, a dick.

Viddy was rubbing a clear sheen of lipstick over her mouth with a dick shaped stick.

Trance, who'd been talking to me, looked over to see what had caught my attention and growled low in his throat when he saw what she was using.

Stomping over, he ripped the offending object out of her hand.

"Hey!" She yelled. "Give that back, Trance."

I wondered how she knew it was Trance, but that paled in comparison when Viddy raised her arm and punched Trance in the shoulder before calling him a 'bully.'

"You have a dick shaped lipstick tube and you're rubbing it all over your lips in front of us. What'd you want me to do? Let you use that in public?" Trance growled.

"A dick?" Viddy asked in surprise. Then her face changed; even behind the glasses she always wore, I could tell she was pissed. "Adeline, you bitch!"

Adeline, who'd been standing in the doorway watching the whole scene in a pair of yoga pants and a sweatshirt, started to laugh hysterically.

"That was for sending me your fat jeans." Adeline glared at her sister.

Viddy started laughing then, too, and the tension between the two was broken before it even got started. Which surprised me, because my sister was a vindictive little shit, and could hold a grudge for months.

She also fought dirty, and these two did not. It was all in good fun, and they knew how to laugh it off.

"My sister would've castrated me if I'd done that." Loki observed from his end of the bookshelf.

I looked over at the man and saw him smiling for the first time in weeks. "Yeah, mine would've, too."

"One of my brothers would've held me down while the other beat the shit out of me. Then they would've salted my wounds. Maybe even drowned me afterwards." Trance smiled wistfully.

We all turned and looked at him, even Viddy.

"Okay then," Adeline said, eyes wide. "Is there anything else you need out today, Viddy, or do you want me to get the rest of it tomorrow?"

Viddy stood there thinking for a few more moments before she snapped her fingers together. "I need Hemi's tennis balls. I go play with him in the morning, and if I don't have those, he'll get mad at me."

I glanced down at the dog in question, saw him lying in the

middle of the floor like a bump on a log, and had to laugh. "This dog will get mad at you?" I asked in surprise.

Hemi was the sweetest dog I'd ever met. He was snowy white with splotches of muddy brown interspersed throughout his coat. His eyes were the warm color of honey, and he was the softest thing I'd ever felt.

He'd worn himself out playing with Radar for the last few hours, and now both dogs were laying in a ray of sunshine that was beaming down through the window curtains.

"Well which box is it in?" Adeline asked her sister.

"A smaller box." She answered as she walked slowly to the couch and sat down carefully.

My eyes flicked to the pile of boxes lining the living room wall with trepidation. They were all the same size boxes.

"Viddy, all the goddamn boxes are the same size and you know it." Adeline growled at her sister.

Viddy smiled widely. "You're the one who packed them, Twinkie, not me. How about you tell me where they are?" She replied sarcastically.

"Motherfucker," Trance sighed. "Do y'all always fight like this?"

Adeline and Viddy both shrugged.

At their non-answer, he threw his hands in the air, and then called Radar's name.

Radar, who'd been sleeping peacefully in the sun, sprung to his feet, quivering in anticipation.

"You got anything that smells like the balls?" He asked hopefully.

Viddy thought about it for a few seconds before she stood and walked to her room.

I shook my head as we all watched her maneuver boxes, furniture, and packing supplies as if she could see the entire room.

"How does she do that?" Loki finally asked.

I turned to Adeline who shrugged. "She counts her steps. Maybe we're just lucky that she didn't have anything in her path, cause if there was, she would've tripped over it. She does that a lot, so try to keep your shit clear of her walking paths."

Viddy returned on the tail end of our conversation with an old pair of pants in her hands. "I do count. I've counted the number of steps four times today. Here, I sat on one of his balls yesterday before Addy packed them. My ass had a ball shaped wet imprint for nearly an hour. They were one of the lasts to be packed. Will this work?"

"Yep." He said holding the pants up in the air so he could see the ball imprint, and then held it down to Radar who appeared at my side. "Retrieve."

We all watched in fascination as Radar started to search in slow, methodical loops until he centered on one single pile of boxes. Then, with his large nose, he pushed the top box off the pile of boxes. Then the second before he got to the third and sat on his haunches.

"There anything breakable in them?" I asked.

"I don't know. Probably not. I don't do breakable real well." She teased.

Sure enough, the one box he didn't knock to the ground was the one that had the balls in it.

"That's still impressive; even after seeing him do it half a dozen times." Loki said with a shake of his head.

Trance smiled. "He's a smart boy, aren't you big boy?" Trance asked Radar with a scratch behind the ears.

"Well my dog has a trick, too!" Viddy exclaimed and jumped to her feet. "Give me those balls. Three of them."

This is how Trance and Viddy started trading dog tricks. Although Hemi holding three balls in his mouth was impressive, it was decided that Radar definitely trumped Hemi in the trick department, much to Viddy's disappointment.

EIGHT

My 34-year-old boyfriend still plays with fire trucks.
-Adeline to Silas

Adeline

I had a phobia.

It had to do with large bodies of water.

There was nothing I hated more than going down the road that crossed the dam and the spillway. The road itself was narrow and had to be at least a mile drop down to the water. If, for some reason, my car happened to career off the side, it'd end up as a folded hunk of metal that would sink more easily once it hit the water. With my luck, my car wouldn't be stopped by the metal barriers that were intended to keep cars safe, and I'd plummet to my death, drowning in my car at the bottom of the lake.

When I'd gotten to the lake, which happened to be Sebastian's house, I'd been okay. However, getting there was a major feat for me.

I'd met Baylee, formally, for the first time.

Baylee was Sebastian's wife.

She was also a paramedic with the Kilgore Fire Department, a town about forty-five minutes west of Shreveport. Currently, she was on maternity leave with only two more weeks until she had to return to work.

She was definitely a talker, too.

We were in the baby's room, and I was trying my hardest not to watch as Baylee was pumping. When I say pumping, I mean she had these medieval torture devices on her tits that were sucking the life out of them. Literally. They started out absolutely massive, and by the time she was done, they were little more than deflated bags that resembled normal breasts again.

Why was I looking at her boobs?

I couldn't tell you. I guess when she'd asked if I minded if she pumped, and I didn't automatically shout 'Fuck No,' she thought it was okay to whip the old fun bags out and start that shit. Yes, the majority of the time they were covered. But still.

"Why don't you work for Benton?" I asked Baylee, trying my hardest not to look at her nipples that were elongating into the slender tube.

Baylee laughed. "First of all, I can't handle spending that much time with my husband. He tends to turn into an alpha-hole when he wants me to do stuff a certain way."

My head turned slightly. "What does alpha-hole mean?"

Finally, she disengaged the torture devices from her boobs, tucked her boobs back inside the shirt she had on, and stashed the milk in the mini fridge; big cones and all.

"Follow me." She said as she walked purposefully towards the kitchen.

"Now, watch." Baylee said as she picked up the cooler that was sitting at the bottom of the porch steps and started walking.

She'd gotten maybe ten feet from the steps when Sebastian

looked up, saw what she was carrying, and yelled. "Baylee! I said I'd get it in a minute! Put it down."

Baylee ignored him and got about five more steps before Sebastian let out an audible growl, tossed the boat electronic thing he was showing Kettle, Loki, and Trance onto the boat seat, and stalked towards Baylee.

You know those red flags you wave at bulls to get their attention? That's what it was like. The cooler being the red flag.

He grabbed the offending cooler out of her hands before she'd even made it fifteen feet from the porch steps, and glared at her before going back the way he came.

When she made it back, she smiled at me. "Does that answer your question?"

"No," I laughed. "I think I need a few more examples. I'm worried I might have an alpha-hole on my hands."

Kettle hadn't let me move one single thing this afternoon. Not even a freakin' bag of clothes. He'd treated me like I was fragile. As if I couldn't handle even the small things.

"Here," Baylee said, shoving a baby bag and a car seat that had her infant daughter, Blaise, already strapped into it at me before pushing me towards the door.

Blaise, according to Baylee, was the one and only thing that could terrify Sebastian.

"Take this down there to the water. Watch what Kettle and Sebastian do. You'll see what I mean." Baylee's eyes were filled with mirth.

Cautiously, I started walking down towards the water, walking carefully down the path that was lined on both sides with rocks. Blaise was incredibly tiny in her car seat, and feelings, ones that only came out when babies were in the vicinity, started swelling in my chest. Making me *want* things.

I'd made it all the way to the dock. Which was further than I'd expected to get. I was in the process of stepping onto the uneven dock when Blaise was out of my arms, followed by the diaper bag.

I looked up into glaring eyes. One pair belonging to the doting father, and the other to Kettle.

Both looked annoyed that I'd even contemplated getting onto the dock.

"Is there anything else y'all need brought down here?" Sebastian asked in exasperation.

I shrugged and turned around without answering.

I found Baylee in the kitchen pouring milk into a bottle.

"How far onto the dock did you get?" Baylee asked without even turning around.

"Not even. I didn't even have a foot onto the dock before she was out of my arms." I told the other woman.

Baylee giggled. "Does that answer your question?"

"Other than they don't want you or me carrying things when they could do it, you mean? I think you still have to show me some more examples."

"Well, I'm sure there'll be more by the time the night's over. Your sister's still on the phone in the den. How much longer do you think she'll be?" Baylee asked as she leaned her hips against the counter.

"Done," Viddy declared as she walked into the room, her large white cane in her hand leading the way.

"Are you ready, Viddy?" I asked her.

"Yeah," Viddy sighed. "He's driving me nuts."

Viddy was currently in a relationship with a man doctor. He saw the students at the same school Viddy worked at. He's also an asshole.

I hadn't liked him from the moment I'd met him four months

ago.

Mostly because he didn't treat Viddy well, and always liked to add emphasis to the fact that Viddy couldn't see.

When we'd gone out to eat the first time, Paul had requested a table, because he wasn't sure Viddy could get into the booth without seeing. Then he told the waitress to bring out water for Viddy, because she was blind, and probably should stick with water, just in case. Then he'd gone about ordering for her because she couldn't see the menu, even though Viddy had been to that restaurant so many times that she knew what was on the menu without being asked.

He'd ended the night by requesting Viddy not wear flip-flops ever again. He didn't want her to fall and break her neck.

I was so used to Viddy's independence, that to see her treated like she was severely handicapped, really rankled my nerves.

Viddy was anything but handicapped. Sure, she couldn't drive a car, but she could get to the bus stop. She could go to the mall if she wanted.

She could make herself dinner.

Viddy's senses were even more heightened due to her lack of vision that she soared over the charts compared to everyone else when it came to hearing, smelling, and perception.

"Your boyfriend?" Baylee asked taking a hold of my sister's hand and guiding her out the door.

"There're five steps here, about six inches tall," Baylee instructed as she walked over to the porch steps.

"Thank you, and yes. My boyfriend. He didn't want me coming tonight, and he's upset." Viddy said going down the stairs effortlessly.

I hung back, grabbed the forgotten bottle on the counter, and thought about how to break it to my sister that I hated her boyfriend.

Actually, hate was too nice of a word. Detested. Disgusted. Those were better.

I'd have to break it to her gently, otherwise it would cause a rift between us, and I hated fighting with my sister.

I wouldn't know what to do without her.

Thus, I kept my trap shut. Even when she said stupid stuff like what came out of her mouth next.

"He's coming to pick me up. Maybe he can tag along next time if it's not too much trouble."

I closed my eyes, willing my opinions to stay in my mouth.

Except it didn't work.

I'd tried. I really did.

It was like a countdown in my head.

Five. Four. Three. Two. One.

Blast off.

"You've got to be fucking kidding me! We helped you fucking move today. Where was his lazy ass?" I erupted.

"He had a meeting at two. He was..." She started.

"Two?" I laughed humorlessly. "We moved your shit at five! It doesn't take that long to meet with anyone. He just didn't want to help you move. He wanted you to move in with him. To punish you, he made up some fictional fucking meeting so he didn't have to help you. Then, to add the icing to the cake, he refuses to let you hang out with your own sister. What's one freakin' night? I haven't had a night out alone with you in over two months. Doesn't that bother you even a little bit?"

The whole time I was ranting, I was following Viddy as she walked out the door and waited for the douche to pick her up in his Lexus Convertible.

He didn't disappoint, either. He drove up in a cloud of dust and gravel, coming to a stop so far away that Viddy had to walk nearly the entire span of the driveway.

A driveway she'd never been to before, and couldn't see.

But did The Douche get out?

Hell no.

He sat his ass in the car, and then honked when Viddy kept glancing back in hesitation.

Then she tripped and fell.

Well, she would have fallen.

Trance saved her like a knight on a shining Harley.

His hands went down and scooped her up before she could even hit her knees.

His strong arms went around her waist, and he cradled my sister to his chest as if she was the finest piece of spun glass that would break if he held her too hard.

Speaking of strong arms, my own pair of strong arms wrapped around my neck and pulled me against a strong, firm chest.

"Your sister's man is a major douche." Kettle observed lightly, watching as the douche in question got out of his car and stormed over to Trance, who still held Viddy against his chest.

Trance bent down until his face was pressed against the side of her ear, and he said something very softly before he released Viddy and took a step back just as Paul reached them and yanked her forward.

I hadn't been aware that I was moving until I stood in front of Paul and pushed him. "Don't yank my sister around. You damn well know her balance is shit. Treat her like she should be treated or I'll..."

Kettle's hand went over my mouth as his other arm snaked around my middle as he physically restrained me from advancing on the stupid man.

The man's face was a twisted mask of disgust as he stared at me, Kettle and Trance. My hate-filled eyes were annoyed as he hustled Viddy over to the car, not even bothering to open the door for her.

Once Paul sped out of the driveway, I whirled out of Kettle's arms and pointed an accusing finger at Trance. "You!"

Trance's eyes rose. "Me what?"

"Get her away from him. You've been charged with your duties. Now make it happen."

I hadn't missed the desire that had flared through Trance's eyes every time he saw my sister. I also hoped that Viddy pulled her head out of her ass long enough to see what was right in front of her.

"Now," I said stomping away. "Take me to this stupid place on the lake. I hope they make strong margaritas. 'Cause I'm gonna need one when I get there. If we don't die on the boat ride over."

Masculine chuckles followed in my wake.

• • •

In fact, I didn't actually die in the water. Sebastian drove slowly, and I actually enjoyed the boat ride.

I didn't see any alligators, or any Loch Ness Monsters.

After a fifteen-minute boat ride, they pulled up at the quaint little restaurant called *Cypress Hideaway Bar and Grill*. I'd never visited here in all my time of living in this area, even though it was the main attraction in the small town.

Kettle and I walked arm and arm down the dock and into the restaurant.

The décor was cute, in a rustic kind of way.

Huge painted catfish and largemouth bass dominated the walls.

Trophies. Lake records. Old tackle. One spot had a flat bottom boat hanging from the rafters.

All the tables were wooden and made out of old timber. The chairs out of wicker.

It wasn't until we were sitting down, after having ordered our drinks that I started to look around at all the patrons. That was when I saw the glaring Detective Hernandez staring at me with barely concealed hatred.

"What's wrong?" Baylee asked me.

I looked towards Baylee, finally breaking eye contact with the blatant hate Detective Hernandez was emitting before answering.

"Kettle's ex-girlfriend is trying to kill me with her eyes."

I didn't ask how Baylee knew I was in a stare down with someone who was very clearly pissed off that I was sitting next to her ex-boyfriend. Must've been the look on my face, but she knew.

I'd seen plenty of jealousy in my time as a high school teacher. Teenagers, high school girls in particular, were notorious for being petty and vindictive about boys that they liked. I'd seen the looks other girls would get when the boy they liked was hugging someone else.

"Yeah," Baylee sighed. "Kettle went out with her all of three times. But she couldn't handle the club or the bitches who like to flaunt the fact that they've fucked our men."

I wasn't stupid. I knew Kettle hadn't been a virgin when we'd gotten together. I also knew the biker lifestyle, regardless of how much my father had tried to hide it. I knew what club whores were. I also knew they were at every club, regardless.

"I haven't had the pleasure of meeting those women yet." I said dryly.

Kettle's arm tightened around my neck, and he gave me a lazy kiss on the mouth that tasted like the Foster's beer he'd been sipping on for the last twenty minutes.

"You'll get to meet those lovely ladies this weekend when you go on the Toys for Tots run with us." Kettle said, before going back to his conversation with Trance, Loki, and Sebastian about the City of Benton's benefits for fallen firefighters and police officers.

"You're going with us?" Baylee asked excitedly.

"Apparently," I laughed.

That was the first I had heard about any 'run' and I had to admit that I was pretty excited about going for a ride longer than a few minutes here and there.

I hadn't been on a long ride since my father had taken me to the ocean, one weekend, before his accident.

To say I was a little excited now would be an understatement.

I only wished my sister could experience it again with me.

"So, what do you do, Adeline?" Baylee asked as she took a huge dip of salsa onto her chip and shoved it into her mouth.

I took a dip of my own salsa before answering. "I'm a high school chemistry teacher at Benton High."

"I'll bet you're the star of all the high school boys' fantasies. It's always the quiet ones that get the most attention." Baylee teased.

Kettle's arm tightened around my neck, drawing my attention away from Baylee.

His blue eyes looked eerily bright with the neon blues and greens from the beer signs shining all around us.

"You let me know if you have any admirers. I'll come for another visit." Kettle told me before returning back to his conversation.

Baylee stood awkwardly with Blaise in her arms. "Alright, I have to go change this girl. She's got an ass like her daddy."

Sebastian snorted but didn't bother to comment.

"I'll go with you. I need to visit the lady's room as well. I've been holding my bladder for the last fifteen minutes." I said and stood.

Surprisingly enough, there wasn't a line, and I was able to get my potty break in just as Baylee was finishing with Blaise's diaper and snapping the tiny snaps on her onesie.

"She's just the cutest thing in the world," I said as I washed my hands and watched her through the mirror.

Baylee smiled. "Yeah, she looks a lot like her daddy. All that pretty hair and big feet." She said, scooping the tiny girl up to her chest. "Will you hold her while I use the bathroom?"

I accepted gratefully and settled Blaise on my shoulder. She made the cutest little sounds that started the little clock to ticking away double-time inside of me.

"He'll never give you kids, you know." A nasty voice said from the doorway.

I looked up from Blaise's cute little face to see Detective Hernandez just inside the bathroom door, glaring daggers at me.

The little voice inside my head told me to not say anything, but then she sneered at Blaise with a look of contempt. "He's fucked every woman in the county, and then some. He's never going to settle down. Even if he does stay with you, you'll never be the only woman. He cheated on me openly while we were dating. You'll always be that stupid woman who sits at home and waits for her man to come back while he's out fucking every woman at his stupid little club."

I was surprised at the intensity in the other woman's voice, and knew whatever I said now wouldn't take away the hurt that the other woman had experienced, so I kept quiet.

Baylee, however, didn't. She came out of that stall as if she'd be been ejected from a jet in a tailspin.

"You bi-witch! Do you have any idea how much your blasé attitude and general butch-ness turned Kettle off? He dated you at first because you were pretty. Then you had to go and whip out your dick to show him that yours was bigger than his. On top of that, you refused to even be around his friends and family. We're not murderers and rapists. We all work for a living, just like you. I'm sorry you couldn't handle that, but that's no reason to take it out on his new girl that he's head over heels in love with. Go take your bad attitude and suck it."

"Oh, you think he's actually going to keep it in his pants? I had it for a month, and the entire time he was fucking someone else. I've got friends, too. They wouldn't lie to me." She sneered.

"I think it's time to grow up." I said quietly. "You have a responsibility as an officer of the law to act properly in public, and cursing and snarling at me when I have a young child in my arms is not the way to go about it. Maybe, if you want to do this some other time where it's not public, we can do that. Right now, however, you need to leave."

Detective Hernandez glared at Baylee, and then me before turning and stalking out of the bathroom.

Baylee was still pissed, and she followed the woman, stomping and glaring at her back the entire way.

I followed more slowly behind the two since I had to grab the diaper bag Baylee had left behind, making sure to stay back just in case the detective decided to start something.

Kettle clocked us as soon as we'd exited the hallway that led to the bathrooms, scooting his chair back and standing.

Kettle was a big, intimidating man, and when someone like him stands up, and is pissed off on top of that, it draws attention.

The icing on the cake was that Baylee had gone to the table

and started retelling what had happened, and I had one pissed off Kettle on my hands.

In an effort to stop conversation I knew he wanted to have, I rushed forward and blocked him in with my body, plopping down so he couldn't go past me unless he crawled over me, which he wouldn't do with Blaise securely in my arms.

He narrowed his eyes at me, but sat reluctantly.

I knew what I saw in his eyes, though.

I may have won the round, but at some point in the near future, he'd be having a conversation with Detective Hernandez, and it wouldn't be ending well for her.

NINE

Like I need a Christian Grey. I have a biker that wears bunker
gear.
-Adeline's text to Baylee

Kettle

"Oh, my God. I can't feel my legs." Adeline groaned as she fell back onto the bed.

I laughed at her and started stripping out of my dirty clothes.

No matter how long you rode, you always had to deal with the fallout of not having a windshield, and that was bugs. I hated bugs. They covered my riding clothes.

Giggling from the bed had me look over towards Adeline. "What?" I asked.

"Did you see Sebastian's face when Baylee brought out his new helmet? I thought he was going to die of disgust." She snickered.

Louisiana law requires motorcyclists to wear helmets; yet, in the years that I'd known Sebastian, not once had I ever seen him with a helmet, until today.

He'd begrudgingly put it on, and Baylee had smiled widely at her husband before putting on her own matching helmet.

"Did he just not like the helmet? I thought it was awesome!" Adeline crowed.

The helmet she was talking about was one that had Batman ears on top.

In truth, the helmet was an ingenious invention that allowed you to see your rearview without turning completely around to look. I'd have to look into getting one in the near future. Sans Batman ears, that is.

When I had about half a grand to drop on a helmet at least.

"It was pretty awesome. It'd have to be, and Baylee knew that; otherwise he wouldn't have worn it. I'm sure it didn't hurt that he could hear Baylee's voice in his ear the whole way, either." I noted.

"He doesn't normally wear one?" Adeline asked in alarm.

That was about the same reaction all the women had when it came to a man not wearing a helmet. For some reason, when they saw us without it, every single horrible thing that could go wrong started playing through their subconscious like a movie, enlightening them on what could happen.

I'd always worn one. I'd grown up on dirt bikes, and it was second nature to put on a helmet. Just like it was second nature to snap on my seatbelt after I got into a car.

"Yeah," I nodded. "He's never worn one before. Doesn't like them, but Baylee's been on him for a long time about wearing one. He said she wouldn't ever get him in one. So you saw a miracle today when he put it on without hesitating."

"Well that makes me happy. Dad's best friend died in a motorcycle crash. I don't know if he would've survived if he'd been wearing a helmet, but he might have had a fighting chance. He was just driving to the store that was just a street down from his place. He left behind a wife and three kids who were devastated."

I had my fair share of motorcycle horror stories, too.

Ones I hated thinking about, so I changed the subject.

"What did you think of your first run?" I asked, dropping down beside her on the bed to take off my boots, and then tossing them to the corner of the room.

"I think I want to just sit right here and let the feeling come back into my lower half." She sighed, closing her eyes.

Once my socks were off, I stood and started working on my clothes.

First the belt, followed shortly by my cut, which I set nicely on the table in the corner of the room.

Then I took hold of the collar at the back of my neck and hunched my shoulders as I pulled the long sleeved t-shirt over my head.

"The feelings are definitely starting to come back into my lower half again." Adeline rasped in a husky voice.

I turned to find Adeline's eyes on me, dissecting my every move.

"Oh, yeah?" I asked, stalking to the bed.

She nodded her head, and then moved her legs, pressing them together for relief.

Reaching my hand down, I grabbed her by the ankle and yanked her down to the end of the bed, causing her to squeal in surprised excitement.

"Kettle," she gasped.

"Tiago. Call me Tiago." I demanded, as I practically shredded her pants in the process of trying to free the button, and ripped them, panties and all, down her legs, leaving her bare to my hungry gaze.

"Do you know what it does to me to have your pretty little tits and your hot little pussy smashed up against me and not able to touch you? To smell your scent for five straight hours? To have you run your tiny hand up and down my stomach and thighs? I'll tell you what. It makes me so horny for you I can't even see straight." I growled.

My voice sounded like it'd battled with gravel and lost with its abrasiveness.

I let my fingers explore Adeline's inner thigh, teasing the sensitive skin with the very tips of my fingers.

"Touch me," she pleaded.

I grinned at her, leaning down into the bed with one clenched fist and used the other to run the length of my palm up the smooth expanse of skin that lined her stomach.

"So soft," I said, leaning down and kissing her skin from the top of her pubic bone until it met the barrier of her t-shirt that was bunched up underneath her breasts.

"Off," I demanded, nudging the shirt with my nose.

She lifted up and ripped the shirt over her head, tossing it in the vicinity of the floor, leaving her in a black lace bra that cupped the perfect swells of her breasts to perfection, and left absolutely nothing to the imagination.

I could see the dark circles of the areolas, and make out the perfect nipples that were hardened to tight peaks.

When her dainty fingers went to the clasp of her bra, I stayed her hands.

"Let me play, first." I instructed her.

Then I showed her.

Using only my mouth, I trailed my lips from one creamy swell to the other. Then I repeated the process with my tongue.

Her hands went to my head, trying to show me the direction

that she wanted me to go; I took her cues and allowed her to push my face until it was centered over one pebbled tip of her nipple.

"What?" I rasped. "Do you want me to lick it through the fabric?"

I didn't wait for her to answer though.

Circling one turgid tip with the tip of my tongue, I blew on her chest to make them harden even more, before leaning down and sucking hard.

Her body, which had been laying quivering on the bed in anticipation, bowed, following my mouth as I pulled, drawing exuberantly on the tiny tip.

When she became impatient with the attention on the one nipple, she hooked her finger on the cup of her bra and pulled it away, exposing the dusty brown nipple on the other side, just waiting for the attention of my mouth.

I obliged, switching breasts as I sucked the other wanting tip into my mouth and drawing roughly on it, eliciting an excited response from Adeline.

When I felt her body urging my own insistently, I let the turgid nipple slip from my mouth and looked at her face.

She didn't wait to explain to me what she wanted though; she scampered out from underneath my large body. She slowly pushed me until I fell on my back.

I went willingly, allowing her to maneuver my pants and underwear off my legs.

My erection sprung free from the confines of my pants in a lunge and bobbed for a few seconds before settling to point at my chin.

"Jesus, I can't believe that thing fits inside me." She observed before leaning down and letting her tongue slip from her mouth to flick the tip of my nipple.

"Don't touch," she warned, as she felt the hand I'd lifted start to run along the inside of her thigh.

I ignored her warning and let my callused hand skim the inside of her thigh, stopping at the brink of touching her outer lips with the outside of my finger.

When she moved forward to run her tongue down my stomach, she'd inadvertently allowed my knuckles to brush against her smooth, wet skin, provoking a groan of torture from her.

That luscious mouth of hers found my jutting erection in the next moment, and I barely bit back a groan of torture myself, when the thigh I was resting my hand on moved as she straddled my chest.

I discovered that there was finally a draw back for me on being so tall and dating a woman that was nearly a foot shorter than I was.

I couldn't reach Adeline's beautiful pussy while she was working my dick with her mouth.

That wasn't to say I couldn't touch with my fingers though, but I found that I could torture us both if I just stilled my hands and waited for her.

My hands went up the back of her legs and came to a stop at the swell of her ass.

Both thumbs dipped inside, and parted her slippery folds, but I didn't do anything more, only watched her pussy in anticipation of things to come as she worked my dick with her mouth.

I could tell it was getting to her though, because only after a few long, tortuous minutes of her trying to swallow my dick as far as she could, she let it go abruptly, turned on my lap, and sat herself on my dick before I could get another word in edgewise.

"Oh, yes." She groaned as my length slipped inside of her, slowly but surely. "Jesus, you've got me filled."

At the husky sound of her naughty voice, my dick twitched inside of her, eliciting a small smile from her face as she started to ride me slowly.

She looked fucking beautiful.

The hair that had been in a low ponytail when we'd started the day, was even lower and large pieces of her hair had slipped free to decorate her chest and shoulders.

The bra she was wearing was still pushed down underneath one nipple to reveal one hard peak fully. However, the one still covered was not to be outdone, and was trying its hardest to slip out between the break in the lace to no avail.

With each bounce of her ass, it would cause the one tit to bounce up and down with the momentum.

My large hands spanned each hip, and the dance of her hips was erotic as hell as I urged her faster and faster.

We were both barreling towards one hell of an orgasm when there was a hard pounding on the door. Whoever it was, was insistent. And going to get their asses kicked.

Especially when Adeline's pace stuttered. Mine didn't. I started fucking up with my hips, as well as pulling down with my hands.

"Yes, yes, yes," Adeline chanted with each thrust of my hips.

Then, her head flew backwards until I could no longer see her face.

Her hair tickled my thighs, and her hot pussy started to convulse around me in waves.

It was then that I realized I was inside her bare, for the first time ever, and I was helpless to stop what happened next.

With a roar, I ripped myself free of her tight clasping heat, and came hard.

Semen spurted from the tip of my dick, splashing onto Adeline's chest, and then her lower belly as I came and came.

When the pounding in my ears finally became manageable, I let the grip on her hips go as I collapsed onto the bed.

Adeline collapsed as well, but on me instead of the bed.

They were both panting hard when she said, "I can't feel my legs."

I chuckled and was just about to reply when the pounding, which I'd somehow forgotten during my orgasm, started up again.

Groaning, I rolled to the side, moving a limp Adeline onto the bed before rolling off the other side, making my way to the bathroom for a pair of sweat pants and a towel.

Wiping off my release from my chest, I tossed the towel in the hamper, shoved my legs into a pair of sweatpants, very aware of the fact that my dick was still just as hard now as it was five minutes ago, and made my way out to my apartment door.

With one look into the peephole, my good mood vanished when I saw who was behind the door.

Wrenching it open, I glared at the disturbance and crossed my arms over my chest, not caring in the least that I was sweaty, and still sporting an erection.

"Can I help you?" I barely contained the urge to snarl. It more came out sounding like a pained hiss.

Annalise stared at me with contempt. "I need to ask you some questions about the fire."

The balls of my fists became tighter, making the knuckles on my hands crack with the effort.

"We both came in and gave statements the day of the fire. You could've called and I would've answered any additional questions you had." I said reluctantly.

Annalise tensed. "What do you mean 'we'?"

"He means," Adeline said as she wrapped one arm around my

bare back. "That we already gave the nice officers and detective in charge our statements. Why isn't he here?"

I looked down to see the woman that should still be laying with me, sated and warm in my bed, standing beside me. She was wearing a gray cotton shirt over her braless breasts.

Something inside of me, a green headed monster for sure, reared its head at the idea of anybody, even my ex, seeing the state of her chest.

I was saved by Annalise's snarl of, "I can see you're busy, I'll come back later."

It was only when I shut the door and turned to Adeline that I realized the gray shirt of mine she'd been wearing clearly showed the wet spots of my come on her belly from our earlier lovemaking.

Which made my anger evaporate just as fast as it had come.

"She's gonna be trouble," Adeline observed as I stalked towards her.

She didn't even realize she was in danger of what was to come until I was right on top of her. "You wanna know what's trouble? What's trouble is seeing you with my come on your chest, and you expecting me to have a coherent conversation." I said, right before tossing her over my shoulder and heading right back to the bedroom.

• • •

"The landlord called and told me I could take the apartment directly across from yours if I was interested in a four-bedroom." Adeline told me as we cooked dinner side by side that night.

I was stirring the vegetables for their stir-fry and broached the subject I'd been meaning to bring up for the past three days.

"If you don't have a problem living with me, I want you here. I know it's really soon, but it makes me happy having you around. Plus, my house will be ready soon, and if you really want, you can keep this apartment when I move back into my house." I said hesitantly.

"You have a house?" She asked sharply.

I nodded. "I do. It's on the lake, catty cornered to Sebastian's. Our property lines butt up against each other, but where his is new and all, mine is old. I had to have the floors and plumbing replaced before I could move in, and that's scheduled to take another two months."

Adeline finished cutting the chicken into pieces and turned to regard me. "I'm told I'm not the easiest person to live with."

I laughed. "Who told you that? Your dad or your sister?"

"Both," she laughed.

"It can't be too bad."

"You're gonna eat those words." She laughed.

TEN

A firefighter lives here with the hottest flame of his life.
-To Kettle from Adeline

Kettle

I didn't have to eat my words. I did have some adjusting to make, both good and bad. Overall, though, I quite enjoyed having Adeline around all the time. Much more than I'd expected to, anyway.

I hadn't realized how much of a neat freak I was until I went into my bathroom one morning, a month later, to find Adeline's bras, in every shape, color, and texture imaginable, hanging off every available surface in the bathroom.

I had to move three out of the shower itself, before I could get in to rinse myself. With cold water, seeing as Adeline had finished her shower about five minutes before, and could spend no less than an hour in the shower and still want more time.

Although, everything paled in comparison to when I woke up last night to Adeline's snake slithering up the inside of my mother fucking leg.

At first, my sleep-fogged brain had thought it was Adeline's hand, but then the temperature of whatever was crawling up my crotch and then further to my stomach, finally registered. I promptly freaked the fuck out.

I really wasn't a fan of her snake.

The next day I'd immediately gone out and purchased a cage with a lock, because there was no way that was ever going to happen again.

Then there were the benefits of having Adeline here.

Like waking up in the middle of the night to Adeline curled around my body with her head tucked into the crease of my arm, or the space where my back met the mattress.

Then there was how my clothes were *always* washed and folded before I needed them. She made sure that my uniforms were hanging up and ironed as well, which was beyond worth the cost of bras hanging from my shower rod right there.

"Hey," Adeline said as I stepped out onto the bathmat after my shower.

I looked up as I bent over to dry my legs with the towel, and had to smile at the glazed look that overcame her face.

She didn't say another word until I stood from drying my back and wrapped the towel around my hips, covering my junk.

"I'm ready to go." She said finally.

A grin tilted up one corner of my mouth as I started walking towards her.

She stayed where she was, leaning on the doorway, and raised up on her toes to get a kiss before I passed her to get dressed in my uniform.

"Are you ready to let me drive myself?" She asked in exasperation.

She'd gotten her car back from Reed the week after the fire, but it'd been sitting ever since. I'd told her about the threat from the two boys that were involved in the fire, but she didn't see the big deal. She'd said that she got threats like that from the kids at the high school all day long, and if she took the threats seriously, she wouldn't be able to live her life.

The high school boys at her school were small potatoes compared to the drug makers who'd gotten out on technicalities less than a week after they'd been jailed.

Although they hadn't heard from the two boys, or the one that had lived there, since the day of the fire that had burned down both apartments, I had a niggling thought in the back of my head that was warning me not to relax.

"I know, Adeline. I just have this," I said shrugging into my shirt. "Feeling that I shouldn't let you drive to work by yourself. Then again, if you really want to, I'll follow you, but that's the only way you're getting out of riding with me."

The boys left Adeline alone while she was at school, but they always had someone there to follow her home, or to the grocery store if needed. If she wanted to go somewhere, they always had a prospect ready and willing to follow her.

And as much as she hated to have a tail, it made me worry about her less, which, in turn, made Adeline happy.

"How long is this going to go on?"

My fingers moved deftly on the buttons of my shirt, and then I started shoving the shirt down into the pants before buttoning and doing up the belt.

"I don't know."

I really didn't. I was just worried about her, especially after what I'd learned last night from Silas.

I stewed on the call from Silas all the way to Adeline's school, agonized over what bad shit Silas was going to throw at me next.

Silas had called late last night after she'd gone to bed and told me he'd found out some things that he needed to discuss this morning before I went to work.

So, after I drop Adeline off at work, I was running to the club-house before my shift started to speak with Silas and Sebastian.

I knew I wasn't going to like it.

Then Adeline did something so cute, that it knocked me off my game for a few short moments, allowing me to smile despite the impending doom.

"Oh! Hey, hold on one second." She said as soon as she got off the bike.

"Adeline, we're both really late." I groaned but stayed where I was.

Out of all things I'd expected her to do, dropping down on her haunches, ass to the back of her legs, and putting on eyeliner wasn't one of them. Using the chrome plated overlay of the bike's air filter, she deftly used the long stick and rimmed the edges of her eyes with black. Followed shortly by mascara on her lashes.

Then, she stood up, leaned in to give me a kiss, and walked quickly to the school building, smiling widely over her shoulder at me from the doorway before she disappeared inside with a tide of high school kids.

I should've known, though, that life was never nice to me, and never had been.

Good things had a way of going bad when it came to me, and I was about to be shown how.

• • •

"So let me get this straight," I said while leaning forward. "Those two-bit criminals were bailed out by Adeline's brother?"

Trance and Silas nodded in confirmation.

"Then what?" I asked.

"From what I can tell, they all left the station together and Mr. Sheffield drove them in a shiny new Hummer to a park where they had some sort of meeting. After that was over, the boys left with about twenty grand lining their pockets and took up a new residence in the old Umber House on the outskirts of Benton." Silas said.

"Okay," I said hesitantly. "What the hell is going on with the brother? Just a few months ago, he'd broken into Adeline's apartment and then went to steal from Viddy. How'd he go from zero to hero so fast? What'd he do?"

Trance shrugged. "The brother, as far as we can guess, is the middle man. He finds the suppliers, gets them what they need, makes sure they get their shipment done in time, and then carries the cargo to the buyer."

"Fuck," I sighed and rubbed my face. "I don't fucking understand."

Trance stood and passed over a file, which I took warily out of his hand.

"A one Jefferson Samuel Sheffield, 27, was penniless up until about three and a half months ago. The day after you had me report the break in of Adeline's apartment, a cool fifty grand was deposited into his account." Trance explained.

"What about Adeline...where does she fit into this?" I finally worked up the nerve to ask.

Silas was shaking his head before I'd even finished the question. "We don't know. Best case scenario is that this is all just a coincidence. Worst case, the brother used her as leverage to get what he wanted. We won't know until we knock some heads together and shake it out of someone. If I had to guess, though, she's in danger up to her pretty little eyeballs and doesn't even know it."

Before, Adeline just had three young kids pissed off that she'd called cops. Now I had no idea who was after her, and that was part of the problem.

And I had no clue what the hell to do.

Sebastian's eyes were hard, totally in congruence with my own state.

My hands found their way into my hair, and I grimaced. "Jesus Christ, I'm lucky nothing's happened to her yet."

Silas nodded. "She's going to need a lot more protection than what she has right now. You and I need to go visit the brother. Then the buyer so we can throw our weight around a bit. Let them know what they're getting into if they go after her. It'd also be better if they know she's an old lady of one of our men. The Dixie Wardens are four states strong. Right now, her being free of your patch just shows that she must not mean that much to you if you're not willing to make her yours. With our colors protecting her, they'll know we won't take shit without retaliation."

I'd already gotten that ball rolling over a month ago with Minnie.

Minnie was the wife of our secretary, Porter. Minnie had done nearly every cut and sewn every patch that covered member's backs; mine included.

When I'd gone to Minnie and explained what I wanted, I knew it was going to be different, but she was extremely excited to get started. I'd never thought it would take as long as it had, but I knew she would make it perfectly, and I wouldn't be disappointed.

"Minnie's been on top of that for a month now. She's been doing it in her spare time, and it's...different. So it's taking her longer than she'd originally intended."

"Different?" Sebastian asked from his position at the other end of the table.

"She's a teacher. She can't really be seen wearing our colors like all the other old ladies wear them. I was worried they'd fire her, so I had Minnie do something a tad unorthodox. She sure as hell thought it was awesome though, so I don't doubt that it was a good decision. She can wear it easily while she's at school without drawing too much attention."

"So does that mean you're asking her to be your old lady soon?" Silas asked after a long pause.

I nodded in confirmation.

"Good," Silas nodded. "Now, let's plan for tomorrow at eight. Meet here, and we'll drive over to Gustavo Amadeus's house together after we visit the brother."

So I had a name.

Gustavo Amadeus.

I was sure it wouldn't be a pleasure to make his acquaintance.

• • •

"Ma'am," I said through clenched teeth. "We need you to back off. This is not helping, and your daughter might die if you don't give us some room!"

I hadn't meant to yell, but the woman's daughter wasn't breathing, and I couldn't do my job if the woman didn't back the fuck off and let me work.

Sebastian was giving an infant mouth to mouth, while I worked on another child around the age of three.

Both of whom had been thrown from the car because this stupid woman ran a stop light and plowed into the car carrying them.

There had been two vehicles involved.

A sedan carrying two passengers; a woman and her teenage

daughter, had run a red light and plowed into another car. The other car had been driven by a young mother who'd neglected to strap her children into proper car seat restraints.

They'd arrived on scene to find two cars in the middle of the intersection with a crowd gathered around the victims.

Then this woman, the woman who smelled of alcohol at eleven in the morning, wanted them to work on her daughter first, when the daughter only had a laceration above her right eye due to some flying debris in the car.

Probably a fucking liquor bottle.

The officers on scene were busy trying to control the traffic, since it was a major intersection, and didn't notice the woman currently harassing me to 'fix her baby.'

"But that baby is dead. No 'mount of work gonna be done for her!" The woman yelled.

The young mother sitting on the curb by the ambulance heard, and of course had to come join the party.

"Motherfucker," I breathed. "Ma'am, you need to go take a seat on the curb over by your daughter. We have more medics enroute. Please go."

My temper was starting to fray.

"I'm not going anywhere." She said as she stomped her foot.

Although inadvertent, when she stomped her foot, she kicked a cloud of dust and debris at my face and I snapped.

Moving quickly, I took the woman by the arm and shoved her bodily away before returning to my patient. I saw her fall out of the corner of my eye, but couldn't scrounge up the urge to care.

The young girl wasn't dead, but she was severely close, and if we didn't get the bleeding stopped, she'd bleed out before I could get her to the hospital.

"Morrison!" I bellowed. "Get this woman out of here."

Morrison, a prospect with my club, obeyed immediately, running from the crime scene tape he was in the process of hanging to the woman who was still blinking stupidly at me for pushing her.

He ignored her and got to work.

"Clear!" Sebastian called from behind me. "Shocking in 3, 2, 1."

I distinctly heard the automated voice from the AED speaking, but I was focused on my own patient.

Starting an IV and some fluids, I loaded the little girl onto the backboard and carried her to the back of the ambulance.

I loaded the patient onto the gurney and was relieved when I saw Sebastian loading his own patient into the medic right behind me.

We were both working frantically to save our individual patients, and I knew they'd never do it if either of us had to drive; so, making a split-second decision, I called Tunnel Morrison over.

"Morrison, get in the seat and drive!" I bellowed.

Tunnel jumped like he'd been poked in the ass with a cattle prodder, sprinting around the ambulance, closing the doors, and then heading for the driver's seat.

"Lights and Sirens, code 1. Go!" Sebastian urged.

Morrison went, slamming his foot down on the gas a little too hard, and then taking the corner a little too quickly.

"Slow down, boy! We'll never get there if you don't get your nerves under control." I said soothingly.

"Goddammit. You're going to have to start an IO. Can't find a fucking vein anywhere. Motherfucker."

I cursed.

Sebastian couldn't legally perform an IO since he was only an intermediate. As I was the acting paramedic, I'd have to perform the procedure. On a tiny baby.

It was hard enough to get an IV on a baby that young, but with as much blood as the infant had lost, while we were on scene, it became almost impossible to accomplish.

An IO was only used on patients that didn't have any other options.

It looked like a little baby screwdriver that was used to drill through the bone and run fluids straight to the bone marrow. Although it was crude, the technique worked. Even on babies.

Stripping my gloves off and replacing them with new ones, I switched places with Sebastian awkwardly and then got to work.

Tunnel slowed his pace moderately, and Sebastian and I worked side by side running fluids, taking vitals, and staunching blood flow the entire way to the hospital.

When we arrived, we took our patients to different rooms before giving our reports to the nurses and walking back out to the medic.

"God, I hate those now." Sebastian sounded like he'd been beaten.

Babies and children were hard for anyone to work on, but when you had a child of your own, comparisons start to be made, and you end up making yourself sick at the potential of your own children being hurt like that.

My eyes flicked to my best friends' before returning to Tunnel who was practically bouncing up and down on the balls of his feet, beside the truck.

"It's never been easy to see babies, but now I'm sure it'll always be hard for you, Ian. I'm sorry." I said, genuinely sorry for my friend.

"Did they live?" Tunnel asked as soon as they were within a distance that he didn't have to yell.

Sebastian snorted. "This kid has to be as green as they come.

What the hell were you thinking?"

I was currently sponsoring Tunnel. Tunnel was his given name, too; one that Tunnel hated with every fiber of his being.

I saw something in the kid that I'd seen in myself quite a few years ago.

Tunnel, like me, had been kicked out of his parent's house when he was eighteen for dating a little Mexican girl and getting her pregnant.

Just like I had...I shut my mind down before it could go back to that dark place. That wasn't something that I wanted to think about right now, especially when I'd just ran a call on young kids.

Particularly one that dealt with a young mother that didn't have the first clue on how to take care of her kids.

What the fuck was that woman thinking not putting her kids in child restraints? Although not 100 percent effective, most of the previous call could've been prevented. All it took was one lone instant in time to change the course of those childrens' lives.

My own baby wasn't...

"Kettle!" Sebastian growled snapping my fingers in front of my face. "Where'd you go?"

"To hell." I muttered before stepping into the passenger side of the medic.

To hell indeed.

"You can drop me off at the station. They took my rig back to headquarters." Tunnel explained quickly.

Sebastian nodded, but didn't comment on the fact that the two places were right the fuck next to each other.

Looking down, I studied my clothes and grimaced. These would need to be sent to the dry cleaning service the department utilized. There was too much blood...and other stuff, to let Adeline wash them.

Speaking of Adeline, my phone started vibrating in my pocket, and I pulled it out carefully, avoiding the blood that practically coated my pants leg.

"Hello?" I answered.

"Tiago?" She coughed.

"Addy, what's wrong? Are you okay?" I asked quickly.

Sebastian's foot let up on the accelerator slightly, gauging what was going on to see what he needed to do next.

"I'm fine," she said. "I'm going home sick, though. I don't feel well at all. My head feels like it's the size of a small turbo jet, my sinuses are killing me, and my body aches."

I relaxed slightly and returned my back to the seat once more and felt Sebastian resume my pace. "Sounds like the flu. Did you get your flu shot?"

She snorted. "Yeah, right. I've had the flu every year since I started teaching and had the flu shot for half of those. What would be the point?"

"Umm," I had the resist the urge to laugh. "Possibly not having the flu right now?"

"Shut up." She sniffled. "Anyway, I need a ride home."

I looked at the rig and the state of my clothing and knew immediately I couldn't give her a ride. She'd probably have a heart attack.

"I'll have to send someone over there. Don't leave without someone from the club." I said harshly.

Much more harshly that I'd intended, but I could just see the stubborn woman calling a cab because whoever was supposed to pick her up took too long.

"Fine," she hissed and hung up.

"Fuck," I groaned.

"Trouble in paradise?" Sebastian goaded.

"Up yours." I said before calling the club to see who could pick up my woman.

Turns out there was only the president in residence; he'd have to do.

• • •

I walked in later that night to find Silas kicked back on my recliner, drinking my beer, and watching my DVR.

"Please, make yourself at home!" I said dryly as I dropped my duffel bag on the floor inside the door.

"Your woman started running a high fever on the way home, and I was worried to leave her alone. She started talking about her papa and thinking I was him." Silas shrugged and took another swallow of beer.

I started stripping out of my clothes as soon as I made it past the hallway, and was down to my boxers by the time I entered my room.

The first thing I noticed as I entered was the TV that was playing Transformers, one of Adeline's favorite movies. The second thing was Adeline clothed in only a pair of underwear that showed the swells of her ass and one of my fire department issued t-shirts.

She looked freakin' awful.

Her hair was a matted mess, pieces here and there clung to the sweat on her forehead, and her face was the color of chalk.

Walking quietly as not to wake her, I felt her forehead and winced at the temperature. 104 at least.

Walking to my dresser, I grabbed the first pair of sweats I found and stepped into them before heading back out to the living room.

"When was the last time she had any meds?" I asked Silas as I walked past him into the kitchen.

"She had a hot toddy and some Ibuprofen at seven." Silas answered.

Looking at the clock on the microwave, I realized that she still had over two hours before she could have that again; I reached for the Tylenol and shook out two pills.

Then I grabbed a glass of ice water before heading back the way I came.

Setting it down on the bedside table, I sat on the edge of the bed and smoothed Adeline's hair back as I spoke quietly to her. "Addy? Honey? You need to wake up and take these pills. You're fever's too high."

She groaned, sat up, and held her hand out for the pills.

Which she promptly dropped.

"Here," I said as I scooted her closer to me.

With my arm around her back and my hand on her tummy, I held her still as I grabbed the pills from the table. I held them up to her mouth and dropped them in before giving her a sip of water.

She grimaced and then dropped back against me in a boneless slump. "Feel like shit." She whimpered.

"Yeah," I agreed. "I'll bet you do."

"I heard you had a bad day. Baylee sent me a text message a couple of hours ago. I'm sorry." She whimpered, kissing my neck softly.

"That's okay, honey. Coming home to you makes everything better." I said softly.

"I know," she whimpered, coughed, and then settle back into my arms. "I love you."

Then she passed out, and I was as high as a fucking kite.

ELEVEN

Sometimes being a bitch is all a woman has to hold onto.
-Adeline to Viddy

Adeline

I woke at five in the morning six days later, finally able to breathe. The first thing I saw when I opened my eyes was Kettle's tattooed back.

He was curled up on his side with his arms stretched up over the top of his head, and he didn't look comfortable at all.

Smiling, I got up quietly and walked into the bathroom to get a quick shower that ended up lasting nearly half an hour.

However, it felt so good to finally be able to stand by myself that I got a little carried away.

When I got out, I dried off with my favorite towel that wrapped around me completely and turned off the light before exiting the bathroom.

Kettle was still asleep, only now he was on his stomach in the middle of the bed. It was almost as if he'd drifted over when he realized I was gone, and instead used my pillow as a substitute for my body.

Dressing quietly in sweat pants and Kettle's fire department sweatshirt, I went out to the kitchen and had my first cup of coffee in nearly a week.

My sigh of bliss echoed in the empty alcove as I grabbed a blanket and walked out to the back porch. I took a seat on the lounge chair Kettle had set up for my viewing pleasure and sighed in happiness.

Pulling up the reading app on my phone, I read for nearly an hour before I heard the house beyond me starting to stir to life.

Kettle tapped on the window as he finally made it into the kitchen, causing me to look up and smile at him. When he waved his iPod at me and made the universal running sign, I held up my thumb in acquiesce and waved as he disappeared from sight.

I saw him twenty minutes later as he ran down the street that lined the back of our building, and of course, I had to whistle at him.

Putting my thumb and pointer finger in a C shape, I placed the two fingers in my mouth and whistled lewdly at him.

Raising his fist into the air, he gave a fist pump as he turned the corner at the top of our apartment complex.

Sadly, today he was covering up that beautiful body of his since it was nearly thirty degrees out.

I stood up and made my way to the front porch when I ran smack into the chest of the man that was standing at our door getting ready to knock.

"Oh," I said rubbing my forehead. "I'm sorry. I didn't realize you were knocking. I was on the back porch. Can I help you?"

The man was older, mid-fifties or so, and in fairly good condition for his age. He was wearing a pair of black slacks with black shiny shoes, and a pale blue linen button down shirt. His hair was black with silver at the temples; the more I looked at him, the more I realized he looked a lot like someone I knew.

I couldn't quite place whom, until I saw Kettle running through the parking lot only to come to a sudden screeching halt where my old apartment used to face.

Once I had the two of them in my field of vision, I knew instantly that they were related; most likely father and son.

Kettle didn't talk about his family much at all, and when he did, it was about Shannon, his sister. I knew that Kettle and his parents had a falling out, but I didn't know about what, and knew Kettle wouldn't allow me to pry into this subject. He'd practically shut down for an hour after I'd asked about his father, and I made it a point to steer far away from that subject from then on.

Except now, I was wishing I knew what the hell to do. Did I slam the door in his face and call him an evil bastard? Did I invite me in? Did I yell and scream at him for abandoning his child?

Turns out, I didn't have to do anything, because Kettle barreled up the walk, pushed me ever so gently inside, and slammed the door in my face.

I could hear Kettle's raised voice, followed by the smoother voice of the older man, and I felt it best to just go into the bedroom in case they came inside. It was obvious to me that Kettle didn't want his father there, and more so, he didn't want me anywhere near his father. I did the only thing I could think of, and that would keep myself the hell out of earshot. I did that by going into the bedroom, closing the door, and cranking up the TV.

• • •

Kettle

"What the fuck do you want?" I snarled at my father.

My father flinched slightly at the pure venom in my voice, but I didn't feel one iota of remorse.

"I came because your wife..." My father started before I interrupted him.

"She's not my wife." I snarled. "You saw to that, didn't you?"

My wife? What a fucking joke.

I'd met my ex-wife when we were juniors in high school. She'd been the girl from the wrong side of the proverbial track, and I'd been the rich boy who got snared in her web.

She'd been looking for a payday while I thought I'd genuinely been in love.

Then I'd gotten her pregnant.

When I'd gone home to tell my parents about the baby, my father lost his mind. He kept telling me to 'take care of it' then shoved some money into my hand like it was a fix all. When I'd refused, my father kicked me out.

I wasn't experienced in the least.

Before I'd been kicked out, my mother had refused to let me work, scared to let her son go just in case something happened to me again. Which meant I had no job, no home, and I had a pregnant girlfriend to take care of on top of that.

I did the only thing I could think of that day, and that was to enlist in the army.

I'd done it without Rosalie's knowledge and paid for it.

The whole situation became a cluster-fuck after that.

Rosalie had agreed to be my wife, and we stayed with friends since neither set of parents allowed us back home. Within a months' time, I was at boot camp, and then six weeks after that, deployed to Afghanistan to help fight in the War on Terror for a year.

In that time, my fiancé gave birth to our daughter, and then found another man, who'd beaten my child to death when he found out it wasn't his. All the while, I was halfway across the world in the middle of a firefight.

When I'd gotten home on emergency leave, my father wanted to make friends like nothing had ever happened.

I'd refused, and we hadn't spoken to each other since.

"Rosalie's been calling us non-stop trying to get a hold of you. She says she has some things to say and that she really wants to talk to you. I've agreed to give you this letter by hand if she stops calling me. So here it is." My father said as he shoved a letter into my hand and left just as quickly as he came.

I stared at the piece of paper as if it was a live grenade and had to physically restrain myself from ripping it to pieces and burning them to ashes.

When I walked into the apartment, I was glad to see that Adeline wasn't there. I needed some time to process; I didn't want to take my demons out on Adeline. She didn't deserve that, but I also didn't think I could hold on to my temper much longer, which was why I did what I did next.

"It's time to go visit the brother." I said to Silas when he answered the phone.

"Meet you at the clubhouse in ten," Silas confirmed before hanging up the phone.

I picked up my cut and shrugged it on over my sweats, grabbed my keys off the hook, and left without another word.

I forgot the letter and all the shit that went with it on the counter next to my key hanger, not realizing it until much, much later in the day.

We arrived at a tiny little house, in the middle of a cookie cutter neighborhood, in Shreveport an hour later.

Silas pulled his bike up to the curb first, followed shortly by Loki, and then me.

I kicked the stand down and stood, stretching my joints out one by one before taking a step up on the sidewalk.

"Jesus, couldn't you have worn a shirt or something? It's cold as hell out." I eyed Loki.

Loki smiled. "Somebody's gotta look like the crazy one. I figure all my tattoos will help. That and my scars make me look manly."

"Silas, why'd you sponsor this joker again?" I quipped as we walked up to the front door.

"Because he can break a man's arm in five places in less than three seconds." Silas said instantly, making us both chuckle.

My eyes went from the front door to the house beside Mr. Jefferson Samuel Sheffield's to see an old lady nearly falling out of her wheel chair as she got a load of us.

"We've got company," I whispered.

"Already taken care of." Silas said in his authoritative way that only dared them to question him.

We didn't.

Silas grunted as he knocked sedately on the door, and the man that answered the door moments later was well and truly...disturbing.

He looked like a douchebag, pure and simple.

Dressed in a pair of creased jeans and a polo shirt with the collar cocked like a real winner, he had the same dark hair as his sisters' but his skin was craggy, and he twitched like he was coming down from a high.

"Can I help you guys?" Jefferson asked warily.

Good, he knew who we were. Now to tell him who belonged to us.

"Yes, you sure can." Silas said as we pushed our way through the door.

• • •

I arrived home a couple hours later to find Adeline in bed, her hands wrapped closely around her knees.

"Oh, Kettle," she whimpered brokenly as she raised a hand up to her cheek and dashed away the falling tears. "Oh, God. Kettle, I'm so sorry."

I looked over at her in confusion.

"What?" I asked.

She held up the letter for me to see, and I suddenly became furious.

"Did I tell you to read my personal letters?" I bellowed.

She'd been in the process of crawling out of bed, but abruptly sat back down on her ass hard and looked at me in surprise.

"No," she said hesitantly. "But I found it next to the keys. I was going to go buy some Christmas presents, but then I remembered you told me I couldn't leave without someone with me. So I hung the keys back up and saw that. I thought it was a letter from you, so I opened it and I just..."

I suddenly didn't care.

I didn't want her to know that ugly part of my life. Didn't want her to know my greatest shame. And she'd stolen that option from me by butting into my business.

"When I leave, I expect you to get your shit and go. I'll call Trance to come pick you up. Leave the key on the table."

Without saying another word, I left. Snatched my keys from the hook and left.

I knew I was being unfair. Completely and utterly unfair, but

I just couldn't wrap my head around that. That moment that was most likely described in that letter was the lowest point in my life. It changed the course of my life, and left me with such a bitter taste in my mouth that I could barely function for the next year. My brain went back to those dark times, and I couldn't claw my way back out.

"Sayo-fuckin'-nara."I said before starting my bike with a roar and spinning gravel in my haste to get out of there.

It didn't take long for my temper to cool down. Not even a ten-minute drive down the road, and I realized I'd fucked up. Really fucked up.

I realized my mistake and was at the apartment within an hour, but she was already gone. Realizing too late that, in my haste to leave, I'd never called Trance to make sure she was safe.

TWELVE

Don't make me mad and tell me to calm down. That's like placing
food in front of a starving man and expecting him not to eat it.
Fuck you.
-Text from Adeline to Kettle

Kettle

"Where's she at?" I asked Trance over the phone.

Trance sighed, and I knew I wasn't going to be too happy with the news.

"She ditched the phone somewhere in Alabama. Took a huge chunk of change out of her 401K in Southern Louisiana, and hasn't used her cards since." He said frustrated.

"Alright, give me a minute. I think I know someone that could help. Don't know where the fuck Silas has been for the past three days, but he sure as fuck's pissing me off." I growled before hanging up and dialing a number that Sebastian had handed me earlier.

It rang three times before a rough male's voice answered. "Hello?"

"This is Tiago Spada. I got your number from..." I started to say before the man interrupted me

"Know who you are, man. What can I help you with?" Jack said with no bullshitting.

Jack was a member of Free.

I'd met him only a few times before, due to Sebastian's sister being married to one of the men that worked at Free.

Jack and his wife, Winter, were the computer whizzes of the Free foundation, and could find anybody, anywhere, at any time; or so I'd heard. Most of the time faster than Silas' contacts could. From what I could gather, Jack and Winter were computer hackers.

Although they were the 'good guys' they still did illegal shit. But I didn't give one flying fuck at that moment; all I wanted was my woman. Now.

"I need the whereabouts of someone."

Twenty minutes later, I was printing out directions off Google Earth of Adeline's coordinates, and walking to my bike when Trance stopped me.

"If you'll give us an hour, we'll ride with you. Wouldn't mind a short ride, if you know what I mean."

I turned and eyed Trance. "Got some groveling to do, man. Not sure I want you to be witness to the shit I'm going to have to do to get her back."

Trance waved a hand in the air as if to clear it. "We'll wait outside until you got that shit squared away. With luck, we can be back tomorrow morning, at the latest.

• • •

Adeline

"How long are you going to lay around and eat like that?" Viddy asked me over the phone.

I looked down at the caramel covered popcorn in my hand and shrugged. "As long as I fucking want."

"You shouldn't curse like that on Christmas Eve-Eve. It's not very nice." Viddy said as I heard fumbling and shuffling while she moved around in the background.

Viddy was a klutz. When her other senses were focused elsewhere, she forgot to pay attention to her surroundings.

"How'd you get there?" I asked, turning my attention back to the Sons of Anarchy TV show I was watching.

I didn't know why I was watching it. It just somehow made me feel closer to Kettle. That, and maybe I was torturing myself.

I shouldn't have read the letter after realizing what it was. I knew within the first three lines that I shouldn't be reading it, but I was so horrified that I kept reading until the end of the page, not stopping to think until I'd finished it.

Paul had invited Viddy to his parents' house for Christmas Eve-Eve, though he'd refused to let me come. Not that I would've gone anyway. I was too deep in my wallowing to think of anybody but myself right then. Oh, and I was in Florida, nearly ten hours away.

"Called a cab," she murmured.

I rolled my eyes. Of course she called a cab. Paul was a world-class prick. What else did I expect? He wouldn't come pick her up. It was Christmas Eve-Eve, and Paul was busy. Why would anybody expect him to go pick up his blind girlfriend for their first Christmas with his parents?

I couldn't stop the snort of amusement. "Your boy's a real winner."

"Yeah?" Viddy asked. "Well yours is a real winner, too. Who kicks his girlfriend out of his house in the middle of the night when he knows she has nowhere else to go?"

"He was upset." I said lamely.

"Whatever," she said. "Listen, I've got to go. I'm here. Wish me luck."

"I love you, Viddy. Merry Christmas. Good luck." I said before hanging up, and then curling up on my side for a good cry.

I told myself I was crying so much because of my period. In reality, I was feeling sorry for myself.

He'd tried to call me within an hour of me leaving to apologize, and I'd sent him a reply text to fuck off. He'd then told me to calm down, and it went downhill from there.

Now I was in a hotel room in Florida, spending Christmas by myself, eating three different flavors of popcorn and watching my new favorite show.

Oh, and ignoring Kettle's calls.

I was doing that very well.

In fact, I'd left my phone charger, and had nothing left but the room phone, which had worked out well in my favor since my sister told me that he'd attempted to track my phone, but had come to a dead end somewhere in Alabama where my phone had died.

Once withdrawing three grand from my 401K, I took it and drove to Florida, paying in cash for a week's worth of groceries and a hotel room that overlooked the beach.

Lucky for me it was the holiday season and it was discounted greatly. Otherwise, I would've had to settle for the crappy place across the street that didn't have an ocean front view and no cable internet.

My room phone rang, and I picked it up with annoyance.

"What do you want? Jesus, I told you I'm fine!" I growled to my sister.

The same sister who'd called me five times in the past four hours to make sure I wasn't hanging myself from the hotel shower stall or trying weed for the first time.

"Really? Well I'm not. Let me in." Kettle growled from the other end of the line.

I slammed the phone down in the cradle and glared at it before deciding the best course of action was to take a shower and ignore him until he went the hell away.

Glancing at the lock to ensure it was properly placed, I started stripping out of the short shorts and tank top I'd bought at Wal-Mart earlier that morning on my popcorn run.

I smiled when I saw the bathroom, thinking that when I finally had enough money, I was definitely going to be buying a shower-head like this one.

After I paid back my 401K loan, and got a new apartment. And new clothes. And shoes. And food.

Damn, but I was broke. I still had student loan debt to pay off, and I really shouldn't have come to Florida. I was mad though; that's my only excuse.

Yanking my hair out of the messy bun on the top of my head, I stepped into the shower and directly under the heated spray.

The water felt divine as it flowed over my face and head, before cascading down my body in rivulets.

Reaching my arms up, I started to lather the water through my thick hair, sighing in pleasure.

Then two arms slithered around my body, and I was eased backwards into a smooth, hard body. Laying my head back, I let myself be held by Kettle, letting my dreams flair to life, and then

I viciously smothered them right before I turned in Kettle's arms, reared my fist back and let it fly.

I hit him in the eye.

The bastard didn't even flinch. Not even a single inch of movement.

"I hate you," I said before the tears started flowing.

Kettle's eyes closed as if in pain, finally, but not from my fist.

He opened his eyes and watched the tears flow from my cheeks, trying in vain to wipe them away with the pads of his thumbs.

"Please," he said hoarsely. "Please stop."

I shook my head quickly. "I can't. You really hurt me."

Then I disconnected from his strong arms and exited the shower. Grabbing the only towel off the rack, I briskly dried off before tossing it at him where he stood, dripping on the mat.

He caught it with a forlorn expression and watched from the bathroom as I roughly started shoving my legs into a pair of sleep pants and shrugging on one of Kettle's sweatshirts.

Then I thought better of it, took the sweatshirt off, and threw it to the floor before going to the bag of new clothes I'd bought and pulled a tank top on instead.

His eyes, watching the whole show, took in the act but didn't say anything until I was fully clothed. Then he went about pulling a pair of jeans up over his naked, wet legs. Then proceeded to zip, but not button them, totally ignoring the underwear, t-shirt, socks, and shoes.

I sat on the bed, and wrapped myself up in the comforter on the bed like armor.

"Tell me everything." I said softly.

His head hung.

"My baby was four weeks old when Rosalie's boyfriend, at the time, found out the baby wasn't his. The man fucking flipped, threw my baby across the room like a goddamn rag doll. S-she didn't make it, but the guy continued to mutilate her little body. Then he beat the shit out of Rosalie. At first, they'd tried to pass it off like the baby never happened. It would've worked, too, if Rosalie hadn't tried to act like the kid didn't even exist to me. I called my mother, because I didn't know anybody else to call. She went over to the house and didn't see any sign of her grandkid. She was able to get to the police before my dad caught on, and they launched an investigation." He said woodenly.

I shook my head. The things coming out of Kettle's mouth seemed so surreal, as if it was a movie or something. Things like that only happened if they were made up for a movie line. That didn't happen in real life!

"So what happened?" I asked sadly.

Kettle shrugged. "My dad had to act like the grieving grandfather. On my mother's part, I feel like it was actually genuine. The detectives launched an investigation. Rosalie's boyfriend buried our baby in the backyard and then started a compost pile on top of it, just in case."

My heart hurt for him. I knew he could really use a hug right now, but we weren't finished. We had a few more things to discuss before I even contemplated the possibility of being together again.

"Why isn't this something you were willing to discuss with me?" I asked as I plucked an invisible piece of lint off the comforter.

His sigh was audible as he took a seat beside me. Not touching, but close enough I could reach out and touch him if I wanted.

"I thought it was the talk of the town, honestly. I thought you knew already. It happened right in the middle of Benton and everybody and their brother still looks at me as if I might break if they're not careful about what they say in front of me. It's not an enjoyable thing to talk about, and it makes me so goddamn mad that I can't see straight. Always has and always will. I'm only talking about it now because you need to hear it." He explained roughly.

I nodded. I could see that.

"Did you read the letter?" I looked at him.

He shook my head quickly. "I'm not going to, either. I don't want to ever speak to her again."

"Would you like me to tell you what she said?"

He thought about it for a couple seconds before shrugging. "I can't promise that I'll like what you have to tell me, but I'm willing to listen to you until I can't handle it anymore."

"There wasn't really much to it. She got out of prison last month. She's sorry for what she put you through. And she was diagnosed with terminal cancer a few months ago. Really, that was about it. She just wanted to apologize for what happened to your daughter."

"So she didn't say anything about what happened before that?"

"No, she talked about the man that did it, and how sorry she was for lying to you about it. She wished she could've told you the truth at the time, and wished for you to forgive her if you could." I said softly.

At the shake of my head, he told me everything. Absolutely every single detail of what happened leading up to him joining the army, and what happened after that when he found out about his daughter's death.

"Your dad sounds like a huge dick." I said into the silence afterwards.

"Massive." He said dryly.

"You haven't spoken to either one of your parents since?" I asked, finally turning to him.

He looked sick. His eyes were haunted. His skin was pale and clammy. His fists were clinched so tightly that I was worried for the state of his knuckles if they got much tighter.

Going on instinct, I reached out from my comforter cocoon and touched first one, and then the other fist with one hand, which he relaxed immediately.

"My mom, one or two times around my birthday. My dad's pretty opinionated though, so it's rare if she breaks through his hold on her and works up the courage to call. I always talk to her though." Kettle explained.

"So where does your sister fit into all of this? How did she get kicked out?" I questioned him.

"My sister's really flighty. She's a great girl, and I love her to death, but I don't know. I guess she didn't conform to my father's wishes on not talking to me or something. He told her it was the trust fund or me. Of course, she was stupid enough to choose me. She's one of the best people in the world, once you get to know her."

I nodded at him. "Your sister must be special to give up something like that. She must really care about you."

"She does, and I care about her." He nodded in agreement.

Moving out from under the comforter, I crawled to him until I was straddling his lap. My front plastered to his. It wasn't sexual though. Not then.

Looking into his eyes, I framed his face with my hands before leaning in slowly and kissing him softly on the lips.

"Don't shut me out again. Please," I whispered against his mouth.

He shuddered. "I won't. I love you."

I smiled widely and hugged him a little harder. "I love you, too."

"I need to tell you about your brother. It's what I was doing after my father dropped off the letter." He said hesitantly.

I sat back, putting some distance between us, but he didn't like it and wrapped his arms around my lower back and pulled me back into his chest.

"Okay," I said cautiously.

His huge hands rubbed my lower back soothingly as he started explaining. "It's a major clusterfuck, but as far as we can figure... your brother's right there in the middle of this whole fucking thing. The boys that were responsible for your apartment decided to play the blame game and tell the big boss that it was entirely your fault. He recognized your name immediately. Your brother owed him for some drug habit he couldn't support fully, and his price was to be the go between with him and the makers. And you."

"Me?" I reared back.

Kettle nodded. "Yeah. Gustavo Amadeus can't let one of his employees get narked on and let it pass. He was set to make an example of you by putting every criminal in Northern Louisiana on your trail to bring you in, but then your brother's debt fell in his lap, and he charged your brother with bringing you to him."

"Jesus."

Kettle nodded. "Your brother was supposed to meet Silas the next day but never showed. Silas is working magic on his end, but other than just starting to turn over rocks, we're not real sure where to find him."

My head collapsed on his chest, and I shivered in dread.

"You were right about the danger." I rasped.

His arms went around my middle and pulled me in tight. "I won't let anything happen to you, I promise. They'll have to get through me, and the entire Dixie Warden MC to accomplish that, and that sure as hell won't be happening."

"Will you come home and spend Christmas with me and my family?" Kettle rumbled against my ear.

I didn't know why I was trying to get out of going home. Maybe I was afraid that if I did, things might change.

"I already paid for the week here." I tried. "It's nonrefundable."

He laughed softly, making me bounce lightly against his chest.

"I already took care of it. They only charged you for two nights. If you get out within the hour it'll only be one." He explained.

"I didn't buy anybody any presents." I tried again.

His mouth widened from a lip tilt to a grin. "I know damn well you did that *weeks* ago. You've been shopping on the internet for a while now."

I scrunched my nose up at him. "They're probably really mad at me."

My laugh was audible now. "They actually think *I'm* the dumbass. None of them has any negative opinions about you, I promise."

"I drove my car." I said weakly.

My lips went from his ear, down his jaw, and settled on his lips.

"I drove my bike, but I think we won't have a problem getting your car back, honey." He said as he stood up, walked to the window that overlooked the driveway and the beach beyond, then pulled the blinds backward.

"Holy shit," I breathed.

Every single one of the men that belonged to the Benton Chapter was on the beach.

The driveway was absolutely filled to the brim with bikes.

Some even had to park in the sand. "How the hell are they going to get that bike out of the sand?" I asked worriedly as I saw one bike in particular buried midway up the wheels.

Kettle's eyes flitted to that particular bike and shrugged. "It'll happen... eventually. There's enough manpower."

Baylee was sitting on the tailgate of Sebastian's pick-up feeding her daughter, and when she looked up and spotted me, she waved furiously.

I returned the wave and dropped the window treatment before turning back to Kettle. "Thank you, Kettle."

He crowded me until my back was plastered up against the window and leaned forward. He was so close that I could see the striations in his beautiful blue eyes.

"So, will you come home with me?" He rasped.

At my nod, he smiled. "I love you, Addy."

My eyes filled with tears. "I love you, too, Tiago."

He leaned forward, closing the last bit of distance between the two of us and gave me a scorching kiss I felt to the tips of my toes before pulling back abruptly.

His heat left me, and I stumbled forward with the loss of his body.

Following my movements, I watched as he walked quickly across the room and stopped beside a large box, picked it up, and returned to the window that I was leaning against.

"I had these made for you. I knew it had to be something different, since you can't be seen walking into school with a huge ass 'Property of Kettle' patch across your back like all the other old ladies wear. Minnie spent a ton of time on these, and I really hope you like them." He said as he took the lid off the box.

Inside was a killer set of boots.

"Oh, God," I breathed. "Oh, my God. They're beautiful."

Black leather, with chrome colored steel accents and pointy heals that were painted blood red; they were the most bad ass looking boots I'd ever seen.

The top half of the boots were fairly plain except for a wraith like woman stitched into the leather with '**Kettle's Property**' in bold white underneath.

Immediately, I started ripping at the sleep pants I was wearing, pushing them off my legs in a rush. Once off, I painstakingly undid buckles, unlaced the leather tie-ups on the inside and shoved my feet into each.

Hastily, I started re-lacing them and then buckling them before standing and dashing to the mirrored glass that framed the sliding glass patio doors.

"Oh, God. They're so pretty!" I said lifting my shirt and turning so I could stare at the beauties from the back.

"I have a vest for you, too. But these you can wear to work. All you have to do is wear your pants over them and they look just like regular boots." Kettle said softly.

I practically melted into a puddle of goo right then and there.

Not giving our fight another moment to ruin anything we had between us, I let it all go and launched myself at Kettle.

He caught me in midair, arms wrapping around my back with his hands settled on the globes of my ass.

"I'm sorry I ran away," I said as I ran my fingers through his hair.

His eyes were focused on me, all-consuming and beautiful. "You're the halligan to my axe. I'd never give up on you."

What we did next wasn't something we'd ever done before.

With no more will power left, Kettle walked forward until my ass and back was plastered up against the mirrored wall.

His lips sought my neck, and he sucked on the sensitive part underneath my ear, making my hips undulate in time to his motions.

"Don't ever leave me again. I don't think I could survive a second time if you left me." He groaned before his mouth crashed down over my own.

The only time my legs left Kettle's hips was when he removed my panties.

Almost immediately, though, they returned to their previous position.

The buckles from my boots connected with Kettle's overheated skin, making him yelp with the difference in temperatures.

Then his mouth hit an extremely sensitive spot at the base of my throat, and my head fell back in defeat. No longer did I care about my boots against his skin. When his mouth was on mine, I experienced out of body experiences that sent my cognitive abilities on a flying leap.

Only one single thing became the sole focus at that moment.

"I want you inside of me," I demanded.

Kettle ground his hips into my own, moving them back and forth, allowing the roughness of his denim covered cock to rasp over my distended clit. The motion elicited a moan to burst out of my mouth, and I squeezed my eyes shut as he went lower and lower, lifting my shirt up to around my neck before capturing one of my nipples with his mouth.

The suction of his mouth was powerful as he went from one nipple to the other with single-minded determination.

"Can you come with just my mouth on these pretty little tits and your pretty, wet, little pussy rubbing against my jeans?" He asked as he pulled back, letting my nipple pop free from his mouth.

Then he blew on it, making my nipple tighten and bunch until it was so tight it hurt.

"No," I shook my head adamantly. "Please."

He gave me a little nip on the nipple before reaching between us and undoing the zipper on his pants. With that one act, his pants fell; he lifted me up with the hand around my back, and sat me back down on his cock, filling me to capacity.

He growled low in his throat as he eased me back up slowly, and the let my weight work against me as I dropped back down, hard, onto his waiting length.

With each fall, our grunts and groans intermingled until you could barely tell whose was whose.

"God I've missed you. Missed this." He said, running his nose along the exposed skin of my throat.

Our combined wetness was making Kettle's cock tunnel into me with such ease that it was nearly laughable. It felt like we'd doused ourselves with lube with the effortlessness it took for his cock to sink inside of me.

Tattoos lined Kettle's chest, and all I wanted to do right then was trace every single one with the tip of my tongue.

He had a killer grin, a mouth to die for, and the hottest body on the planet. One look at the man had my core hot and wet for him.

I was in the process of licking his left pectoral when a small tap on the window beside us had Kettle freezing, staying my hips with his large, callused hands.

Both of us together looked to the side to find Loki standing there with a shit-eating grin, and Trance a little further down the stairs, back towards the door, contemplating the para-sailors in the distance.

That was when I realized that, although we were inside, those that ventured too close to the deck got an eye full. Just as Trance and Loki had done only moments before.

Kettle growled in frustration before shuffling, as best as he could, with pants around his ankles until my back was on the far wall instead of the door.

Did he stop though?

No. Hell no.

He just sped up.

"This is gonna be quick. I've left them alone too long and now they're wondering how things went." He growled as he started thrusting harder.

Then he grasped one thigh, pressed it up and out, fairly plastering it to the wall, before he started working me in hard, deep strokes.

The rasp of his pubic hair against my throbbing clit was making me barrel towards my orgasm at a high rate of speed. It came on so fast that I skyrocketed out of oblivion with very little air in my lungs. Emitting a small squeak as I went.

My hot core clamped down on his cock, working him like a hot, wet, pulsing fist as my orgasm overtook me.

Kettle's growl of completion escaped against my mouth, and our tongues dueled as our orgasms tore through us. It hurtled me into a pleasure I'd never felt before.

"Fuck," he panted a few minutes later as he let my legs drop from around his hips to the floor.

My boots hit with a soft clicking as I shifted positions slightly, feeling the leaking of his seed as it dripped slowly out of my pussy and slipped down my thighs.

"I've got to hit the shower," I said before dashing into the bedroom, leaving Kettle to deal with our little problem.

Then I snickered to myself.

I was such a hoe.

THIRTEEN

There's a fight in your firefighter. Just be there for him when he needs you.
-Silas' words of wisdom

Adeline

Fifteen hours later found us all gathered around a huge table in the middle of the clubhouse.

All the couches and chairs I'd seen on my previous visit were pushed to the side of the room in one corner.

Rock star Christmas Pandora Station was playing through Kettle's iPhone that was connected to the speakers, and I was having a fucking blast.

I'd been to many parties with my father's club, but I was a young kid, and kids didn't have the same participation level in a club as adults did.

So here I was in the middle of the table with Baylee on one side of me, and Kettle on the other.

Baby Blaise was in my arms, dressed adorably in her tiny little onesie that said, 'Merry Christmas ya Filthy Animal' on it, and it made me have those ideas again.

Baylee was currently going over a call they'd caught last week, and Trance snorted when he heard her recount.

"What's the craziest call you've ever had?" I asked Trance.

Trance thought about it for a few seconds, eyes going distant, before he smiled widely.

"Well, there was this one time I was called by dispatch for officer assistance. They had a man masturbating at the local Wal-Mart on one of those benches that sits by the checkout lanes. He was just doing it right out in the open for everyone to see. Anyway, the first cop to get on scene was a rookie cop who'd never been on a solo call before. Of course, he picked that one up. So, he goes about trying to persuade the man to stop, but there's such a crowd around him that he really can't do much of anything besides talk to the man." Trance started.

He picked up his beer, took a sip, and set it down before continuing.

"Anyway, he called for backup, and two seasoned beat cops show up. Of course, the same thing happens. The guy's still stroking his meat in front of God and country while the three cops try, calmly, to tell him to stop. They can't really do much about it, because the guy was high on meth, and they know he's going to have to be brought in. Then the show started when the rookie lost the quarter toss and was forced to actually put the guy in handcuffs. As soon as the rookie touched the guy, he fucking flipped. Switch thrown, I'm saying. One second he's calm and just slowly stroking, and the next he goes fuckin' wild and starts attacking the cops and the crowd. Let's not forget that he's still working his cock." Trance laughed.

The men around me were all laughing their asses off, Kettle's top half was bent over the table as he wiped tears from his eyes, and Sebastian and Loki were leaning against each other laughing full throttle.

The scene made me so fuckin' happy I could scream.

These men had a soft spot in my heart a mile wide.

"So they call me. By the time I showed up, there were twelve officers on scene all trying their best to stop the guy, but none were brave enough to get close to the man because the fucker's still jacking off, more furiously than before. They'd tased him numerous times, and he shrugged it off like the goddamn Hulk. So my old K-9 partner, Elixir, and I walk inside the Wal-Mart and follow the crowd to find the fucker scrapping with the rookie cop while a few of the other cops are standing back videotaping it. At one point, the man that was high on meth got the upper hand and straddled the cop, aiming his dick right at the rookie cop's face. Needless to say, I let Elixir go to do his job and the meth head still wouldn't fucking stop jacking it. It did hold him still long enough for us to get some restraints on him and shit. They shoved him in the back of the rookie's police car where the meth addict proceeds to use the fucking seat to finally get off. Then he goes to fuckin' sleep. Like it never even happened."

"That's..." I said shaking my head. "Crazy!"

"I used to live in Vegas. It's a big city. Lots of crazy shit going on." Trance nodded.

"So you're telling me he fought them off single handedly?" Sebastian wheezed.

Trance nodded solemnly making the entire table erupt in laughter.

I shook my head and then looked at Kettle. "What about you?"

He wasn't able to answer before his name was bellowed from the other end of the table.

"Kettle!" Porter yelled. "It's time"

Porter was holding up a black case in the air that resembled the shape of an instrument and shaking it wildly.

"Hey, careful with that!" He said standing abruptly and walking quickly to Porter.

"Oh, yeah. Get ready for a show!" Baylee said, as she rubbed her hands together vigorously.

"What's going on?" I asked, as I moved the baby until she was propped up on my shoulder with her little baby bottom in my hand.

"You'll see," she said cryptically.

Kettle, Porter, and another man I'd seen, but didn't know right off hand, took a seat in the very corner of the room and started tuning their individual instruments.

Porter pulled out a worn and battered acoustic guitar, the other guy, who I'd finally placed as Torren, pulled out a harmonica type device that was connected to some sort of cord or something. Then there was Kettle, who'd pulled out a gleaming wooden fiddle that was beautiful.

"Are they going to play Christmas carols?" I asked

Sebastian, who was on the other side of Baylee, heard my comment and snorted. "Do they look like they're going to play Christmas carols? They'd all have to be really, really drunk to do that. Kettle doesn't normally play too often, either, so they wouldn't piss him off by asking him to play carols. He'd never play again, and it's an awesome thing to witness; it's best not to piss him off just in case."

I stayed silent as I watched Kettle check his instrument, and then his bow. He ran his fingers over the strings, testing the long fibers of hair.

"Can I have ice cream now?" Johnny, Sebastian's four-year-old son, asked from across the table.

All our eyes went to the plate in front of him, noticing for the first time it was empty of the carrots that Baylee had put on his plate when they'd started dinner.

He'd been complaining for nearly an hour now about 'hating carrots' because they were 'rabbit food' and he was a 'human fucking being.' When he'd asked for ice cream, Sebastian had flat out told him no, he sure as hell wasn't getting any 'fucking ice cream' until he finished his 'goddamned carrots.'

I'd winced right along with Baylee at the curse words coming out of Sebastian's mouth knowing Johnny would turn around and repeat each and every word at a later date in time. Most likely when they were around other people that would be highly offended by a four year old cursing.

Sebastian leaned forward and looked at his plate. "Let me see your hands."

Johnny lifted up his hands and showed his father they were empty.

Then Sebastian bent down to look under the table. Upon seeing no stray carrots, he nodded at his son. "I'll go get you some ice cream. Thank you for eating the carrots."

When Johnny smiled, I saw a small piece of orange in his mouth, but then music from the direction of my man started to fill the air, making me look up to see Kettle perched on the very edge of the bar stool. One foot on the ground, and the other on the lowest rung.

His eyes were closed, and he was letting the fine hair of the bow run lightly over the strings of the fiddle.

The other two were warming up as well, but my eyes were glued on Kettle. On the peaceful expression on his face. On the slight quirk of his head as he leaned his chin on the black pad of the instrument.

After about ten minutes of them fiddling around, adjusting things, and basically tuning their instruments to their liking, Mike started playing a few soft notes. Then Porter started picking at his guitar with his large, blunt fingers.

Then there was Kettle, who waited.

His foot tapped along with the music, and instantly, I knew what they were going to play.

"Callin' Baton Rouge?" I asked Baylee. "Isn't it against a motorcycle club's religion to play anything but rock and roll?"

Baylee laughed.

"Wait for it," she said, sparing me a small glance before she returned her gaze to the impromptu concert ahead of us.

Blaise stirred in my arms, making me miss the part where Kettle actually started to play, but once I looked up again, my eyes were laser focused on the sexy beast of a man rocking it out on his fiddle in front of me.

"There it is," Baylee smiled as Kettle's brilliance started pouring out through the music.

Kettle was dressed in dark faded jeans, a black t-shirt, and his cut. His hair was shaved back down so his Mohawk was once again perfectly a half inch long with the sides shaved cleanly down. Then there was the fiddle. It looked so tiny in his large hands.

Words could not explain what I felt as I watched Kettle play.

My arms and hands, as well as my legs, feet, head, and torso were moving with the beat.

What once started as a perfectly lined bow was now sporting broken pieces of hairs as Kettle fairly attacked his instrument in his exuberance.

His fingers were moving so freakin' fast that it was hard to see, and by the time they were into the last beats of the song, my heart was pounding.

"Holy shit," I breathed as I watched the boys finish their song.

The men around the clubhouse were all drinking and having a good time. There was family and fun, and I was so very happy.

The only thing missing was my sister, but as long as my sister was happy with her life, I was, too.

"Finished!" Johnny declared as he set his spoon down and then promptly spit out every single carrot that had been on his plate earlier in the meal back onto his plate and left the table.

I had to laugh when I realized that the boy had obviously had the load in his mouth the entire time, throughout eating the ice cream and all.

"I can't say that I'm not impressed." Sebastian said dryly.

"I cannot even fathom how he was able to do that..." Baylee said as she shook her head in awe.

Standing up and leaving them to their discussion, I made my way around the large table and sidled up to Kettle who was drinking a beer.

He had sweat beading on his forehead and running down his face, but he looked happy. His eyes had tracked my movement as soon as I'd stood, and watched as I made my way closer and closer to him.

"You did well, Tiago." I said as I got to within hearing range.

"Yeah," he said. "My parents paid for me to do well. I still love it anyway."

"Got a little rough with your bow, there, didn't you?" I teased.

He snorted. "You're not putting enough emphasis into it if you don't break a few hairs."

"So are you guys taking requests?" I asked, eyes turning from Kettle, to Torren, and back to Kettle.

He looked at me skeptically.

"As long as it isn't any of that shit I heard rolling through your car when I'm the one following you around, we'll be good." Porter glared at her.

I laughed.

"Hey, I resent-"

Kettle's pager went off. Followed by about half the men in the room. Cell phones started ringing. Alarms started sounding. Then all the men receiving those calls were standing.

"Here, baby. Will you put this away for me? I'm getting a call out. Hang here with Baylee. I'll come back for you as soon as I can, okay?" Kettle said as he handed me his fiddle and started running away without even a backwards glance.

In short order, eight men out of the twenty nine members of the Benton Chapter, four from the fire department, and four cops, were hauling ass out of the door.

I knew it was something big. Something so big, that they needed every off duty cop and firefighter on the force there, and they needed them quickly.

I shuffled back to the table with Kettle's fiddle in one hand and Blaise in the other, until I came to realize that Baylee was on the phone with someone, as was Silas and Dixie.

With no other option, I laid the instrument down on the table where there was a clean spot and went to the playpen in the corner that Baylee had set up when she'd arrived earlier in the day to cook and prepare.

The baby stirred slightly with the movement, but fell back to sleep promptly, allowing me to put the fiddle away and then started clearing the plates and trash.

I was a worrywart, and with nothing else left to do but that, I started cleaning to try to distract myself.

Minnie started helping as well and in no time, every single piece of trash and food was cleaned away, and we started guiding the men that were left to replace the furniture back to its previous position.

"Get him out! Get him out!" Silas yelled into his phone. "Don't let him go into his place. Don't let him. Take him out before he can get there...forget the motherfuckin' snake! Don't let him go in there."

The sound of Silas' voice sent shivers down my spine.

I knew they were talking about Kettle. How many snakes could there be in Benton? Certainly not many. And absolutely none that anybody would risk their life for.

"I'm not saying don't send anybody in there. Just don't let it be him. You do it. I think..." Silas said glancing in my direction. "I think the sister was in there when they doused it. I saw her go in and not come out when I went over the feed."

I dropped the pretense of pretending to listen and walked slowly to the bar where he was sitting with his laptop open in front of him.

On the screen was a live video of what was happening.

From the location, they'd set up a camera on the light pole across the street from Kettle's apartment.

Although the fire trucks were mostly obstructing my view, I could tell Kettle's apartment, as well as the one directly above Kettle's, was on fire. Something shooting out that much flame had to mean the place was toast.

"I've got eyes on the back, too. She didn't come out." Silas explained roughly.

Silas head dropped, and he ran his hand over the back of his neck.

"Trance, there's no way she could be alive in that. I'm watching the feed as we speak. There's no way." Silas explained.

We both watched, for what felt like hours, as men worked to

put the fire out.

At one point, one fire engine moved to allow another one to move in closer behind it, and my breath hissed out of my lungs at seeing the apartment just...gone. Right then they were attempting to save the apartment beside Kettle's. They were trying to contain what was left of Kettle's to keep it from spreading to any apartments beyond.

My heart sank.

"What happened?" I finally asked.

Silas hit a few buttons, and then suddenly I was watching the feed from about an hour before.

I watched in horror as Shannon parked her little Ford Focus in the spot in front of where I used to park, got out, and walked to the front door.

After knocking, she waited for exactly four minutes and fifteen seconds before pulling out her keys and unlocking the door, closing it softly behind her.

"Oh, no." I moaned.

She stayed in there and didn't come out.

"No, no, no, nooo," I whimpered brokenly.

My heart was in my throat, and I could feel the movement of bile slowly rise and settle at the base of my tongue; I could taste the bitterness of it.

"Please, no." I whimpered.

I hadn't realized that tears were leaking out of my eyes until Silas put his big arm around me and pulled me deep into his chest, allowing my cheek to settle on his massive chest.

His big beard tickled my cheek, but I didn't care.

I was too busy watching the devastation in front of me, horrified, as a Hummer that was sleek and beautiful pulled into our lot, turned around, and then stopped right outside the apartment.

One man got out with a giant gas can in his hand, walked up to the front walk and started pouring it out on the wooden paneling that lined the outside the apartment.

The man was of average height and build, dressed in an impeccable pair of slacks, pointy-toed shoes, and a red silk shirt.

His face was covered by a black ski mask, so any other identifying markers couldn't be detected.

"Why isn't anybody saying anything?" I asked in surprise. "They have to see what he's doing, and who the hell wears ski masks anymore?"

I hadn't meant to yell, but I couldn't help it.

While Kettle and I were eating a Christmas meal, his sister was being burned alive.

I couldn't keep my eyes open any longer. I knew he was about to torch the place. With Kettle's sister inside. Oh, God. Oh, God.

"Oh, baby." I said as I thought of Kettle. "Oh, Tiago. I'm so sorry."

Silas' hand came up and cradled my head in his big palm, stroking my hair as he watched the rest of the video.

A whimper behind me had me turning to find Baylee standing very close with Blaise in her arms. Minnie stood beside her, holding Baylee to her body. The rest of the MC stood behind them, all watching the scene unfold on the computer in front of me.

"Time to show our hand, Silas. You know exactly who it was." Dixie said as he came up close to Silas' free arm and watched a little more closely.

They were heading to a room at the back of the bar. A room that had a large table with chairs surrounding it. There was nothing else in it. Other than the large Dixie Wardens mural on the wall, nothing else decorated the room.

Although I'd only been to the clubhouse for the first time today, I knew instantly that this was where they had all their club meetings. What had my dad used to call it, gospel?

"Yeah," Silas agreed, giving me a reassuring squeeze before letting me go and standing. "Let's go to church. Minnie, darlin', how about you bring out a couple cots. I think we're going to be a while. No reason y'all can't all catch some rest while you can. It's time for us to bring our family together. Kettle's gonna need the support when he gets back."

Church was a MC's version of a business meeting between the members. It's where all the important decisions were made. Who was told to do what. Where problems were brought forth to be worked through. I always compared it to a judge's chambers. It was where all the important things were ruled on. Some of them even life and death.

Knowing that arguing would be futile, we all started setting up cots in between the splayed couches and recliners. Some even behind the bar.

I had no intention of sleeping, however. Exactly the opposite, in fact. I wasn't sleeping until my man was home safe in my arms. Where I could hold him, because I knew he wouldn't be all right when he got back.

And I was right.

He wasn't.

FOURTEEN

Pain is weakness leaving the body. No, pain is my fist when it hits your fuckin' face.
-Kettle to his father, age 18.

Adeline

It was the sound of glass shattering that jarred me out of my in between sleep and awake state.

I'd laid down on the cot that was against the far wall hours ago.

My eyes blinked open blearily and I looked around noting all absence of light in the huge room, minus the sliver that was coming from a door at the back of the bar.

It took me a few more minutes to get my bearings, but I knew it was Kettle who'd done the glass shattering.

Sitting up slowly, I took the phone off the floor and pressed the button to light up the screen.

4:27 A.M.

Friday, December 25, 2014.

A sick knot of dread filled up my stomach, and I swallowed

convulsively to keep the bile from exiting my mouth.

Bending at the waist, I slipped my feet into the boots from Kettle, being sure to tuck in my sweat pants that had been thrown at me from Silas earlier that night.

'Here. These are Kettlle's. Might be too long, but the boy probably wouldn't like seeing you in some other man's clothes.' He'd said.

Using the light on my phone, I worked my way through the maze of cots and couches until I got closer to the sliver of light.

That was when I heard the men, and what they were talking about.

"Have to do something. He's not going to stop. He already took my sister. What do I do now? Wait for him to take my woman while she's at school? The fucker took out three other apartments beside my own today. Three adults in the first. Two adults and one eight year old in the other. Five kids and one adult in the last. Luckily, they all got out. Though, he's not going to care about a couple of kids that get in between him and his goal. He's already done that tonight." Kettle snarled.

Something low and vicious was said by another man, and then I heard them all get into it.

"All right, settle down boys. Now, day after tomorrow we'll figure this out. Spend your Christmas' with your families. Kettle your house good enough to go home to?" Silas asked.

I didn't hear Kettle's answer but he must've confirmed that, yes, it was because Silas next comment scared me a little.

"Okay. Now that that's settled, Kettle, you won't be going with us. It's too new for you. Too personal."

Then there was more crashing as well as rage pouring out of that room, and my hesitation at the door vanished. I went into the room like I had every right to be there.

I lost the desire to know the word as soon as I saw Sebastian pushing Kettle up against the wall with Trance on one of his arms, and Loki on the other. In fact, I was kind of pissed.

My man was hurting and what he needed was vindication. Not someone telling him that he couldn't go with them, effectively denying him the one outlet that he needed to make peace with the fact that his sister was gone. He'd just lost the only blood-family member he spoke with, in one of the most horrific ways possible. If they thought he wasn't going to go, they didn't know him at all.

"Fuck you," Kettle was bellowing. "I'm going and you can kiss my fuckin' ass."

Silas was back at the head of the table sitting down calmly as he watched the men. "This right here is why I don't want you to go..."

Kettle just started struggling more, and I had enough.

Stomping into the room, I started elbowing members out of the way so I could get to Kettle. One by one, they either moved or I squeezed by them until I was standing behind Loki's left shoulder.

Loki's shoulders were straining hard, and I knew he really had to work to keep Kettle from destroying the room or taking a swing at one of them. Kettle was straining so hard that veins in his neck and arms were distending the skin. Kettle's eyes were pinned to Sebastian as he kept telling the man to get off him in such a deadly low tone that it made my insides feel like jelly.

Looking around, I found a rolling chair pushed off to the side of Loki's legs, so I went to it and moved it to where it was directly in Kettle's line of sight before standing on it and using Sebastian's back as a stabilizer.

Sebastian, who'd been directly in Kettle's face backed off slightly to see who was at his back, and when he did, it gave Kettle a clear view of me and he froze.

"Addy," he rasped brokenly. "My sister's gone."

I launched myself at him, going over Sebastian's right shoulder and Loki's left shoulder to get to him. Since Kettle's arms were still pinned down to his sides, I did the next best thing, and wrapped my arms around his neck, and held on tight.

"I know, baby. I know." I said consolingly.

When they realized he was no longer struggling to fight, but to get his arms around me, both Trance and Loki let go of him, leaving me over Sebastian's back, and Kettle's arms now wrapped around us both.

It actually would've made a funny picture under different circumstances; but now, it was just what he needed. His best friend and the woman that loved him. I could tell he needed it just by the way he clung to us, refusing to let go.

"What do you need me to do, baby?" I asked Kettle.

Kettle shook his head, but didn't say anything. "Are you hungry? Do you want me to go get you something to eat?"

Kettle shook his head furiously. His arms got tighter, saying without words that he didn't want me to go.

"Do you want me to leave?" Sebastian asked quietly.

Kettle didn't answer, only squeezed his arms tighter in answer.

Therefore, that's how we stayed for what felt like a long time. Me on my chair, leaning over Sebastian's back, and Sebastian sandwiched in between us.

After a long while, Kettle finally loosened his hold on our bodies, allowing the both of us to step back out of his arms.

"How 'bout I go get you something to eat, and then you head to one of the rooms. Baylee said the one on the furthest end was empty and had clean sheets. No need to go home tonight. I'll bring your food to you." Sebastian said quietly.

When Kettle nodded, Sebastian left quietly, leaving me standing on my chair staring at the man in front of me. I had no clue what I was supposed to say to him. Everything that came to mind seemed to be inadequate at that moment. Saying 'I'm sorry' just didn't seem like it was good enough.

So I got down carefully, while he looked at me hauntingly. I grabbed his wrist before guiding him out the door.

Surprised to find the room empty, I was even more surprised when I saw the hallway.

It was a normal sized hallway, but the way each member of The Dixie Wardens stood with their backs leaning against the wall made it look tiny.

Then there were the women that belonged to those men sitting beside them. Some were sitting on their bottoms. Others were holding on to their men, giving Kettle the silent support that a family did when one of their own was hurting.

I smiled at each and every one of them while we walked down the hallway towards the rooms I'd seen earlier when I'd helped Baylee with replacing sheets, cleaning and straightening.

Some of the men gave head nods, others gave pats on the back, but every single one of them gave silent support, showing that they cared.

I was humbled.

I'd seen the camaraderie over the last few months, but this was a whole new level of trust. Friendship.

Love.

Once we were in the room, I stripped Kettle's smoke filled clothes from his body and walked with him, hand in hand, to the shower where I washed his body and hair with shampoo, and then did the same for myself.

Once we were done, I walked with him to the bed, and tossed him a pair of underwear that had miraculously appeared. They were lying beside a plate of food for us both.

As I ate in silence, I could feel Kettle sinking more and more into himself. He was going back to where I didn't want him to be, so in an attempt to pull him out of it, to bring him back to me, I took the plate of uneaten food out of his hand, placed it on the nightstand, and pushed him to his back.

Then I made love to him.

It was all about him.

I started at his collarbones. Pressing soft kisses along his neck, and then down to his chest. One over his heart where an angel was inked into his skin. Then to his ribs, and down further to the hard muscles of his belly.

That's when I started using my tongue. Trailing it down over each deep ridge of his abdomen, causing his stomach to quiver in anticipation.

Then my lips met the trail of hair that started just below his belly button. I followed it down with my lips until I reached the gray elastic band of his Fruit of The Loom boxer briefs.

The hard ridge of his cock was pushed down, held down tightly to his right upper thigh by the tight elasticity of his underwear.

I could see it pulse with each beat of his heart, and my mouth watered to take his length into my mouth.

"Please," Kettle rasped as I lingered too long at the waistband of his underwear. "Take 'em off."

I ignored him, instead letting the tip of my nose trail down onto the soft cotton of his briefs until I reached the base of his hard dick. His smell was musky and warm, all hard and horny male.

Pressing a kiss to the hard column of his cock, I trailed my lips down the length of him. My lips met the skin of his thigh, and the tip of his cock that was still covered by the material.

Opening my mouth over the head of his cock, I let my breath

fan out and warm his length. His hard cock jumped with the different sensation, and I used my nose to nudge up the leg of his underwear until the very tip of his cock was uncovered.

My hands, which had been idle at my side before now, started moving up the outside of his thighs until they came to rest on the notched edges of muscle that formed the V on his lower abdomen.

As I flicked my tongue over the tip of his cock, I stroked my fingers along those ridged muscles, teasing him with my just barely there touches.

His tummy, which had been sculpted but pliable before the touching had begun, now resembled a slab of stone.

I could make out even more muscle now than there had been before, and it was a tossup on what I wanted to lick. There were just too many options to choose from.

In the end, he was the one who decided for me.

With one hand in my hair, he yanked me back, making my flicking tongue, which had been circling the head of his dick and running around the crown, lose its plaything as he roughly threw me back to the bed.

The low throb that had been pulsing softly before now started to burn with need. Warm slickness started seeping out of my channel, lubricating my entrance for him.

I hit with a soft bounce and watched as he shucked his underwear, moved in between my legs, pushed my panties aside, and thrust his hard cock deep inside of me. Bottoming out before withdrawing and slamming home once more.

The hard thrusts were not nice. They were jagged. Unbreakable. Desperate thrusts that showed just a hint of what Kettle was feeling right then.

His breath sawed in and out of him in ragged gasps.

The panties that were bunched at the base of his cock rubbed against my clit coarsely but, strangely, it worked for me.

The rough lace felt so foreign, so utterly wrong, that it was surprising that it would also make my pleasure all the more intriguing.

"God, yes," I panted as one particular thrust had my head smacking into the headboard.

Normally, Kettle would've backed off, moved me to the end of the bed so I would be in no way uncomfortable, but Kettle was gone. In his place was a ravaged man who needed me to take him away from the horrid things that happened that night.

Which was why I was letting him use my body as an outlet. He was fueling our coupling with the rage and hurt he was feeling. Punishing both of our bodies.

"Hold on," he said coarsely, before abruptly pulling out of me and roughly flipping me over until I was on my belly. "Get your knees up under you. Keep your shoulders and face on the bed."

I did as I was told, following his directions implicitly.

Once in the desired position, he got a hold on my hair again, pulled it back roughly, and slammed his length back inside of me.

"Fuck," we both hissed.

He was fucking me so hard now that I practically felt it in my throat.

His huge length was tunneling inside of me so hard that our flesh was making a loud smack each time our hips met.

Then the hand that was not busy pulling back on my hair went to the cheek of my ass and squeezed. Hard.

He took his thumb and ran it along the seam of my sex. Gathering my wetness on his finger, and then he thrummed the very tip of my clit, making my orgasm crash through me.

It wasn't until his thumb, coated in my juices, found the hole of my ass and pushed inside that I realized what his goal was.

The feeling, so very, very foreign, made that orgasm that had previously been a ten on the Richter scale, smash through the fuckin' charts, blowing every other orgasm I'd had before to smithereens. My eyes squeezed tightly shut, so hard my head hurt. My mouth turned and closed on the fleshy part of Kettle's wrist, biting down roughly to withhold the scream that threatened the very structure of the room we were in.

My head moved forward until the sting in my scalp went to a burn, and my heat clamped down hard on the raging cock that was pummeling it, squeezing it like a fist.

He groaned low in his throat, and with three more sharp thrusts, he came. Pushing into me so hard that my knees went out from under me and I collapsed onto the bed.

Our hearts were pounding, and the rise and fall of our chests were rapidly diminishing the amount of oxygen in the room.

However, neither one of us spoke.

Kettle just disengaged from my body and pulled me into his side.

I could tell he was still upset. He was still in his head. But he was holding me.

I had *him*, and that was all that mattered right then.

FIFTEEN

Life's a bitch and then you die.
-Silas to Kettle

Kettle

Two days later

2:49 P.M.

"You good?" Sebastian asked me as we got off our bikes in front of the old warehouse the club owned.

I shrugged. No, I wasn't good, but I'd deal. It was harder than hell to leave Adeline earlier, and knowing I'd go home to her with blood staining my hands, made my chest tight.

I'd do it anyway, though. That sadistic bastard had killed my baby sister. The one who I'd promised to look after forever and always. The one who would never see motherhood. Never walk down the aisle. Never bear a child. Never again give me a call in the middle of the night telling me she needed a ride home from another douchebag's place.

Gustavo Amadeus had some explaining and atoning to do, and I was just the man to make sure he received it.

We were meeting at the warehouse that Sebastian, Loki, and I all had offices at. Where we also held parties at that were too big for our clubhouse to handle.

Today, we were meeting all the members of the Dixie Wardens at the warehouse before going in for a little discussion. My hope was that we were going to raid Gustavo's front business, take every single one of his crew, and hopefully, lure Gustavo out in the process. Then, I could show him the business end of my fist. Repeatedly.

However, Trance and Loki showed us the error of our ways, giving us a better option that would take out every single member of Gustavo's crew without making The Dixie Wardens have to kill over one hundred people in the process.

I must've taken too long to answer because suddenly Sebastian was in my face, grabbing each side with his mitts and glaring at me. "Are. You. Good?"

I glared right back at him, but nodded. I was as good as I was going to get.

"Alright, let's get this meeting taken care of. I want to eat some leftovers." Sebastian said dismissively.

The tone of Sebastian's voice might have come out sounding blasé, but I knew the man was a live wire, just like me. Sebastian may not have liked Shannon very much, but she was family, and the Dixie Wardens protected their own. God help anybody who fucks with something of ours.

We might be 99% law abiding, but we didn't condone disrespect. And we sure as fuck didn't tolerate a murder of another brother's blood sister. Not without one hell of a retaliation.

"Let's do it." I agreed.

• • •

Adeline

3:15 P.M.

"Hello?" I answered my phone.

"Ummm, hi. This is Ray Platt from The Bayou Funeral Home. I'm the one in charge of getting a Ms. Shannon Spada's funeral planned. I was given this number by your husband, Mr. Tiago Spada? Is that correct?"

My heart leapt at the mention of being Kettle's wife, but fell just as quickly when I realized just why he was calling.

"Yes, that's me. How can I help you, Mr. Platt?" I asked softly, looking at my toes that were in serious need of a coat of polish.

"This is quite unusual, but I contacted Mr. Spada since he's the primary contact. However, we have the deceased's parents here trying to plan the funeral, and since Mr. Spada advised us to speak with you on the matter, since he was otherwise occupied, I'm calling to see just what you would like us to do. He said, and I quote, '*Tell her she's got full sway. Make it pretty, baby.*' Now, what would you like us to do?" Mr. Platt asked.

I wiggled my toes in the 70's carpet in the clubhouse's bedroom that Kettle and I'd stayed the night in, and came to a decision.

"I'll be there in less than thirty minutes. Can you stall them?" I asked him.

"Certainly, Mrs. Spada, I'll see you momentarily." He said primly before hanging up.

I growled in frustration. What kind of parents would disown their own daughter, and then show up to plan her funeral? What sick bastards they must be.

Then I was shoving my feet into socks, followed by my boots.

I made sure to tuck in the pleats of my pants so the boots looked smooth where they met my jeans, and stood. I pulled another piece of borrowed clothing on, this one donated by Trance, much to Kettle's vexation, and then shrugged my beautiful vest that declared me 'Kettle's Property' over that.

By the time I exited the bedroom where I was reading my book after a large leftover-filled lunch, I was feeling mean.

I wanted to kick Kettle's parents' asses. Although it was more like I'd probably just yell at them.

I was sadly deflated when I made it into the clubhouse's main room only to find Tunnel, the prospect who was such a sweet man that I still couldn't see how he fit into this group of bad asses.

That's not to say that he probably couldn't be badass, he just didn't act like one each and every time I'd been in his company. I was also sure that Kettle's parents wouldn't be too intimidated by the man. He was like a sweet, baby cop who'd hesitate on doing anything that might harm someone. However, I had a feeling I could probably convince him to go with me...or at least let me out.

"Tunnel?" I asked sweetly, stopping just short of batting my eyelashes at him just in case he noticed my ruse.

He turned around quickly from where he was shoving a fat piece of ham into his mouth the size of a small horse and cocked his head slightly. "Yes?"

"Uhh," I hesitated. "I'm in need of a favor."

Life has a way of being...tragic.

A mistake, by definition, is something you do that is misguided or wrong.

Going to that funeral home was a mistake.

I should've known better. Should have listened to that inner voice begging me to listen to what Kettle had commanded that morning before leaving.

Don't go anywhere. No matter what. It's not safe.

Why didn't I listen?

• • •

Kettle

3:55 P.M.

"Why, out of all the places in the world he could use as a front business, did he choose a funeral parlor?" Dixie asked as he shook his head.

"You got me." I murmured.

"Nobody's going to check out a hearse and coffin for drugs. Hell, most people down here pull the fuck over for a hearse. Some even have police escorts. What better way than that? The man's a relative genius. I can't believe I've never even thought about that before." Trance said shaking his head.

"We doing this in plain sight, or are we going in through the back as not to draw so much attention?"

I snorted and got off my bike. The bike's engine ticked as it cooled down from our hard ride over from the warehouse district, making me take a second glance at it and then at the area surrounding us.

"Fifteen bikers just pulled up in downtown Benton in the middle of the afternoon. It's safe to say we were noticed." Silas drawled dryly. "Which was the point, wasn't it?"

I ignored them and started to head into the funeral home. Then came to an abrupt halt when a familiar license plate that read 0SPADA0 in a handicapped parking spot near the front of the door caught my eye.

Mother. Fucker.

"That's my folks' car." I told Sebastian who was directly behind me.

Oaths and curses sounded at my admission, and I ran my fingers through the short spiky strip of hair that lined the top of my head.

"It was a good plan, having The Bayou Funeral Home take care of the funeral arrangements. Never expected your parents to show at the parlor though." Sebastian observed.

"Yeah, well they've fucked absolutely everything up. Why stop now?" I said as I yanked the front door open.

Loki's plan was to call in to the funeral home and ask for them to start the never-ending process of burying my sister as an excuse to be there. Once inside, they'd take over the front, then move to the back where there was an extra 10,000 square feet of space that the fire station didn't account for.

Each fire station had blue prints of the local businesses on file in case of a fire so that the on duty captain could plan accordingly. The Bayou Funeral Home's plan didn't match up, making it obvious to me and the rest of my club that they had a little extra room unaccounted for, and reason to hide it.

As a firefighter, that ticked me off. The firefighters that went into burning buildings had a right to know what they were getting themselves into; Gustavo Amadeus was a selfish prick who deserved what was about to come at him.

Just one more nail in Gustavo's coffin.

"This doesn't change the plan. Does it?" Silas asked as he walked around me and opened the door to the building.

Sebastian gave me a hard pound on the back as he passed, making my feet come unstuck, allowing me to follow them inside.

Trance was to come in later with Radar, who would alert

Trance to the drugs, effectively signing the warrant that allowed him to search any facility, and take each and every one of Gustavo's employees into custody. Followed shortly by searching his properties and other businesses for more evidence.

We just had to get back far enough to provide Radar the opportunity to alert, first.

Of course, nothing ever works as it should. The best-laid plans always backfire when your father's the ultimate douche on the planet.

The first thing I observed was the sickly sweet stench of flowers as we walked into the front room.

It was elegant with deep maroon and hunter green coloring. There were sedate paintings of forests and bayous, as well as some wildlife moderately interspersed throughout. The carpet was plush and hunter green, allowing my shoes to sink into it as soon as my feet entered the room.

The desk in the front of the room was covered in fliers of the upcoming viewings happening in the next four hours, as well as a guest list. A woman, all of twenty-five at most, was dressed in a prim black pantsuit with her brown hair styled into a partial up-do that kept the fly-aways out of her face.

I knew immediately that she hadn't worked there long. She was too sweet. Her eyes showed every single emotion she was feeling, and right at that moment, it was remorse.

She didn't seem to care that fifteen men had entered the room wearing their Dixie Wardens cuts, or that most of them had tattoos that were very colorful. Color and language wise.

No, her eyes were trained on my father who was in the corner of the god-forsaken room crying about his 'precious girl' being gone.

Of course, it could've been genuine. However, he didn't have the right to that anymore. Not after everything he'd done.

My mother was sitting down next to my father. Her hands were clutched tightly to her chest, and she'd clocked me as soon as I'd walked in, causing her eyes to widen. Mother's intuition or some shit.

She wasn't crying now, but I could tell by the deep bags underneath her eyes and the paleness to her skin that she had been.

"Ma'am?" My disgusted voice brought the woman's attention from my parents to me, and she smiled warmly at me.

"Can I help you?" She asked me.

"Name's Tiago Spada, I'm here to checkout some of the rooms, get some things ironed out before the viewing of my sister in a couple of days." I told the woman.

Her eyes widened. "Of course, I'll be glad to show you the way." She said as she hustled in the direction of the back room.

Ignoring the call of my father, I followed, knowing for a fact that my brothers would keep them from following me.

I didn't know how I did it so calmly, but I walked behind the pretty woman at a sedate pace as she led us into a back room.

• • •

Adeline

"What do you think?" I asked Tunnel, as Mr. Platt walked into a back room to take a phone call.

Mr. Platt looked so familiar. Like I'd seen him before from somewhere.

Tunnel's eyes, which had been on the retreating man's back, turned to me. "Something isn't right. Kettle's parents, although they were upset, didn't look like they were trying to take over any funeral plans. I tried calling Kettle on the way here, and he didn't answer, which means that his phone was turned off. They'd told me the phones were going off as they left the parking lot this morning. How was Kettle supposed to relay a message to you if he couldn't have answered in the first..."

I was too absorbed in watching the side room where Mr. Platt had disappeared. If I hadn't been, I might have been able to tell Tunnel that he had a lead pipe headed towards his head.

One that was in the hands of my own frickin' brother.

"Tunnel!" I exclaimed as he went down like a sack of wheat. "Jefferson! What the fuck, what are you doing?"

"Quiet," my brother hissed. "You're in so much fucking danger that it's not even funny. I've done everything in my power to keep you out of this shit, but you keep shoving your head back in there. Jesus Christ. I don't even know what the fuck to do anymore."

"What are you talking about? I don't understand!" I said as I dropped down to my knees to check Tunnel's pulse.

It was strong and steady, allowing me to take a deep breath for the first time since I'd seen him drop.

"The guy you were talking to is a very dangerous man. Do you know who that was?" He asked as he glanced nervously at the door Mr. Platt had disappeared through.

Jefferson looked different. Almost...normal for him. What he used to look like before dad died. Although I could still tell he was a little underweight, he wasn't so sickly looking that I could see his cheekbones. Was he getting clean?

"Jefferson, what are you doing here? What's..."

"Jefferson. Get her in the locker. With any hope they won't find her and she'll be dead before anyone's the wiser. We've got company in the parking lot." Mr. Platt said as he came out of the room he'd disappeared through earlier.

The haughty, pompous attitude made me realize where I knew him from. He was the man who'd 'accidentally' entered my lab the day I'd stayed late catching up on my work.

It had been such a fleeting moment. He was there one second, and backing out of the door the next, apologizing for interrupting.

However, now that I thought about it, I'd also seen him at the grocery store a few weeks ago when Kettle had gone down the ice cream aisle. Then again at the phone store when I was paying Viddy's phone bill.

I didn't let on that I realized who he was though, I just stared at him blankly, not even realizing my own brother was about to hit me over the head with a goddamn steel pole until I saw his arm lift in my peripheral vision.

I turned my head just in time to see the bar to descent towards my temple, a blast of pain, and then nothing.

Lights out.

• • •

Kettle

Our plan worked out perfectly.

After going through the motions of looking at the rooms, and listening to the woman's spiel about how they like to make the family's last moments with their loved ones to be special, Trance showed up with a very anxious Radar.

Trance walked in with Radar on his heels, restrained only by a long black leash. Radar was going nuts, barking and snarling furiously. His strong, lithe body was straining towards the back wall trying with everything he had to get at the door.

"How do you get to the back?" Trance all but snarled at the poor woman.

She started at the question, stepping back until her back hit the podium and she could go no further.

With a shaky hand, she held up her finger and pointed towards a door that was partially covered by a long curtain.

Trance's big arms strained to hold the dog back, and finally, he just gave up, releasing the dog from the confining leash and letting him go.

Radar dashed off, shooting like an arrow towards the door, only to come to a stop with barely restrained patience.

When Trance arrived at the door, he cursed and bellowed at the woman who was still in the same position as before, fear etched across her features.

It wasn't because of Trance's snarled question, though. It was because of Loki who'd strode in moments after Trance.

He'd trimmed his hair since I'd last seen him the day before. Gone was the shaggy cut, replaced by a shorter buzz that no longer resembled a preppy surfer boy's hair. His beard, though, which had been trimmed, remained.

He was wearing his badge on his left hip and his semiautomatic Colt .45 on his other. He had a black polo shirt tucked into his jeans, and black sunglasses sitting on top of his head. His eyes were all for the dog though, completely disregarding the woman who was staring at him in pain.

"Ma'am," Trance snapped at the woman. "Come open this door."

The woman, finally tearing her eyes away from Loki, snapped to and came to punch in some numbers into the keypad.

I saw the moment Loki noticed the woman, which caused him to freeze.

After that, I didn't see much, because I was already through the doorway, on the heels of Trance.

I heard pounding boots behind me as we wound down a narrow hallway to the embalming area. It was a large room about the size of a large dining hall of a restaurant. There were tables about every ten feet, and on the far wall stood a bank of upright freezers that he'd guessed were for the bodies of the deceased.

A man, mid-thirties, wearing a black button down shirt and black pants was standing beside the drawers where they kept the bodies of the deceased.

Adeline's brother.

Another man, near the same age as Adeline's brother, wearing a polo shirt over khaki pants, stood beside a plain gray door that most likely led to the alley in the back of the building.

Which was proved true moments later when he jerked open the door, and sprinted out, not sparing his partner even a cautionary glance before he disappeared.

"Retrieve, Radar!" Trance commanded.

Radar looked torn, but ultimately followed Trance's orders, slipping out of the door just before it closed. Which also remained locked due to the keypad on the side of the doorframe.

"Fuck!" Trance yelled as he turned and ran at a full sprint, going after Radar through the front room.

Loki, who powered into the room just after Trance left, took Adeline's brother by the arm, turned him around, and started reading him his rights.

"You have the right to remain silent," Loki said, as he snapped one cuff over Jefferson's hand. "You have the right to an attorney. If you cannot afford an attorney, one will be appointed for you."

He said as he snapped the other cuff on, then pushed him forward, leading him out of the door they'd all come in through, still stating his rights.

I, however, stayed.

Something inside of me made me stay. I didn't move. Not a single muscle. I moved only my eyes around the room, scanning over it for any hidden doors, cabinets large enough to hold a person, but I didn't find one. Until my eyes landed on the freezers, and the feeling in my heart grew until it beat an erratic tattoo against my ribs.

Why was her brother standing at the doors to the coolers? Was someone in there? Was someone hiding in one of them? Was there a fucking bomb just waiting for every single cop in Benton to show up before it detonated?

Moving quickly, I jerked open the bottom right corner drawer.

After finding nothing, I moved to the one above it. That one, however, did have something in it.

Ripping the bag open, I was slightly startled to see the charred remains of...something... in it before I moved on to the next body.

Dixie, seeing what I was doing, joined me in the search, opening the doors one by one on the other side.

The next two were more of the same, and it wasn't until I got to the first row on the far side of the room that I found Tunnel's massive body shoved inside.

What the fuck? Why was he here? He was supposed to be at the clubhouse with...

His eyes were closed, and a dark purpling goose egg was welling on the side of his temple, indicating that he'd been hit by something before being shoved into the small opening.

Leaving the door open, I frantically reached for the last drawer as bile rose from the pit of my stomach like a tidal wave. It wasn't until I was at the very last box at the bottom left corner that I found her.

Adeline.

She was on her back, eyes closed, and an ugly bruise was oozing blood just above her right eye. The blood was running steadily out of the cut and into her hair, then further down to the hard surface beneath her where a small puddle was forming.

A steel bar about the size of a crowbar was in the drawer beside her.

Cursing low, I first checked to make sure she had a pulse.

After feeling the slow steady pound of her blood pumping through her veins, I removed the small pen light I always carried with me, lifted her eyelids, and shined it at her pupils. First one, and then the other.

Luckily, they were both equal and reactive.

Her eyes fluttered a few moments after that, and opened, blinking sleepily at me.

Then she winced, raising a hand to her head, saying, "Owww!"

Relief poured through me, making the breath in my lungs leave me in a rush, and I sagged. My elbows caught me as I leaned more fully into the drawer, laying my head against the softness of Adeline's belly.

"Jesus," I whispered.

The sharp bark of a gun report tore through the room like a thunderclap, tensing my spine once again, making me look at the closed door that led to the outside alley.

"Oh shit," Dixie uttered the same words that were on the tip of my tongue.

"What's going on?" Tunnel groaned from the drawer below Adeline.

I watched as the young man stood, and then winced as I got

my first good look at the size of the goose egg. "You're gonna be going to the hospital with us."

Adeline sat up with my help, and then stood.

We were making our way out to the main room when Loki found us.

He looked a little worse for wear and the grim set to his face let me know that something more was wrong. Well, more than what I guessed was the love of his life working at a funeral parlor belonging to a known drug dealer, was wrong.

"Nelson Platt is now in police custody. He shot Radar though. Luckily, it was in the vest that Trance got him last year. Saved his life. Found the crew in the room we suspected they'd be in. They're all outside waiting to be taken in on charges for drug trafficking." Loki said, sounding exhausted.

Seeing Adeline sway on her feet, I picked her up, one arm underneath her legs, and the other around her back. We followed closely behind Loki as he weaved his way through the bowels of the funeral home and out into the morning sunshine, passing a massive amount of cops in the process. Probably more than we'd had on duty that day.

Carrying Adeline straight towards the ambulance, I sat her down on the cot and started to dress her wounds with more than just tissues and paper towels, ignoring the weird glances I was getting from the medics, as well as their verbal demands.

They were ones I hadn't met before, which was weird because I knew practically every medic within thirty miles of Benton. Which meant they must be new.

"Sir, we can do it." One said to him.

I ignored them as I cleaned off her skin around the wound, purposefully not speaking with her, just in case I went insane and lost my temper.

Lucky for her, she stayed quiet too. She must've sensed how very annoyed I was with her, because she barely even looked at me the entire time.

"Do you need a ride to the hospital?" The medic asked snidely.

My eyes turned to the rude man, staring at him, letting him know that I was in no mood to deal with his shitty comments.

"No," I said. "I'll be driving her myself. Thanks for the offer though."

"You're refusing transport, too?" The other medic, the one who was looking at Tunnel's goose egg, asked.

"Yeah, I have a car here. Can't leave it." He explained tightly.

Tunnel was pissed. Most likely at himself. Which was good, because I was mad as hell at him, too. Served him right.

"You do know that you've got a goose egg the size of a Burger King Whopper on your head." Paramedic number two clarified.

"Yeah," he said. "My wife's a nurse. She'll take care of me."

We left shortly after that.

After taking a closer look at Adeline's cut, I decided that there wasn't much to be done for it. It wasn't deep enough for stitches and other than prescribing her headache meds and being told to wake her up every three hours, there was nothing that they could do at a hospital that I couldn't do at home.

Adeline still didn't speak, and I could sense her unease. I knew she thought I was upset with her, and I was. She was trying not to say anything in order to keep my temper in check. Which was good on her part, because my temper was eager to go.

I didn't take the road home, instead deciding to ride. I knew Adeline was probably cold, but she didn't complain, only buried her helmeted head into my back and held on tight, moving into the turns with me, making me feel as if we were one.

I thought about a lot of things during that ride.

Mainly about how I'd lost a lot of stuff in my life, and I didn't want to lose anymore. I didn't want to waste any more time. Didn't want to wake up one morning and regret what I'd done with my life. What could have been.

When we finally pulled into the driveway of my lake house three hours later, I'd come to a few decisions.

One, I was marrying Adeline.

Two, I was having kids with her. Soon.

Three, it was time to talk with my parents. Have a relationship with my mom. My dad, I couldn't give a rip about, but I'd seen the longing in my mother's eyes. I knew she'd wanted to hug me. Talk to me.

If I was truthful with myself, I wanted the same. I missed her.

"This is a beautiful place," Adeline said softly.

I looked at my place through her eyes. Eyes that only saw beauty in the world. Or had until tonight.

"Yeah, Shannon loved it out here. She'd come and tan on the dock in a vain attempt to get Sebastian to pay attention to her." I laughed.

It still felt raw inside, to speak about her in the past.

I didn't know if the feeling would ever subside, and thought that maybe it was a good thing that it didn't.

I still thought of my child in the same way.

An aching longing poured through my chest at the thought of never holding her.

Hell. I couldn't do this right now.

"I left because they said your father was trying to arrange the funeral. I didn't want him to fuck anything up, and the guy that called told me that you relayed a message to me. It sounded like something you'd say." She whispered brokenly.

I shook my head. "It doesn't matter anymore. Just, don't ever do that to me again. I won't be able to handle it if I lost you, too."

My voice sounded raw, and it was.

I was feeling pretty raw, too. Sleep sounded like a good thing, and that's what I declared when I unlocked the door and held it open for her.

"Let's get to bed. I don't want to do anything else right now but sleep, if that's okay." I said as I locked the door behind us and flipped on the front room's light.

It was piled to the brim with the furniture that belonged in the rest of the house. The only thing that probably resembled livable space right now was the one bedroom where my bed was, which was a good thing. That's all I really cared about right now.

"Okay," she said, as she followed me into the bedroom.

I showed her to the bathroom, stripped out of my clothes until I was in only my briefs, and then walked to the back door and pissed off the side of the porch.

I chuckled a little when I saw Sebastian doing the same thing. At least I'd had the decency to leave the light off, unlike Sebastian.

After we both waved, I went back inside, locked the door, and walked to my bedroom to find Adeline asleep on the four-poster king sized bed directly in the middle.

I had to smile as I walked to the dresser, opened the top drawer, and pulled out the engagement ring that I'd had for nearly a week now. At least I was lucky enough to hide it here with the rest of my valuables, or those would've been gone, too, after the fire.

Replacing it back in the drawer, I walked to the side of the bed, lifted the covers, and crawled in beside my woman. She was soft and willing as she turned into my body. Fortunately, I was too exhausted to think about anything that had happened in the past couple of days. Unluckily, I woke up in the middle of the night to a nightmare that was sure to be recurring.

The dream. The most god-awful dream I'd ever had. It had me sweating bullets as I was jarred awake by Adeline's hand.

Adeline was up on an elbow, looking at me in concern.

I hadn't given it a second thought earlier, but my unconscious hadn't forgotten, and now I couldn't slip the mental pictures of the bodies in the drawers. One of those that had been burned could've very well been my sister.

Logically, I knew they weren't my sister. My sister's remains were being examined by the BPD coroner. Was that what she would've looked like?

"Kettle?" Adeline asked worriedly.

My eyes snapped to hers, nearly black in the pre-light dawn. The time of day where you knew the sun was about to come up, but it was still practically dark outside.

"Wanna go watch the sun rise on my dock? It's the only thing that's finished." I asked as I threw the covers off myself and stood.

My body ached, and I stretched my arms up high above my head, feeling my tired and sore muscles stretch and ease. My spine crackled and popped, making the tension in my body ease a small bit.

"Sure, but I've got no clothes, and from the looks of it, you don't either." Adeline said, staring around the empty area.

I snorted. "I've got a blanket. That'll be enough for now. Moreover, I remember hearing last night that today is supposed to be in the 70s. Can't be too cold out there." I said as I grabbed the blanket off the bed.

It wasn't until we were down at the dock that I realized we didn't have any chairs, and the deck was wet with the morning's dew. "Well, shit!"

"We should go steal a few of Sebastian's," Adeline said as she eyed the other man's dock with its numerous chairs. All dry, due to the gazebo he had over the top of his deck.

"He's probably awake right now watching out the window like he usually does. He'd kick my ass." I teased.

"He wouldn't kick my ass." Adeline affirmed before she got up and started in the direction of Sebastian's dock.

She'd gotten her hands on one of Sebastian's favorite chairs before he came out in his underwear with a coffee mug in his hand. "Hey!" He said indignantly.

Adeline ignored him and continued down my dock before she came to a stop right next to me and thumped the chair down.

I sat down with a wave to Sebastian, who was glaring at me, and wrapped my arms, comforter and all, around Adeline as she sat in my lap.

The sliding glass door followed on the heels of Sebastian's stomp into his house. Making us both laugh at the inventive language he'd just used.

"You've got a nice place here," Adeline said a few moments later as we watched the sunrise.

"Yeah, I like it." I agreed.

A lone fish jumped about fifty feet ahead of us, making Adeline jump in my lap.

Before she jumped, she was sitting to the side, most of her butt resting on my thigh. The new position had her flush against my cock. Which, inevitably, led to it getting hard, because it was morning, and Adeline's fine ass really made me hot.

Making me very aware of the state of our clothing, and the fact that Adeline wasn't wearing any pants. Nor panties for that matter.

She giggled when my erection went from soft to harder than a steel pole in two seconds flat.

My hands, which had been wrapped around her tightly, release her and started smoothing down her front.

At first, it only started with smooth circles on her abdomen.

It was only when she started squirming in anticipation that I let my hands roam.

One went underneath her shirt, and started plucking her nipple. The other went down to slip in between the lips of her vagina.

"You're wet," I observed when my finger slicked over her entrance.

"God, I was wet as soon as I sat on your lap. You make my body do these things. I don't think it's normal." She moaned.

I chuckled, switching from one breast to the other, plucking her nipple, pinching and twisting.

"You make me hard when you walk in the room. I remember the first time I saw you stepping out of your car in your fuck me heels and your tight pencil skirt. I wanted to fuck you up against your car. I guess we're even." I rasped, as I trailed my lips down the outside of her neck, sending shivers coursing through her body.

The heel of my hand rubbed against her clit, moving in slow circles until her hips gyrated with the movement of my hand. Her hips thrust forwards and backwards, side to side, slowly, before picking up speed as she got closer and closer to her orgasm.

"Do you want me inside of you when you go?" I asked, teasing her pussy with the tips of my fingers, spreading the moisture around the lips of her sex.

"Yes," she growled, freeing my dick from the confines of my briefs.

She did this under the boundaries of the blanket, keeping her movements as inconspicuous as she could under the circumstances.

"We need to build some walls on this bad boy. We can't keep doing this out here. There could be people watching."

I ignored her, instead lifting her ass up just high enough that I could position my leaking cock at the entrance of her body.

Slowly, with both of my hands on her hips, I eased her down over my turgid length, until I bottomed out inside of her.

My hands moved to span her waist, and I started to move her body, as well as thrust my hips, pulling and pushing, until we were both panting and on the verge of release.

"God, you feel like you're so deep." She breathed.

"This is a good angle. This chair is perfect. I wonder if Sebastian will notice if I keep it." I grunted, pushing her forward and yanking her down, more roughly now.

"I'll just keep stealing it." She gasped.

"What do you need?" I groaned pulling her down until my chest was flush against her back, letting me free up a hand so I could move it to the little bundle of nerves between her splayed thighs.

"That. That right there. Ohh, yes. Right there. Fuck me." She growled, swirling her hips in time to my finger.

Then she clenched down hard, and the hot, wet, pulsing tunnel of her pussy clamped down on me, working my dick until it exploded inside of her.

Hot spurts of come shot out of my dick, seeming to emanate from somewhere deep, branding her with everything I am.

She cried out as my thrusts became jerky, panting and gasping for air.

"Oh, my god." She said as she collapsed against my chest, barely having any energy to breathe.

"You should go off the pill." I said after I caught my breath.

Adeline turned in my arms, stunned.

My length, which had still been inside of her, slipped free of her wet heat and I felt the combined fluids of our coupling leak out of her.

"What? You want to have more kids?" She asked, looking into my eyes.

My eyes moved over her face, studying it closely. "Yeah, that okay with you?"

She nodded emphatically. "To be honest, I wasn't sure if you would ever want to after...your baby was taken."

My arms tightened around Adeline, minutely, before I told her what was on my mind. "I don't think I did before. Now, though, well I don't want to be half a man for the rest of my life. I've lost too much, and I don't want to lose anything else. I want to have babies with you. Grow old with you. Watch my grandkids jump off our dock and swim. To be honest, I've lost too much *not* to try. I have to have hope that life won't keep taking from me. It's time to live again."

SIXTEEN

A Halligan Bar is one of the most versatile tools used in the fire service industry. If you can't get in with a Halligan, you're fucked.
-Kettle

Adeline

Two days later we had a full list of things we needed to do. The morning went surprisingly well, even though both of us had no clothes or food due to the fire. Still. We'd been living on the bare minimum for the past couple of days. Wearing what clothes Sebastian had at his place. Most of them were summer clothes, which worked out well since it was unseasonably warm for this time of the year.

Kettle had gotten a call that morning saying Shannon's remains were released to us, and we could plan her funeral accordingly. Most of it had already been arranged as we were just waiting on her remains to be released before we scheduled a final time.

Not having any food had made us venture out earlier than we'd intended to the local diner for breakfast. After stopping by the church to settle on a time for Shannon's funeral, we'd stopped at a store on the way home. We had to take his truck seeing as he had nothing in his house. And by nothing, I mean absolutely nothing.

Pots, pans, dishes, food, silverware, bathroom supplies, cleaners, towels. The list went on and on. The total that Kettle had to pay at the end of the excursion was close to a grand, and made me cringe when I thought about it.

Luckily, it was a nice day to carry bag after bag of groceries and supplies into the house. It was nearly seventy degrees out, and the perfect day in my opinion.

We'd just gotten the last bag out of the truck and in to the house when the doorbell rang, causing me to turn and regard it with trepidation.

Kettle didn't show the least bit of reluctance, though. Instead, he dropped his bag with the others, and walked to the door sedately before opening it for his mother.

I made it to the door to lean into his back just in time to see the tears start to shimmer in her blue eyes. The same color as her son's.

Kettle's mother was beautiful. Her hair was brown, and hung in a trendy bob just underneath her chin. Pale silver strands were interspersed throughout her locks. She was wearing jeans and a fitted shirt, showing off her curvy, slim body, despite her age. I could only hope to look that good after two kids and thirty years on me.

"Oh, Tiago. I've missed you so." She wept.

Kettle's back tensed slightly before tapping my thigh and moving forward, taking his mother into a hug for the first time in sixteen years.

Her weeping turned to sobs as her son enfolded her into his big arms, and I backed away, letting them have the moment that they so desperately deserved.

Needing something to do, I grabbed my cell phone off the table and walked outside. I went out onto Kettle's deck that had seen better days, and walked down to the dock. The chair that I'd stolen from Sebastian was gone, and I sighed as I dropped down to my haunches before taking a seat on the deck, letting my feet dangle over the sides.

Luckily, the deck was far enough off the water; otherwise, my feet would be dipped into the freezing lake below.

My eyes trailed over the water, watching the beauty of it sway and roll gently in the wind before turning to my phone and punching in my sister's number.

"Hello?" She answered.

"Hey, Vid. Merry Christmas." I replied snidely.

I could hear the TV in the background as Viddy listened to the morning news, as she always did.

"Hey, sister. How was your Christmas?" She asked distractedly.

My jaw clenched, and my anger started to rise.

I'd called my sister the night of the fire, knowing I needed to talk to someone; she'd always been my first choice. But she hadn't answered, and I'd needed her desperately.

I'd called four more times in the past two days, and this was the first time she'd answered in all those times. She'd replied with a text message each of those times. *'Busy, I'll call you when I can.'*

"What's going on with you? Why didn't you call me back?" I asked in exasperation.

"What?" She asked sharply. "What are you talking about?"

My eyes narrowed at a point across the lake where a deer had walked out through the trees and started drinking from water's edge.

"I've called you a bazillion times in the past couple of days.

You never called me back and always replied with the same message. I needed to talk to you." I sniffled.

"Adeline, I never got any of your calls. I didn't even have my phone. It died as soon as I got to Paul's parents' house, and I gave it to him to charge in his car. Every time I'd ask for it, he said to leave it. Said that it was rude to talk on my phone when I was visiting with someone. So I left it there." She replied, sounding very confused.

I refrained from telling her that her boyfriend was a massive dick, and most likely had her phone the whole time. He'd had to have been screening her calls. Why else would he have replied with anything? I'd let her draw her own conclusions, though.

"You didn't even call me for Christmas. What the hell was that?" I asked, as my anger evaporated. Knowing my sister would never do anything to hurt me willingly.

"I did call you. I called Kettle's house phone. I didn't know your cell phone number off the top of my head, and that was the only one I remembered since it was so easy. I would've left a message but the answering machine never picked up." She explained, worry starting to rise in her voice.

That's when I clarified what had happened in the last couple of days. What she'd missed with the fire. And then further with what happened at the funeral home, and what our brother had done.

"Your apartment burned down...again?" She gasped. "What the fuck? Do they know who did it?"

I was shaking my head, even though she couldn't see it. "No. They had a video of it. That's it though."

"What about Monty?" She asked hesitantly.

My throat closed again, agitated with all the life that was lost in the fire.

From what I'd learned from Kettle and the news, over ten pets,

Monty included, had been lost in that fire, along with Shannon. Luckily there were no other human losses, but the one was enough.

"He didn't make it. By the time everyone arrived, the whole place was fully engulfed in flames. That's why Shannon wasn't able to be saved, either. It just burned too hot. The person that set the fire used what they think was jet fuel. It caught fire and burned so hot that nothing was left."

"Jet fuel? Where the hell would you get jet fuel?" She asked, mirroring my own question I'd had when I'd heard Sebastian and Kettle talking about it that morning when I'd walked outside to find them on the dock together.

"I don't know." I replied truthfully.

"And what is all this with Jefferson? He hit you over the head, Adeline. Did you press charges against him?" She asked sharply.

Again, she was mirroring my own worries. "I don't really know anything, Vid. I'm just as in the dark as you are. In fact, more so. I have all of this swirling around me, and I haven't the faintest fucking clue what the hell is going on."

"I don't know what to say." She said after a while.

I didn't either. In fact, I was utterly flabbergasted that any of this had touched my life. I was a teacher for God's sake. What did I ever do to warrant this? The worst thing I'd ever done was steal a couple of animals from a testing facility.

"Me neither." I replied.

Looking for a change of subject after the silence ensued for too long, drew circles in the air with my foot and asked, "What did he get you for Christmas?"

I heard her murmur something in the background, but it was so low and garbled that I had to have her repeat it three more times before I actually understood.

"What was that?" I asked for the last time.

"He got me a picture of him." She snarled.

I couldn't help it. The laugh that burst free from my gut had me falling backwards in glee. I was wheezing and tears were streaming from my eyes. I could hear my sister snarling at me, and then the click of the phone as she hung up, but I still didn't stop laughing.

"A picture!" I wheezed. "What the fuck is she gonna do with a picture of him?"

A large pair of boots stopped where they were straddling my head, and I looked up. Past a pair of blue jeans, past the most glorious package on earth, and then up further until I could see Kettle's face. He looked happy. Smiling widely at my laughter.

"What are you laughing at?" He asked from above me.

I snorted. "Paul got Viddy a picture of himself for Christmas."

Kettle rolled his eyes and held his hand out for me. "Dumbass. What'd your sister have to say about it?"

I reached for his hand and he yanked me up, making my body crash into his.

Breathlessly, I said, "She hung up on me. I wouldn't know."

"I like seeing you laugh like that." He rumbled, eyes zeroing in on my lips.

"I like laughing like that." I replied, moving up on my tiptoes until my lips collided with his.

Both of us were breathless by the time we pulled apart. His smile was soft as he disentangled our bodies until he had a hold on my hand and pulled me towards his back door.

His mother was in the kitchen putting away the copious amount of groceries when we finally made it inside. She had a delighted smile on her face when she saw the both of us together, and I couldn't help but feel the same way. I was glad that she was here, and that Kettle had her back in his life again. I just wished it wasn't under such horrid circumstances.

"Alright, I have to get ready for work. We had three call in's and I'm next on the list. Mom's going to hang out with you and run to the church later on to help you with the final details. Is that okay?" He asked me with a raised eyebrow.

My eyes turned from his mother to him, and I nodded in affirmation. "Yep, that sucks that you have to go to work though. Do you have to stay the full 24 hours, or is it just until one of the others can get there?" I asked.

He shrugged. "I don't know, but I'll call when I find out, okay? The funeral is still on for tomorrow afternoon, though. I'll be done in plenty of time."

I nodded in understanding. "Wait, what about uniforms? You don't have anything to wear!"

"Jeans and a t-shirt. They've ordered me some more this morning. They should be here by the time I have to go back on shift Saturday morning." He explained before walking out of the kitchen.

Not before he gave me a kiss on the cheek, followed by one for his mother.

I watched her as she watched him walk out of the room. She looked broken. Torn.

"You okay?" I asked in worry.

She nodded. "Yes. I've made some huge mistakes in my life. That boy wasn't one of them, though."

"And for that, Mrs. Spada, I will thank you for the rest of my life." I replied.

She smiled at me sadly. "Call me Helene."

• • •

Kettle

"She thinks you're at work?" The man sitting across from me asked.

The man was big. Not as tall as me, but his muscles could definitely compete with mine.

He also looked so much like Sebastian that it was uncanny.

Which made sense. Sebastian was his brother after all.

I nodded firmly at Sam. Sam was the head of an organization that helped women get out of abusive situations. He owned a bike shop where he customized bikes, as well as repaired them. He used his business, Free, as a front. To all intents and purposes, he was just another mechanic who'd gotten out of the military and started up a shop to make a living.

To everybody else, especially the women he helped, he was a goddamn hero.

"Yes," I nodded. "I have until noon tomorrow before she'll start asking questions. Did Silas fill you in?"

Sam nodded. "Jack did a little poking around to see if he could get anything else. He hit the same wall though. Amadeus was thorough if nothing else. The transfer went through earlier this month. Absolutely nothing is in his name anymore. Even his house is under a different name. He had every bit of it transferred to his woman. Everything except for the funeral home. That was transferred into Platt's name. It was like he was tipped off somehow. Like he knew it was coming. We've got absolutely no legal leg to stand on."

My hands went to my eyes and I rubbed them. Hard.

"Goddammit. This is such a fucking clusterfuck. I'm so out of my league." I rasped forlornly.

Silas, who'd been quiet up until this point, spoke. "There's more son."

My hands dropped, and I looked at Silas blearily. "How much worse could it get?"

Do you know that saying... never borrow trouble? With that one statement I'd just uttered, I'd completely fucked myself. I'd opened a can of worms and they were all spilling out wiggling in opposite directions.

"The woman they transferred it to was named Rosalie Espinoza." He said quietly.

I sat back in my chair, closing my eyes.

They all knew what happened to me when I was younger. Knew I'd lost my daughter. Knew about Rosalie. I'd never told them in detail, but they knew what had happened just by listening to the town gossip.

"That's just perfect. Transfer everything over to her. She dies like she's supposed to in a few months, and he gets it all back. Easy as pie." I growled in defeat. "How the fuck did she get tangled up with him?"

Jack spoke for the first time. His deep voice resonated off the walls of the clubhouse's conference room where we held all our meetings.

"From what I can understand, she was married to him. Has been for over a decade. They stayed married all through her time at the women's correctional facility in Huntsville. She was released a year and a half ago. Gustavo was there to pick her up as soon as she got out, according to the guards." Jack's explained in low tones.

I'd known she'd gotten released. They'd invited me to the parole hearing, yet I'd declined to go. I didn't want to see her for the rest of my life. She was dead to me, and always would be.

What I hadn't known was that she was married.

However, now that I did, things started falling into place.

Things that had never made sense all those years ago.

Like why she moved on from me so fast. Why she let that happen. How she'd let that happen to our child.

Then a thought occurred to me. "Wait a minute, when does it say she got married?"

Jack started flipping through a pile of pages in front of him before stopping, when he'd gone through nearly half the stack. "It says here October 3, 1998. Why?"

A sick curdling feeling of dread started to swell in my stomach.

"My daughter died August 12, 1999. She was three weeks old." I said woodenly. "Her boyfriend of nearly a year killed her. But it's not making sense. If she was married, why would she have a boyfriend? Gustavo's not the type to let that pass."

When the last sentence slipped from my mouth, I stood and started moving towards the safe on the far wall.

It was a large safe nearly as tall as me. The keypad was the old-fashioned type that you had to turn with a dial.

Grabbing the lock between my thumb and pointer finger, I started the painstaking task of spinning the dial and stopping at the appropriate numbers.

After the third was inputted, I stopped, turned the large lock, and swung the door open.

The letter I'd set in my file folder at the top shelf was exactly where I'd put it.

Flipping it open, I began to read.

Tiago,

If you're reading this, know that I'm too sick to say it to you in person.

I've been agonizing over this for sixteen years now, so I'm just going to tell you.

Gustavo Amadeus is the man who killed our child, not Mario Martinez.

I fell in with the wrong crowd before you left.

I can't tell you how sorry I am for doing what I did. I didn't know what else to do, I swear to God. I hope one day you find it in your heart to forgive me, but I know that I will be gone from this place when that happens. I'm sorry.

When you left for boot camp my parents welcomed me back home. I'd told them I'd lost the baby. They said I could move back in if I agreed to marry my father's business partner's son. Not knowing what else to do, and having nowhere else to go, I did. I moved back in with them, and a month later I wed Gustavo.

I never told them that I was still pregnant, and thought that if I got married fast enough, I could just act like I was pregnant by Gustavo.

I was naïve. I didn't think he'd figure it out. I didn't think about you sending any presents for our baby. I was just thinking about myself. I was being selfish, and I will forever pay for that mistake.

He had his suspicions when she was born. I never said anything, but when the package arrived that you sent for our daughter, he flipped. I had to tell him then what happened. When he left, I thought it was going to be okay, but he came back drunk, and so very angry.

He killed her in a fit of rage, and told me that if I told, he would find a way to kill every single person I'd ever loved. My parents and you included. I played along with the story that it was my boyfriend who'd done it. He made up a scenario to where my new boyfriend did it, and you know the rest.

God, I'm so sorry.

Please know that I have never forgiven myself, and never will.

Rosalie.

The piece of paper slipped from my hands and fell to the floor.

I watched it in dismay as my fear was confirmed.

That man had killed my daughter. Killed my sister. Attempted to kill my woman. What else could he take from me?

All this time I thought the rightful person was serving a life sentence after he'd killed my baby. My precious, innocent child. She never got to take her first steps. Never got to crawl. She'd be nearly sixteen right now. She'd be driving.

My heart hurt. It was like reliving the moment I'd found my child was dead all over again.

"Kettle?" Sebastian asked after the silence continued for way too long.

I looked up into the eyes of my VP, and every single doubt I was feeling earlier disappeared. In its place was cold, hard truth.

Resolve in its truest and purest form.

The man was going to pay, and I was going to make sure of it. Tonight.

I knew what I had to do.

SEVENTEEN

Never underestimate the power of an extremely pissed off
woman. They're the ones that'll kill you in your sleep.
-Kettle to Trance

Adeline

2:53 P.M.

I walked into the diner and found my sister at our usual booth.
I had to laugh when I saw she was wearing nearly the same thing I was. Dark washed blue jeans, a white t-shirt, and her hair in a ponytail. The only difference was my tattooed arms compared to her tattoo free ones.

"Hey," I said dropping into the booth. "You're wearing the exact same outfit as me!"

She smiled at me. "Yeah? I did it on purpose."

I snorted. Sure she did. Most likely, she just reached into her closet and removed a hanger like she always did. I made sure to match her outfits for her, and then hang them up in the closet. I was nice like that.

"Did you order for us yet?" I asked curiously.

There were no menus on the table, but I knew what I wanted by memory, so it really didn't matter if they were there or not.

"Yes, I got you a burger and fries. For me, I got a tuna melt." She said as she leaned forward, placing her elbows on the table and her chin in her hands. "Who brought you here today?"

"Santa." I replied just as the waitress brought us over some tea.

She looked at me weirdly after I said that, but I smiled and didn't explain. Viddy knew I was talking about Dixie, and that was all that mattered.

"The waitress gave me a dirty look. What'd you say to her?" I asked when the waitress glared at me from across the room.

Viddy shrugged. "I told her the table was sticky, and the floor under the table felt gross."

"What's the big deal with that?" I asked, studying my sister's features.

She looked different. Tired. She had bags underneath her eyes that showed she wasn't sleeping very well again.

"She tossed a rag at me earlier thinking she'd just leave it there for me to clean up, except I hadn't realized it was there, so she did it herself, but then went to complain to Martha, who then told the woman that I was blind. Needless to say, she's mad at me now because Martha gave her an ear full." She said before taking a sip of her tea.

I snorted. Martha was a good woman. She was a mother of four, and her husband was a firefighter at the fire department with Kettle and Sebastian. I'd met them a few times at different get togethers that the fire fighters had every couple of weeks. She was a busy woman, and I got along with her well.

"Dumbass. How would she not know you were blind? I mean the glasses..." I trailed off. "Hey! You're not wearing your glasses!"

I felt stupid for not noticing that right away. No wonder she looked different. It wasn't very often that I didn't see her with them.

Viddy grimaced. "They make my head hurt."

I understood that all too well. I hated wearing anything on my head whether it be sunglasses, a headband, or even a tight pony-tail. Although I hadn't been aware that Viddy had ever had that problem.

"Is there something else going on?" I asked warily.

"Not really, no. But I've been seeing things lately. Shadows. Some lights. Movements. It's really quite weird. Yesterday I woke up, and I swear to God I could see. Not great, by any means, but I could make out my dresser and the window. But then it was just all gone, and I haven't seen anything like that since. A couple of days ago the pressure of the glasses on my head started to really hurt, and I haven't worn them since."

"Have you called Dr. Robbins?" I asked, trying my hardest not to show the excitement I was feeling.

She was shaking her head. "And tell him what? That my glass-es give me a headache and I thought I saw something the other day?"

As I opened my mouth to reply, the waitress interrupted us, dropping our plates down in front of us, making them clatter.

"What is your problem?" I asked, alarmed.

"I was told to tell you this meal is on the house, and I'm sorry for your loss." She ground through clenched teeth.

I watched her walk into the back of the kitchen before turning to Viddy. "What the fuck?"

Viddy was shaking her head, confused as well. "I don't know."

It wasn't until Martha came over with the tea pitcher that we understood. "I'm sorry to hear about Shannon, Adeline. I still can't believe she won't be here anymore."

Then I realized that this was where Shannon worked. This was also where Kettle and I had had our first meal together.

"Oh," I breathed. "Thank you."

God, just when I thought I was doing pretty well, I had to be reminded that I had a funeral to go to later for Kettle's sister, and my good mood shot out the window.

Martha smiled sadly. "Yeah, it's going to suck working with Tillie over there all the time. Shannon always had a smile on her face. Tillie, on the other hand, can't stand people. Especially you." She said, tilting her head in Viddy's direction.

"Viddy?" I asked in surprise. "Why Viddy? Viddy doesn't even know that woman."

"Oh, you sure did. Viddy talked to her ex, and she hates her on principle." Martha snickered.

"Her ex?" Viddy asked perplexed.

"Oh yeah, remember a few months back when you came in here to eat? Tillie was tending the counter that night and watched you speak to Trance for the entire two hours y'all were here. She hates your guts." Martha said excitedly.

"I'm thinking that maybe we shouldn't eat our food." I observed dryly, staring down at the food Tillie had placed in front of us with a forlorn expression.

"I watched her bring it out here, she didn't do anything to it. That's not to say that she wouldn't have, though, if I hadn't been watching." Martha said as she bustled away.

"You've got a hater. Way to go, Viddy!" I teased.

She rolled her eyes, and I had to laugh. She used to do that a lot before the accident, and that was the first time I'd seen it since. It made me happy that she was doing it. That was the first I'd seen of the old Viddy in a long time.

Our hour went fast, and soon Dixie was walking up to the table in no time, offering to usher me out the door. "I've got an appointment I have to get to. Are you about ready, darlin'?"

Viddy smiled when she heard his voice and turned in his direction. "Hi, Dixie. How are you doing today?"

Dixie smiled down at my sister, and I couldn't help thinking how awesome it was that the club accepted my sister just as they had me. It made me feel good that Viddy would have the full support of every one of the Dixie Wardens if she was ever in need.

"I'm doing alright, sweet pea. Do you need help to your car before we head out?" He asked her.

Viddy scowled at him, and Dixie snickered.

"Okay, okay," he said, holding his hands up and backing away from the table. "It was good seein' you girl; make sure you come out for the New Year's party this weekend."

With that, he left, and I looked at the smile still on my sister's face. She looked happy. "Will you come?"

Viddy turned her smile on me, and answered. "Absolutely. I think a party is in order after everything that's happened in the last couple of days. That and I'm due for some fun, don't you think?"

I was happy on my way home from the diner. That was until I realized I was missing my purse.

"Oh, Dixie! I forgot my bag, can we go back and get it, please?" I said urgently.

He played like he was annoyed, but swung the truck around back in the direction of the diner. Luckily we were only about five minutes away.

Nearly five minutes too late.

The first thing I noticed was my sister walking towards the direction of the bus stop.

That had me cursing up a storm because she was supposed to

be picked up by Paul.

"What is she doing walking?" I growled, pointing my sister out to Dixie.

He turned his head to the side as he swung into a handicapped spot illegally, at the front of the diner. Which was why we saw the black Hummer stop on the road just in front of Viddy and cut her off. She startled and froze at the sound of the large truck screeching to a halt beside her, waiting to see her fate.

However, I was nearly out of the car before Dixie grabbed a hold on my hand in an iron grip and held me so tight I cried out in shock and pain.

"Dixie, what are you doing? Let me go!" I screeched.

He silenced me with one look that had me freezing in my tracks before pulling out his phone and dialing. He then set it on the seat between us and reared out of the vehicle, leaving the door wide open as he took off as fast as his big body would allow.

He didn't make it in time, though.

The man who'd stepped out of the Hummer grabbed Viddy by the hair, opened the passenger side door, and threw her bodily into the Hummer before slamming the door shut.

His pace quickened when he saw Dixie coming towards him, but he didn't need to, he was in the Hummer and shooting down the road before Dixie had even made it halfway there.

Dixie growled in frustration before turning around and running back towards the truck.

It was then that I heard Kettle's frantic voice as he yelled for Dixie to answer him.

"Dixie!" He bellowed hoarsely.

"They-they have Viddy. They have my sister, Tiago!" I screamed.

"Where are you?" He barked.

"The diner." I said in horror.

"We'll be there in five. We're right around the corner." He growled before hanging up.

That five minutes was the longest of my life.

As soon as they'd gotten there, they'd set up a command post of sorts, put out BOLOS, and questioned nearly everyone at the scene.

All the while, I stood back, watching with my heart nearly torn in two.

"Kettle?" I asked, suddenly remembering a joke between Viddy and me when she'd gotten stranded by our brother all those months ago.

"What?" He said distractedly as he looked at a map on his car.

The man with the scar under his eye was standing next to him, listening to every word he said.

"Kettle!" I said urgently, making him finally turn and look at me.

"What?" He snapped.

"Do you remember when I joked about getting Viddy a GPS tracker? Well, I did. It was one of the ones you stick on the stuff you don't want to lose. I saw it on a commercial that had it on a dog's collar, and they found him when he was lost. If Viddy was actually carrying hers, as she told me she would, wouldn't that work right now?" I asked desperately.

The Native American man who'd been standing on the opposite side of the truck stepped forward, looking at me intently.

"Did she set it up?" He asked me.

"Yes, I did. But it's one of the one's you have to keep charged. And I don't know if she's been doing that or not. How would I know?" I asked worriedly.

"Did you set it up on the computer or your phone?" He asked.

"My phone." I said, handing it to him.

He started punching in buttons, and then let out a curse of exhilaration. "Fuck yes, I got her. It's giving me coordinates. Hold on," he said as he placed my phone on the roof of Dixie's truck and pulled his own phone out before he started typing. "Bingo. They're on I-20 East Bound heading towards Alexandria."

"Dixie, make sure she doesn't leave. Take her straight home and sit on her if you have to. Adeline, I'm counting on you to not make me worry about you." He said before kissing my lips, and roaring off, followed by eight more bikes and the truck with the Native American man and the one with the scar under his eye.

I watched with my heart in my throat as the love of my life set off to bring my twin home. The other half of my soul.

"It's going to be okay, honey. They'll bring her home. No matter what." Dixie said as he pulled me in close.

That no matter what was what bothered me.

· · ·

Kettle

6:59 P.M.

"They stopped at Lake Darbonne. They took Lake Darbonne Road, and then onto Lake Road from there. I have the property listed as belonging to a Reese Madison. That's Gustavo's married sister's lake home. It's empty and on the market, according to the realty records." Jack said where we were stopped on the side of the road.

We'd stopped nearly a mile and a half away near some dumpsters.

"How are we going to do this?" Silas asked Sam, yielding to

the judgment of the most experienced man on the team.

Sam looked taken aback at his father's trust in him, but quickly took charge.

"We wait for dark. It's only thirty minutes from now, and that should give your friend time to get here with his dog. You said he was another twenty minutes..." He trailed off as Trance's personal truck started to zip past them before locking the brakes up and backing up until he was in front of the dumpster.

He hopped out of the truck and walked determinedly towards us, his face a mask of fear.

"Do you know where she is?" He asked apprehensively.

He visibly relaxed at our nods, calling Radar out of his truck, before he collapsed against the bumper in relief.

"Tell me what we've got." He rumbled.

Sam started outlining what he'd like done; telling us who went where, and then we looked at the blue prints of the house and grounds.

"He hasn't been here long enough to have anything set up. From what I can tell, he used his cell phone to call the sister in Iowa, where she lives now. They were on the phone for ten minutes before they hung up, and Gustavo's course veered from Alexandria to Farmersville within two minutes of that call. It looks like he's just looking for a place to hide out until he can figure out his next move. If we're lucky, he'll have no safeguards in place at all." Jack said as his eyes flicked over the computer screen in front of him.

I couldn't help the manic smile that overtook my face in that instant. It was really good to have that man on my side. 'Cause working against a man of his caliber really wouldn't be good.

"So do we walk in?" Silas asked once we got the logistics of what the plan was. "I think that's best. Although, I think walking along the outer tree line that lines the lake would be best." Sam rumbled.

We all nodded in confirmation.

"Now, I want to be sure that we all understand that this is going to be a police operation. Loki, Trance and Radar need to be the only ones that fire anything or offer any deadly force. It's going to be the only clean way any of this can be done without pulling strings." Silas noted from his position at Sam's side.

Although he said it to all of us, his eyes were pinned on me, making sure he got the point across.

I gave him an assuring nod, and we set out down the tree line.

The walk was less than a mile and a half walking distance through the woods, since we were able to cut off nearly half the distance that it took to drive there.

Everything that happened once we reached the property line was just this side of anticlimactic.

Viddy was sitting at the kitchen table with her hands and feet bound to the chair.

Gustavo was pacing and yelling into his phone, nearly the entire kitchen's length away from Viddy.

Warily, Trance and Loki advanced on the door while the rest of us fanned out around the property.

I took the side door that led out from the dining room while Trance and Loki both took the sliding glass door that led into the kitchen.

Even better, the glass door was open, allowing the cool night breeze in through the screen door.

Allowing us to hear every bit of the conversation. Which was how we knew that Gustavo was alone, weaponless, as well as pissed way the hell off that he'd grabbed the wrong sister, risking everything to kidnap this woman which wouldn't even get him anywhere.

I was inside the house and rounding the edge of the hallway, just barely able to see into the kitchen as Loki stepped inside, when Gustavo turned away in his pacing. He had his back to the door allowing Loki to step entirely into the kitchen before he turned and even saw that anyone was there.

Then he tried to run. Directly towards me.

Ignoring the earlier warning from Silas, I reared back my arm and punched the smaller man with every bit of fury that had built up in the past sixteen years. Releasing every single bit of it on the man, and then some.

The punch took him on the cheekbone.

I clearly heard the crunch of a bone shattering, and then he went down. Hard.

His head hit the tiled floor first, followed shortly after by the rest of him.

It took every ounce of self-control I possessed to keep from rearing my leg back and kicking him, beating the ever loving shit out of him until his face no longer resembled anything human.

But then Sebastian's hand curled around my shoulder and hauled me back from temptation, practically dragging me backwards until I was back outside and standing in the cool winter air.

"You're okay." Sebastian said to me, and it was only then that I realized just how quickly I was breathing.

My lungs were billowing like a freight train, and each puff of my breath filled the cold night air like a cloud, surrounding me.

"You piece of shit. You stupid, goddamn piece of shit. I should fucking kill you. You've taken nearly everything from my sister. You don't deserve to live." Viddy screeched, making the tension in my shoulders ease slightly.

"Who are you calling?" Sebastian asked as I walked to where

I could see the show unfold in the kitchen.

"My soon to be wife."

• • •

9:37 P.M.

"Cameras are off, but I don't know for how long. Keep it under control though. The captain won't like this if you beat the shit out of him. Try to keep a lid on it, eh?" Loki confirmed as he showed me to the interrogation room Gustavo was in.

I walked into the room without saying a word of affirmation to Loki, and immediately clenched my hands into tight fists as not to pummel the little weasel's face.

Gustavo grinned at me, instantly knowing who I was as soon as I stepped through the door.

I walked sedately into the room, trying with all of my ability to keep the fury I was feeling back.

"So you finally came to find out what my motives were, yes *cazzo*?" Gustavo asked.

Cazzo. Dick. Glad he could be original.

My father had said that often when I was growing up

"Yes, cameras are off," I said staring at the man. "Tell me why."

"You got a letter. I would've left you alone if it wasn't for the letter." He shrugged.

"You wasted your time. I never even read the letter." I growled in frustration.

"It doesn't matter, *cazzo*. I've been meaning to find you and say thank you for years now. I would've never known if you hadn't sent that package from Iraq. I never intended to hurt your *bastardo* that bad, but once it happened, well, it just happened. Rosalie was kind enough to keep it quiet, although I did have to threaten her a wee bit." He said holding up my fingers a short distance from the other.

"Anyway, I thought for sure when your papa delivered that letter to you, that you would read it, but you didn't. Only that girl of yours did. Of course, then I had to kill her. I used her brother. Those stupid little twit kids. Nobody could follow through, so I had to do it myself. Sorry about your sister, though. That's too bad." He grinned and bared his teeth.

Hearing what I needed to hear, I started to leave the room, but stopped when I reached the doorway.

"Just remember this, *cazzo*. Don't drop the soap. I hope you enjoy playing the bitch." I hissed before crashing out of the room.

• • •

10:18 P.M.

I watched as Adeline and Viddy reunited, keeping my mouth shut and letting them have their moment.

"So she was kicking him?" Adeline giggled. "Did Trance toss her over his shoulder before or after she kicked him in the face?"

"After. Trance had her nearly outside before she squirmed her way loose, heading for the downed man. Then, she reared back and kicked him in the face, breaking his nose and spraying blood absolutely everywhere."

"Yeah, I think it got in my hair." Viddy groaned from the couch beside Adeline.

Adeline giggled even more as she pulled her sister towards her, and buried her nose in Viddy's hair.

"I can't believe you did that. Thank you." Adeline whispered.

"I guess you should really thank yourself. You're the one who bought me that dog tracker thing. Worked out well, too. I had it around my neck." She said as she pulled the object that was on a chain around her neck from beneath her shirt.

It was a circular medallion type thing that was the size of a quarter.

"No, that was you keeping it charged. Without that, it would've been useless."

Viddy waved the comment away with a flick of her hand. "Whatever."

"Squeeze you to pieces, Viddy." Adeline said as she curled a little more into her sister.

"Squeeze you back together." Viddy replied.

EPILOGUE

Ride with me forever.
-A note from Kettle to Adeline on their wedding day.

"Alright, I'll be back momentarily. I want you to start reading the lab manual, and then we can get started on the lab. Rebecca, can you..."

Beeeeeeep.Beeeeeeep.Beeeeeeep.

The fire alarms started ringing, making my heart lurch up into my throat. Although I'd known we were doing a fire drill today, it still scared the crap out of me. The fucking thing was louder than hell, and on the verge of giving me a seizure.

"Alright ladies and gentlemen, line up at the door. Leave your things. Cell phones too." I said to the class before heading to the door.

As they filed out, one by one, and started heading for the nearest exit, I counted my class until I was sure I had them all, and then followed behind them. "Head to the football field. We're at the thirteen yard line, remember?" I called up ahead.

They all grumbled their acknowledgements as we made our way down the hall and outside into the cool spring air.

It'd been two months since that horrible night my sister was abducted, and I still woke up in night sweats just thinking about how she'd been taken right in front of me.

Viddy, on the other hand, had seemed to come out of her shell. She'd started coming to more of The Dixie Wardens' Barbeques, as well as any party that they threw. I was enjoying each and every minute of having her back, too.

"Gentlemen, stop holding up the line. Please continue to follow the crowd to the field. Jackson Freeman, what did I say...oh, my God." I gasped.

The boys I'd been yelling at moved all at once, and there in front of me, down on one knee, was the love of my life. Decked out in his bunker bottoms and helmet.

It took me a while to get past the fact that my man was down on one knee in the middle of a fire drill, but then I happened to look down in front of him to see '*Will You Marry Me*' written out in fire hose.

I looked at the man; staggered for a few stunned seconds before I took off running, tackling him to the ground and giving him kisses on the face, nose, and mouth. Practically any part of his body I could reach without it being indecent.

"So I take that as a yes?" He asked happily.

"A thousand times. Yes." I squealed back, just as happily.

"Ms. Sheffield, I sure hope you know what you're doing." Mrs. Threadgill said from beside me.

I looked up at the prim woman's face and grinned at the pleasure I saw emanating there.

"Oh yes, he's the halligan to my axe. How could I say no?" I teased.

"I'm not sure I like those types of words used in front of my students."

And the lady dragon was back.

• • •

Four and half months later

I looked around at the finished project of Kettle's house. No, scratch that. Our house.

Kettle and his friends from both the Dixie Wardens and firehouse slaved day and night to make this place presentable for today.

I couldn't help the surge of excitement that coursed through my veins as I looked out our kitchen window at Kettle, my fiancé and soon to be husband, standing on the newly remodeled dock.

In less than an hour, we'd be married.

"Sis?" Jefferson called from behind me.

I turned to find my brother in the doorway. He was looking so much better lately. But that had a lot to do with the woman he had his arm currently around. Detective Annalise Hernandez.

She was fairly glowing, and that wasn't surprising since she was nearly four months pregnant.

Jefferson's hair was cut into a sharp cut that showed off his features perfectly. His royal blue polo and khaki pants looked great on him. His muscles were starting to thicken and spread, and my heart started to weep. He was looking so much like my dad that it made my heart hurt.

A good kind of hurt.

My dad would've been proud of him.

Turns out that when he realized what kind of trouble he was in when it came to Gustavo, Jefferson did the smart thing and went to the ATF instead of the stupid thing and bending to Gustavo's will.

He was working with ATF to bring Gustavo down, all the while The Dixie Wardens and the Benton Police Department were doing the same thing. They didn't realize they were all working on the same team until the night Kettle got my sister back for me.

Annalise met Jefferson during the huge explanation that took part between both the police and the ATF.

From there, their relationship grew, despite the huge differences between the two.

Which only went to show that love's blind. You don't choose who you love, you just try to ride the wave.

And Annalise and Jefferson definitely rode that wave if Annalise's pregnant belly was anything to show for it.

"Jefferson!" I squealed happily. "I'm glad you came. How are you?"

Jefferson's eyes bulged when he got a load of the front of my dress, and I couldn't help the laugh that escaped my throat. Annalise was smiling widely as she saw it though. She knew the score.

"Wow your wedding dress is very...red. And where's the rest of it?" He asked in surprise.

I snickered as I answered. "You know I don't do traditional. That's not my style at all. But this...this is me. Kettle might have a small heart attack, but I think he'll like it."

The dress was red on top with a plunging neckline that slowly bled to white. It was a corset style with black satin ribbon criss-crossing at my back. Swarovski Crystals lined the top, accentuating my voluptuous breasts perfectly.

Oh, who was I kidding? Kettle was going to have a cow, but I planned to tell him something later, and I wanted him thoroughly distracted until I did so. It would be picture-perfect! I just hoped the photographer was able to get his face like she assured me she could when I told him.

"Yeah, I can see you're definitely not traditional. Nor did you offer your bridesmaids traditional." Jefferson trailed off as Viddy and Baylee entered the room.

Baylee was a bridesmaid, while Viddy was, of course, my maid of honor.

Both of their strapless dresses were made out of black lace that came to a stop at just above the knees, fitted tightly to their bodies. There was a deep scarlet ribbon high across their waists that tied their colors in with mine, and I absolutely adored them. I couldn't wait to see the looks on Sebastian and Trance's faces when they saw my beautiful ladies, just as I couldn't wait to see the look on Kettle's.

"So how do I look, 'cause I can't see?" Viddy teased as she twirled around.

Jefferson, Annalise and Baylee all laughed as Viddy had intended, but I just stared. She really did look stunning. Which also made me mad because her body looked better than mine did, although my boobs could totally kick her boobs' ass.

She was wearing flats, but they worked well for her. The dress was exquisite with her lean hourglass shape.

"Adeline?" She asked when she didn't hear my laugh.

How she knew that, I would never know. She just did.

"Yeah, Vid?" I asked, walking up close to her.

"What's wrong?" She asked.

"Nothing. You look beautiful." I whispered, really wishing she could see herself.

"I know. I feel beautiful, therefore I look beautiful." She teased.

"Alright, who's ready to get this show on the road?" Jefferson exclaimed.

"Yes, I'm ready. Is everyone else?" I asked the group.

"Wait! You forgot your garter! Here, lift your dress and let me get it on." Baylee ordered as she squatted down at my feet.

I bunched my dress in my hands and lifted it, watching as Baylee slipped the little slip of frilly lace and fabric over my boots and up my thigh. Once done, she gave my outer thigh a pat and stood with a nod. "Let's get this done. I can't wait to see Kettle's face when he sees you!"

. . .

Kettle

"Holy Shit," Sebastian growled from beside me.

My heart was slow and steady as I watched Baylee come down the dock towards us.

Then came Viddy and I tensed.

She walked sure and steady, cane-less. Once she reached the edge of the dock, she stepped up lightly and walked smooth and steady down the dock towards us.

Trance, who was also at my side, visibly relaxed, as did I, once she made it to Baylee's side.

"Jesus Christ," Trance hissed.

Trance had it bad. Although, I was just as worried as he was, despite Viddy having practiced it no less than a hundred times.

We decided against having any ring bearers or flower girls because of having the wedding on the dock itself. We didn't want to have to go fish little children out of the lake, so the next one out was Adeline.

And what a fucking sight she was.

She was walking out on the arms of Silas and Dixie. She'd bonded with them both over time, and told us she couldn't decide who to ask, so she asked them both, and they had both readily agreed.

Then, as she got close enough, I could see the plunging neckline, and about fell off the goddamn dock.

"Goddamn." I said shaking my head. Then a smile overtook my mouth as she walked down the dock towards me. She was so fucking beautiful it made my heart hurt.

Once she got to the designated spot, Reverend Spano began.

"Who gives this woman's hand in marriage?" He asked.

"I do." Dixie and Silas said at the same time.

They both let her go with kisses on her cheek, releasing her to my waiting hand.

Once she was close to me, I whispered to her, "You look beautiful."

Although I might have said it to her boobs and not her face, but who could blame a man? They were just right there for the world to see.

She giggled and smacked my chest before we both turned to Reverend Spano.

It was when we'd said our vows and Reverend Spano was wrapping up the ceremony that Adeline stole my heart for the second time.

"Tiago?" She whispered quietly, trying not to interrupt Reverend Spano's words of wisdom.

I turned to her, looking deep into her eyes. "Yeah, baby?"

"I wanted to tell you something." She whispered.

"Now?"

"Yeah, now." She said nodding.

I raised my eyebrows and waited for her to explain. "Well?"

"Do you want a boy or a girl?" She asked.

It took a few moments for my brain to catch up to her question, but when it did, I all but burst with excitement.

Totally ignoring everything Reverend Spano was saying, I hauled Adeline into my arms and started to spin her. "Are you fucking kidding me?"

Chuckles filled the air around us, but I ignored them as I waited for her to answer.

She shook her head. "No. I found out this morning."

"Fuck yes," I said.

"I know pronounce you husband and wife. You may kiss the bride." Reverend Spano said with a smile in his voice.

He was too late though. I had Adeline's mouth to my own, ravishing it, before the words even left the reverend's mouth.

• • •

Adeline

9 months later

"And for you, sir?" The waitress asked Kettle.

"I want that 2 for $20 meal. I want both of them steaks. One with corn and mashed potatoes. The other with fries and a baked potato."

I closed my eyes and tried hard not to laugh. The man was a fucking eating machine ever since he'd gotten me pregnant. Now, at nine months pregnant, I could barely fit anything into my stomach. However, Kettle more than made up for it.

When she started to leave, Kettle called her back with a loud, "Wait!"

"Yes, sir?" She asked nervously.

I snorted. The man intimidated everyone, but holy hell was he hotter than sin.

"You didn't take my wife's order." Kettle said patiently.

"Wait, you're going to eat both of those?" She said, stepping from foot to foot.

At Kettle's serious nod, the young server turned to me expectantly. "What can I get you, ma'am?"

"I'll have the Molten Lava Cake, a hamburger, and onion rings. Bring the cake when you bring their salads." I instructed her.

When the young girl looked at me as if I'd lost my mind, Baylee and Sebastian, who were sitting in front of us, started laughing.

I glared at the couple, but held my tongue until the waiter walked away with our order.

"Why are y'all laughing at me? He's the one who ordered two full meals for himself." I growled.

Sebastian started to guffaw at that statement.

"Did you know he had to go up a pant size in his uniform pants?" Sebastian asked Baylee.

Baylee's wide eyes turned to Kettle and her brows raised. "Really?" She asked.

Kettle shrugged unapologetically and then took a sip of his beer. "At least it isn't the morning sickness anymore. That was a killer while I was at work."

Did I forget to mention that Kettle experienced all the same symptoms I was feeling? It was awesome. Not. He whined more than a child about everything! 'Adeline, I'm hungry.' "Adeline, I'm tired.' 'Adeline, I'm horny.'

Well okay, if I was being truthful, the last one wasn't a problem. My desire for sex went through the roof once I hit the four month mark, completely making up for the first three months when I didn't desire it at all.

A very obnoxious scent started to waft through the air, and I knew for sure it wasn't the fajitas that just passed by a few moments before.

"What is that smell?" I asked, eyes turning accusingly in my husband's direction.

He shrugged. "Not me. Now that you mention it, I smell it, too."

Every single head at the table turned to Blaise, who was now a little over fourteen months old.

She was innocently munching on some puffy Cheetos looking to all the world like she was a little princess.

Then the loudest, most abhorrent fart passed from the girls' ass that I'd ever heard; man, woman, and child included.

What happened next was as if it was out of a movie. *Shit* like that didn't happen in real life.

Poop started to ooze from the back of the girls shoulders, over her shirt, and then even further to reach down to her stomach.

Then all hell broke loose, as it started to bubble out. The only thing stopping the noxious ooze was the strength of her little Harley onesie.

We all starred in horror, as the patrons around us ate their dinners, completely oblivious.

"What do we do?" Baylee gasped in dread.

"Take her outside to the truck. I have a couple liters of Coke in the back." Kettle offered, surprising everyone.

It wasn't that he suggested pouring gallons of coke to wash the shit off a toddler. It was that he even had a suggestion in the first place. Kettle was the epitome of non-helpfulness when it came to child rearing. He was the 'cool' guy when it came to all the kids he was around. Didn't want to do something? Go find Kettle. He won't make you.

"I can't say that Coke would be the first thing I'd like to use, but it'll work for now. I have some baby wipes to wipe off the stickiness once we get her hosed down." Baylee nodded as she stood.

When she reached down to grab Blaise, she stopped, looking around the area for the best place to put her hands without actually touching any shit.

She finally settled on the straps to her overalls and lifted her.

Baylee was the first to leave, followed shortly by Sebastian, and then it was my turn to try to un-beach myself from the booth. Luckily, I got it on the first try, all the while Kettle laughed behind me.

"You're such a shit head." I said to Kettle.

Kettle ignored my comment and reached into his back pocket for his wallet. Grabbing the nearest waiter's attention, he told her to bag our food and keep the change as he handed over a hundred dollar bill.

"We'll be in the parking lot, just send it on out when it's ready, please." He instructed as he walked up to my back and then grabbed my hand.

"Mrs. Spada!" A screechy teenage voice yelled from my side, startling the ever-loving shit out of me.

Sighing, I turned and found Amanda, one of my students, facing me. She was wearing her Benton Bulldogs cheerleading uniform, and she had her hair so tight on her head that it looked painful.

"Amanda," I said smiling at the girl. "How was the game?"

"Oh, it was great! You should've seen it! Jimmy Lee scored in the last fifteen seconds of the game, tying his all-time record. Then Boomer..." Amanda droned on.

I didn't listen though, because a contraction hit me out of nowhere, nearly stealing my knees out from under me.

Kettle's eyes narrowed on me as he took in my sweating brow, the hand clutching my stomach, and the claws I currently had sunk into Kettle's left forearm.

"Contraction?" Kettle asked in concern.

"Yes," I panted as the pain ebbed, allowing me to breathe once again. "Jesus, these Braxton Hicks ain't no joke!"

I had already been to the hospital twice in the last two days, and both times, they'd sent me home because I wasn't experiencing real contractions, but Braxton Hicks.

If these were the fake contractions, they'd have to be administering that epidural at the check-in desk. I'd already threatened Kettle with a gelding if he got me knocked up again. There was no way in hell I could go through this twice. The last nine months had been pure hell.

Morning sickness. Motion sickness. Light sickness. Husband moaning sickness. Anything I could have, I did. Gall bladder attacks. Kidney stones. Allergic reactions to something I'd never been allergic to before. You name it I had it.

And don't even get me started on the fucking stretch marks and how my body no longer responded to my will. I'd peed on myself more times from sneezing in the past nine months than I had my entire thirty years of life.

Pregnancy really had a way of making you humble.

"Alright, well if they get worse or closer together, let me know. It was nice seeing you Heather." Kettle said absently.

"Amanda," she corrected, not caring in the least that Kettle had called her by the wrong name.

"Sorry, Angela. Have a good rest of your day." He said before pulling me by my hand out the door.

I got a wave in just before the doors closed. "Tiago, you butt head. You damn well knew her name!" I absently slapped him on the ass.

He grinned at me. "Yeah, so?"

I rolled my eyes, and then laughed as I came up on the scene going on in the back of Kettle's truck.

"Hey! You guys better be taking my truck to the car wash tomorrow!" He yelled as we came to a stop beside Baylee who had a hold of Blaise's hands.

"Is it working?" I asked.

Baylee snorted. "Yeah, it surprisingly works better than a shower. Why do you have so many cokes in your truck, Kettle?"

Sebastian moved into the bed of the truck as he poured yet another bottle of Coke onto Blaise's back and answered the question. "Kettle has a craving for Coke. He doesn't like to run out."

I would've replied, but the wind picked up, blowing sand through the air, which I inevitably inhaled.

Then sneezed.

Then promptly peed all over myself.

"Mother fucker!" I yelled as my hand went down to my crotch.

I held on for dear life as I crossed my legs. "It won't stop!" I yelled as it continued to pour down my legs. "Oh, my God! It's like a waterfall. What do I do? What do I do?"

At the time, I didn't find it the least bit funny.

There I was, standing in the middle of a packed Chili's parking lot, while I watched two of my best friends in the world pour Coke over their child, all the while I leaked all over my clothes, Kettle's boots, pants, and the side walk.

It wasn't until Kettle grabbed my face and made me look into his big blue eyes that I finally calmed down enough to realize that no woman in the world could hold that much pee, let alone a pregnant woman who had a bladder the size of a shot glass.

"I think my water broke," I whimpered fervently.

Kettle nodded, eyes serious, as he put his hand to my tummy. "Any contractions?" He asked as he looked down at my belly, and then further to my legs.

"No," I said just as I was slammed hard with a contraction that stole my breath.

He looked down at his watch and calmly timed it as my eyes crossed. "That one was four minutes thirty seconds after the one you had inside. Think it's time to get you to the hospital."

They say that first labors take hours. Even days.

I knew within ten minutes of my water breaking that it wasn't going to take hours. I'd be lucky to have minutes.

Just moments after we got into the truck and headed for the hospital that was fifteen minutes away, I knew I wasn't going to make it.

"Tiago?" I asked as I leaned forward and panted.

"Yeah?" He queried as he turned down a side road that led to the interstate.

"What would happen if I had the baby right now?" I asked through clenched teeth.

"You're not. We'll get there in time." He assured me.

"I don't...think...we have time."

Then I was struggling with my pants, yanking them from the top of my belly, over my hips, and down to pool at my feet.

"What are you doing?" Kettle asked in surprise.

My hand went down between my legs where I felt something that *really* shouldn't be there. "Uhh, there's something between my legs."

"That would be your twat!" Baylee said from behind my seat.

I was shaking my head, and slapping at Kettle's arm to get his attention. "No really, look at my vagina!"

I hadn't meant to yell.

Nonetheless, I couldn't help myself.

I really hadn't meant for the old man in the pickup next to ours to hear me, but inevitably, he did, and sure enough, he tried to get a look.

Lucky for me he couldn't see over Kettle's window, unlucky for me, the man on the opposite side of us could, and he screamed.

"Jesus, Mary, and Joseph. That woman has a bloody alien coming out of her cooch!"

"Why are the windows open!?" I screeched.

Kettle, who'd been waiting for the traffic to move at the stop light, looked over, and his eyes bulged.

"Mother fucker!" he yelled as he cut across two lanes of traffic to pull over in the nearest parking lot. Which happened to be a Wal-Mart.

"Oh, my God! Don't pull over here! I don't want to be a 'people of Wal-Mart' statistic! Go one more over to that Dairy Queen."

However irrational it was, there was no rhyme or reason to my madness. If I had to have my baby in a truck without drugs, I was damn well having it where I wanted it.

He obliged, too.

As soon as the truck was in park, Kettle was out of his side and running around the front of the truck while Baylee crawled over the console to look down.

"Do you have a go bag?" Baylee asked Kettle once he got the door open.

Kettle's eyes were on the disaster that was going on between my legs, but his answer was crystal clear and precise. "Never carried one. You have one; you're obligated to use it. There're some gloves in the console that you're sitting on with a pocket mask, though. Call 911."

"Already did when I noticed you cut off four lanes of traffic."

Sebastian said from behind me somewhere.

Maybe later I might find the mortification that I should be feeling, but right then, it was nonexistent. Why, you ask? Because my hoo-ha had a baby's head the size of which my vagina had never seen before (even though my husband was no slouch in the penis size department) coming out of it.

"Oh, for the love of all that's hol-arghh!" My sentence was abruptly cut short by the arrival of another contraction, this one having an intense urge to push coming on its heels. "Have. To. Push."

"Adeline, look at me now." Kettle snapped, making my eyes open.

I stared into his eyes as he calmly leaned the seat back until I was lying flat on my back, and then started studying the head that was slowly making its way out of my body, no matter how much I tried not to push.

"On the next contraction, I want you to push, okay Adeline?" He said firmly.

I nodded, closed my eyes, and then waited for the next agonizing feeling to overtake me.

It did moments later, and I bore down and pushed, just as I was instructed to do.

"Head's out." Kettle said softly.

I could feel his hands moving around down there, and I severely hoped with all my being that he didn't remember this the next time we had sex. There was just no coming back from this. My husband had seen my vag emit a baby's head the size of a grapefruit. I didn't see how he could ever forget.

"Sebastian, go get the present we were going to give them later. It's in the truck in front of Blaise's seat!" Baylee ordered from the seat beside me.

"Oh my God," I yelled as I felt the next contraction crest.

"Push!" Baylee and Kettle yelled.

I pushed.

"Just, whatever you do, don't drop him." I pleaded between pushes.

Kettle rolled his eyes. "I've delivered fifteen babies. Every single one has managed not to be dropped. I think I'll manage with my own boy. Now push, you've almost got him all the way out."

I couldn't say how the next three minutes went, but I pushed with all my fucking might, screamed, cursed, and yelled. Most of it was directed towards Kettle, but I saved a few jabs for mankind as a whole.

"Ahhhhh, your goddamned demon spawn needs to get the hell out of my vagina! He's being evicted! Jesus, it burns!"

"One last push, honey." Kettle said softly, not even the least bit affected by my threats.

"Excuse me sir, we can take over from here," An authoritative voice said from directly behind Kettle.

My eyes went to the woman who was trying to take away my lifeline and I snarled. "Back the fuck off, bitch. He's delivering this kid, so help me God. I will take pleasure in gutting you if you even *try* to interfere."

Later I'd be told that I resembled a demon as I snarled at the poor lady, but now, the struggle was very real.

Kettle chuckled, and then suddenly, everything, every single thing I was feeling was suddenly gone. The pain abruptly vanished, and in its place was the crying squall of an infant cradled against her daddy's chest.

"Oh, my God," Baylee breathed. "You had a girl."

My eyes, which had finally shut in relief, snapped open at that, and I stared in stunned surprise at my little girl smeared with blood and gore curled up against her daddy's cut.

"She's getting your vest bloody," I said absently.

Kettle smiled. He smiled so wide that I forgot about all the embarrassment I would be feeling only momentarily. I forgot about everything but the happiness on my husband's face, and I was whole.

"What's her name?" Sebastian asked from some point that I couldn't see him.

Thank God.

"Saylor." I said jovially.

Kettle snorted and I glared at him. "What?"

"You knew all along didn't you? Gave me the hope that I'd get to name him after my favorite National's player, and then you rip the rug out from under me. Get to use your name even after you assured me we could name him Jason." He glared back.

"Guess you'll never know!" I said cheerfully.

• • •

Three months later

"Your baby's awake." Kettle said as he walked into the room.

He was dressed in his uniform, which inevitably meant he'd be leaving me here shortly, and I'd be up all night with our little Saylor again.

"I know. I'm too tired to move, though. Maybe you should feed her." I said tiredly.

"I don't have the fun bags that Saylor wants." He teased.

"I've heard that men can produce breast milk with hormone treatments." I replied wickedly.

He snorted. "Yeah, right. I'd look real good with tits."

"You were the one who said you wanted a baby." I said into my pillow.

Kettle smacked my ass. Hard. Then left to retrieve Saylor.

I stayed exactly where I was until Kettle brought our squalling child into the room and settled her down on the bed.

I flipped to my side and stayed still while Kettle unsnapped the buttons on my nursing gown, freeing one of the fun bags in question, and laid Saylor down gently.

She hurriedly latched on, going from wailing like a banshee to her hungry food grunt in point four seconds flat.

Kettle chuckled as he ran his large finger down Saylor's cheek.

"God, I love you." He said, moving his eyes from his daughter's hungry mauling to my eyes.

My mouth tipped up in a grin before my eyes drooped heavily. "I don't hate you."

He snorted. "I don't hate you either." He replied dryly. "I've got to go to work. I'll see you when I get home. Mom's coming over later. Don't forget."

I restrained the urge to laugh aloud. I wouldn't forget. That woman became a lifesaver our first few days after bringing Saylor home. Now, at three months old, she came to watch Saylor every Wednesday evening so I could get papers graded, and any household chores done. Or even on the rare occasion, go out on a date with Kettle.

There'd been a lot of adjusting when Saylor arrived in our lives.

At three days old, Saylor was pronounced deaf. She'd failed not only her newborn screening, but also her follow up screening.

I'd scoured the internet for days after she'd been pronounced deaf, but the one thing that kept me from totally freaking out was Viddy.

She explained to me that being deaf wasn't a death sentence. With the advancement in technology in this day and age, Saylor could live a full and happy life without one single thing holding her back.

As I looked down at my perfect little girl, I knew that was true.

She was a very special little girl, and she was absolutely adored by everyone.

Most assuredly her daddy, whom she had totally wrapped around her little finger

Which was why when he came back into the room five minutes later to place one last kiss on his daughter's cheek, I wasn't in the least bit surprised.

"Bye baby." He said as he left for the second time.

I smiled and closed my eyes. Perfect indeed.

• • •

Kettle

7 months later

"Can she hear me?" I asked the audiologist, Kathy, who'd just put the transmitter on to my baby girl.

Saylor was ten months now and the light of my life.

She was so chubby that she had to waddle when I held onto her fingers when we practiced walking. Her black hair matched her mama's, but unlike Adeline, she had ringlets. They covered her head from the tips of her roots to the bottom of her hair.

I was never one that liked curly hair too much, but on my little girl, it was the cutest fucking thing I'd ever seen.

"Yes, sir. As soon as I turn them on she should hear you."

Kathy said with a smile.

Saylor had her cochlear implants put in six weeks ago and today they'd be turned on for the first time.

Adeline, who was holding Saylor in her lap, reached out and clutched my hand, tears already dripping down her face.

When we'd learned in the hospital that Saylor was deaf, it was a huge blow.

Surprisingly, the one to snap me out of the dread I was feeling was Dixie. The man who always had a laugh on the tip of his tongue.

What'd he say that made me realize that Saylor being deaf wasn't the end of the world? Something so simple, yet exactly what I needed to hear.

She's freakin' perfect.

And she was.

Now we were sitting here, moments away from turning the implants on, and my baby girl hearing for the first time.

"Okay, I'm turning one on in three, two, one..." Kathy smiled and pointed at Adeline.

"Saylor, I love you." Adeline said softly.

Immediately Saylor turned to the sound of her mother's voice... and screamed bloody murder.

Adeline was smiling, I was smiling, and Kathy was beaming.

"Saylor Rae, why are you crying?" I asked my little girl.

Saylor turned her watery, big brown eyes that could melt my heart, towards me and smiled. Instantly the tears dried, and swear to Christ, I dropped a tear or two for the first time in my life.

As we were driving home later that day, we finally got the chance to play Saylor's favorite movie's soundtrack on the radio, and even I got into the act, singing and dancing at the top of my lungs.

A badass biker belting out Disney songs at the top of my lungs, and not a care in the world as to who would hear.

By the time we arrived home, I knew one thing for sure.

Our life was beyond perfect. I couldn't ask for anything more.

Hope you enjoyed Kettle and Adeline's story. Up next is Viddy and Trance's story in ***Kevlar to my Vest***.

Turn the page for a sneak preview.

WHAT'S NEXT?

KEVLAR To My VEST

THE HEROES OF THE DIXIE WARDENS MC, BOOK 3

PROLOGUE

Please don't leave me. You're my best friend.
-Viddy

Viddy

"Trance?" I cried into the receiver.

"Viddy? What's wrong? Are you okay?" Trance yelled into my ear.

I clutched Hemi closer to my chest and gasped in pain.

"C-can y-you c-come over? P-please?" I cried out.

I heard the sound of a car door slamming shut, and then the roar of an engine as it sped off in the background.

Normally, I'd nag at him about going too fast, but I was about ten seconds away from losing it, and I needed him here. Fifteen minutes ago.

"What's going on, Vid? What happened?" Trance asked urgently.

He sounded like he was in a tunnel or something, which meant he'd put me on speakerphone. Which also meant he was at work, 'cause he couldn't be caught with a cell phone to his ear while he was driving his police issued vehicle.

"Hemi's vet called. They told m-me he h-had cancer and he needed to be put to sleep. I knew it was something bad, but I couldn't take him in until today. I didn't have a ride, and Paul refused to take him for me." I cried.

Oh, God. What was I going to do without him here? He was my best friend!

Hemi had started acting strange a few days ago. After several frustrating attempts to get my boyfriend, Paul, to take me to the vet so I could get Hemi checked out, he still refused. My sister was on vacation and there was no way I'd call her to come home for this. She and her husband deserved a little alone time before their baby came in a few more months.

This morning, when I'd finally gotten frustrated and called a cab, I'd never dreamed that it'd turn into this. First, the cab had nearly refused to transport us due to company policies about pets, but when the dam on my emotions broke, he'd relented, but only barely.

Then, as soon as we'd walked into Dr. Tucker's door, they'd yanked him away from me so fast my head spun. I could practically feel the condemnation pouring off them at the state he'd been in. Yet, I'd called the vet numerous times in a vain attempt to get one of them to pick him up, and they'd said they didn't offer those services.

That was when I started calling other vets, but with him being a new patient to them, they'd refused as well.

"Oh, baby. I'm so sorry. I'll be there in just a few minutes. I'm on duty in the residential district right now, but it shouldn't be more than ten minutes at the most." Trance's velvety deep voice said through the receiver.

Mellifluous.

That was the word that came to mind every time I heard it. So deep. Smooth. Rich and flowing. I wanted to put my lips up against his throat to feel the vibration that poured out with each word that was let loose from his mouth.

Trance was a very good man. When I'd had the privilege of being in his company, I felt alive.

It wasn't often that I got to see him, though. He was a very busy man. He was a member of the police department as well as a member of the local motorcycle club, The Dixie Wardens.

"Thank you, Trance." I whispered and then hung up.

Hemi was a nine year old English Setter with the silkiest fur I'd ever felt. He was a gentle, mid-sized dog with curly locks around his ears, flank, and face. I'd been told that he was snowy white with brown splotches, but that wasn't what made him beautiful to me.

What made him so perfect was the way he'd help me wind through the house, moving little things that might trip me up. On our walks, around the apartment complex I'd just moved into, he'd steer me in the right direction, and always lead me back to our door.

He never barked unless someone was at the door, and always stayed close to my side.

Until he started acting weird.

He still stayed by my side, but he didn't move as easily. I'd gone to fill his food bowl up and found it still just as full as it was the night before, and the day before that. Then his bathroom habits started to dwindle. He was going out more and more, staying out longer.

Then, yesterday, he stopped drinking water.

Now, Hemi had his head pillowed in my lap as I stroked his

coat, and tried to do my upmost best not to freak him out with my crying.

"Oh, Hemi. I don't want you to leave me." I cried, tears dripping down my cheeks and most likely onto his face.

Fifteen minutes on the dot, after my phone call to Trance, I heard the front door open and Trance walk in.

The click-click of nails on the hardwood floor let me know that Radar was with him, too.

I could feel his presence like a shock, and knew instantly when his body was close.

He hunkered down beside the couch where I was sitting with my legs folded underneath me. Hemi's tail thunked furiously on the couch beside me, making the whole couch vibrate with the intensity of it.

I felt the glasses covering my eyes lift to rest on the top of my head, followed by Trance's thumbs wiping away my tears. "I'm here, baby." He said reassuringly.

Any and all hope of not crying my eyes out fled, and I curled down until my head was buried into Hemi's fur.

"What am I going to do without him?" I cried.

I could feel Trance as he stroked Hemi's head, and finally Trance moved, shifting me and Hemi until we were both situated on either side of him.

I curled into his side, moving as close as I possibly could.

My head was pillowed on his chest, one arm around his back and the other around his front, clutching at Hemi's head.

Then I felt Radar's head lay down on my leg, and I cried all the harder.

I'm not sure how long we stayed like that. I know it had to be quite a while, because once I was done with my crying, only little hiccups remained.

"What do you want me to do?" He asked softly, sifting his fingers through my hair.

I felt the rumble of the question vibrate through his chest, and a low deep thrum of contentment coursed through me. One that I never felt when I was in Paul's arms. Never.

Which was why I'd never slept with him, despite his nagging about it.

"Will you take him to the park with me? I want him to play..." I started to ask, but the hard pounding at my door startled me out of finishing.

Then the yelling started. "Hey, Elise! It's time to go. Remember? It's Tuesday, we have to meet my parents for dinner!"

Why did he insist on calling me by my middle name? What was wrong with *Viddy*?

I didn't move, and neither did Trance.

Radar did, however, go over to the door and started growling low in his throat.

"Hey, is that guy in there with you again? Is that his stupid fuckin' dog? What did I tell you about him?" Paul snarled.

I lost it again. After everything he'd done to me lately, I just couldn't handle his shit anymore.

Paul was not a nice man. He'd threatened me on more than one occasion on what he'd do if he caught me with Trance again. Not that Trance and I had ever crossed that line, but Paul didn't care, and wasn't willing to listen. Everything I did pissed Paul off, and I really just didn't give a flying fuck anymore.

Paul could go fuck a duck.

I stomped hard towards the door.

Counting my steps, I got to seven and held my hand out, making contact with the door.

"Move over, Radar, I've got to get rid of the trash." I said to the big boy who was still growling low at my door.

Turning the knob, I felt the full blast of Louisiana heat belt me in the face, as well as Paul's anger.

"What the fuck have you two been doing in there? Your face is flushed, and you're not wearing your glasses. You know how I hate that." Paul chastised me.

Paul was an asshole. I'd started dating him a little over a year ago, and I've been nothing but disappointed since. My sister hated him. My sister's husband hated him. And Trance hated him.

Yes, it was definitely time.

"My face is flushed because I've been crying, you idiot. Hemi isn't well, and I'm putting him to sleep later this afternoon. As for you, I would like you not to come back anymore. We're over." I said as harshly as I could.

Silence greeted me after that statement.

Paul's silence wasn't in my best interest, because before I could even blink, Paul had me by the wrist. "What are you talking about? You know we're not through. You've said that three times in the past four months, but you always come back."

"Stand down." Trance's beautiful voice said from behind me.

I wasn't sure if he was talking to Paul or Radar until, suddenly, Radar's low growling abruptly quit at my side.

Then I felt Trance's heat at my back, and I involuntarily leaned backwards into him.

His hand went around my waist, and he pulled me backwards until I was flush against him with his arm pinning me to him tightly.

"You heard her. Please leave." Trance's authoritative tone booked no room for argument.

"You can't tell me what to do. This is my girlfriend's place. How about you leave? Hmm?" Paul replied snottily.

"I want you to leave. Now. Oh, and lose my number." I said stiffly, before yanking my wrist from Paul's grasp and closing the door in his face.

A snarling snap from Radar had me jumping, and then Paul's squeal of indignation followed.

"What was that?" I asked in surprise.

Trance snorted. "He tried to sneak his hand into the door before it closed all the way, but Radar convinced him not to continue with that line of thought."

"Good," I whispered.

Neither one of us moved.

My head was still pillowed against his chest, and his arm was still wrapped tightly around me.

We stood like that for long moments until Hemi's heartbreaking whimpering from the couch broke up the moment, bringing us both to the couch.

"He needs to go outside, I believe. Would you mind doing that? I want to gather some of his things to take with us before we take him." I said, looking into the direction I thought Trance was standing.

His warm hand cupped my face until he moved it up and to the left, before he replied. "Okay, baby. Just let Radar lead you out when you're ready. I'll be outside near the grass."

"Thank you," I said softly.

He broke away after that. I heard the click of the door handle unlatching, followed by the clicking of Hemi's nails as he walked out the door, before it closed softly behind them both.

"Radar?" I called.

When Radar's cold wet nose touched my hand, I smiled and patted his head. "Can you find me the balls?"

I'd heard Trance ask Radar that once, the last time he was over with my sister, when they helped me move six months ago.

I'd had the balls packed in a box, and I'd wanted to show the guys Hemi's trick at putting three balls in his mouth. Since I'd had no idea where exactly the toys were, I'd been about to give up when Trance had said that Radar could find them. And find them he did.

Walking stiffly forward, I went to Hemi's bed and picked it up.

A loud bark came from my side as I opened the front door.

· · ·

Trance

"Listen, you need to leave. Things aren't going to be pretty if you make me remove you. I have things I need to do, and if you make me arrest you, I will not be a happy person." I said to Viddy's boyfriend.

No, make that ex-boyfriend.

Thank God.

I didn't know how much longer I could follow my moral code when it came to taking some other man's woman.

"We always get back together, though. We'll be back together by tomorrow afternoon at the latest." He sneered, before he angled into his car that had to be a compensation for a small dick.

I took the high road and didn't reply, even though it went against every bit of my ingrained nature to throw the words at him that were sitting on the tip of my tongue.

The main one being, *over my dead body*.

The door behind me opened as I watched Paul back out, making me turn and watch as Viddy dragged out what looked like every single thing Hemi ever owned.

Jogging up to the door, I stopped and surveyed all the million balls that were now lining Hemi's bed.

"That's a lot of balls." I observed as I scooped up the entire thing and walked back towards my police issued patrol SUV. Opening the back door, I dropped all the contents inside and slammed it shut before returning to the passenger side door.

I resisted the urge to offer Viddy help, even though it annoyed the ever-loving shit out of me to do so. It was like rubbing fur in the wrong direction, or walking with sand in my shoes. It wasn't right, but Viddy hated the fact that she was blind. She hated it even more when someone dwelled on the fact.

"Trance?" Viddy called when she was three feet away from me.

Her face seemed to lose the determinedness to it and she held out her hand for me, making my breath ease out of my lungs.

Taking her hand, I led her around the car's door and helped her settle in her seat.

"Where is Hemi?" She asked sadly.

In answer, I picked Hemi up from where he was laying in the grass and placed him on Viddy's lap before closing the door softly.

Radar, who was sitting on his haunches beside Viddy's door, came instantly when I whistled and hopped into the back door of the car before I slammed the door closed behind him.

"What's on your agenda?" I asked her once we were on the road back to town.

"I want to take him to the water park, and then I want to get him a steak dinner from the Salt Grass Steakhouse. Then, well then, we can take him to the vet's office." She explained quietly.

I took my eyes off the road for a split second to regard her, and a pang of sadness poured through me as I saw the haunted look to her face.

It was pale and clammy. Her eyes were red, having still not returned the glasses that usually covered her sightless eyes.

I'd met Viddy through her sister, Adeline.

Adeline was married to a member of The Dixie Wardens MC, Kettle. One of my brothers.

Adeline and Viddy were twins. Both of them had dark hair, nearly black. Their skin was pale and creamy. However, that was where their similarities ended. Adeline was well rounded in all the right places. Well, more so now that she was eight months pregnant; but even before that, she'd always had more curves than Viddy.

Viddy was more what I liked to call...delicate. She was small, fine boned, and trim. Although she did have some meat on her, she really could stand to gain more. Her hair was always braided and out of her way, except for today.

Today, the black strands were loose and flowing around her shoulders and back.

Normally, I would never catch her in anything less than what I liked to call her combat clothes. Loose jeans, a plain monotone shirt, and a jacket of some sort or another.

Today, she was in a fitted tank, a pair of black yoga pants that said *Pink* across the ass, and tennis shoes. This was the most I'd ever seen of her skin, which made me aware of another difference between her and her sister.

"You don't have any tattoos like your sister?" I asked in surprise.

Her head, which had been bowed, tipped up and regarded me. Her eyes moved over my features as if she could see.

Then her beautiful mouth tipped up into a smile. "Can you imagine what my sister would put onto my body if I took her with me? I would never really know if she put something offensive on me or not. I can see her doing it, too. She talked me into it once, but we were both drunk. I'm not even sure if it says what she says it does. Luckily, mine's on my ribs."

I returned my eyes to the road, trying my best not to roll my eyes. "You and your sister have the weirdest relationship. My brothers would kick my ass if I ever tried to do something like that. Although, they've kicked my ass for less, so it's nothing new.

"How many brothers do you have?" She asked as she turned her attention back down to the dog in her lap.

I turned down Main Street and went to the park she'd indicated; glad it was still too early for the spray park to be open. Luckily, I knew quite a few of the city workers, one of which I'd called on the way, who'd told me the code to get in the gate.

"I have two brothers. Miller and Foster. They're both SEALS." I said as I pulled the car into a parking spot directly in front of the gate.

"Like the bad ass ones that have to survive being water boarded before they become SEALS?" She asked quizzically, as I shut off the car.

I rolled my eyes as I got out of the car, opened Radar's door, and then went around to Viddy's. She was still sitting there patiently with Hemi in her lap.

Scooping the dog up easily, I backed up until I was out of her way, and watched as she stood, unfolded her cane, and closed the door behind her.

"There aren't any steps. Only smooth concrete once you step up on the curb that's about six inches in front of your left foot." I instructed her.

She followed my directions, and we walked into the splash pad, only stopping once to input the code.

I set Hemi down on his feet, walked over to the button that

I'd seen Sebastian's son hit multiple times during his last birthday party, at this very place. Sebastian's the vice president of The Dixie Wardens. He'd rented the entire place out for his son's fourth birthday.

Mostly, he rented it out because The Dixie Wardens tended to be off putting to the normal population. Therefore, to save themselves time and heartache, Sebastian rented the place so no other kids, nor parents, could attend while we were there.

"Is he playing?" Viddy asked me.

I watched as Radar got right up next to Hemi, nudging and urging until, finally, Hemi started walking slowly towards the spraying water.

Once the water hit him, renewed vigor started to pour through Hemi, and he started moving a little more jovially until finally he was trotting, keeping up with Radar as they both frolicked and played.

"Yes, Radar's playing with him. He looks happy, honey." I told her, watching her face.

The next four hours went about as expected. Radar and Hemi played in the water for a good hour before Hemi finally lost his battle with the exhaustion. Once they were efficiently dried off, we took him to go get a steak dinner. Sadly, he only ate about a quarter of it before he lost the desire to eat, and nudged the rest in Radar's direction, who'd refused to eat it.

Then the final moment came as I pulled up to my house that was set off in the woods.

At first, I'd been willing to take Hemi back to his doctor to be euthanized. Then, I'd heard about Viddy's treatment, and knew that I'd never take them there.

Instead, I called my good friend, who took care of Radar and my other animals, Kosher, Tequilla, and Mocha. All three were

German Shepherds. Radar being the oldest, at nine, followed by Kosher, who was two, and finally to Tequila and Mocha who were still small at nine weeks old.

I trusted my good friend, Dr. Zack Toler. Zack had taken care of Radar when he'd been sick or needed a check-up for nine years now, and had taken very good care of him.

"Where are we?" Viddy asked when she heard the crunch of gravel underneath the tires of my cruiser.

"How do you know we aren't anywhere we're supposed to be?" I asked as I put the car in park and slid out.

I let Radar out, and then made my way around the car to Viddy, who had her feet up in the seat to allow Hemi to sleep on the floorboard.

"The sounds are different. Nowhere I know has that kind of gravel. So, where are we?" She asked as she turned in her seat and placed her feet on the ground.

Not thinking about the fact that she hated being led around, I grabbed her by the elbow and took her hand to guide her to the front porch and then to a seat.

"We're at my house. I have a friend who's a veterinarian. He's coming over now to help." I explained as I walked towards the front door, opened it, and moved to the side as Kosher came barreling out.

Kosher was a bundle full of energy, which was why I'd moved Viddy out of the way as I'd done. He wouldn't have understood that she wasn't able to play like all the other people that came over. When my boys weren't on the job, they were free to play and have fun just like any other dog. Which included jumping up and licking faces.

Viddy, however, wouldn't have been prepared for the massive dog, and it was best for all if I moved her out of the way, just in case.

Kosher didn't come barreling out, however. He came out slow. Much slower than he normally did, and walked straight to Radar who was standing beside Viddy's open car door. Both of my boys watched as I went to the car, lifted Hemi out, and took him inside to lay him on the couch.

Hemi lay there, not moving, exhausted from all that he'd done in the last four hours.

Feeling the sadness well up, I started to walk back outside but stopped once I saw Kosher and Radar leading her in. She had a hand full of fur from each dog, and was walking slowly forward. She was reading Radar and Kosher's cues as if she'd done it a million times before.

"Your friend is here. I heard him pull up." She choked out.

I walked up to her, pulling her into my body and hugged her tight. She was shaking, and very near to tears.

"Do you want to be there with him?" I asked into her ear, breathing her scent in with each inhale.

She felt perfect in my arms. The only thing I wished was different were the circumstances. I wish she hadn't called because she was in a bind. Especially one such as this.

"Yes," she breathed, looking up at me.

Not liking that she wasn't looking at my eyes, I took her face in my hand and moved her until her eyes were connected to my own.

Eyes so close to mine. One blue and one green. Both pale. Hypnotizing.

That was how I'd gotten my road name. Trance.

Loki had given me that name one day when a woman had turned him down after seeing me.

"It's like they're in a trance. Once they get a look at your pretty

fuckin' eyes, they don't want to see anything else!" He'd whined.

Loki was another member of The Dixie Wardens, and my best friend. We'd met first on the force and, shortly after, prospected for the Wardens together. Both of us had been sponsored by Sebastian, only a year after Sebastian had become a member himself.

"Trance, is it okay that I come in?" Zack asked from my front door.

I looked up to see him watching Viddy and me.

He was a short man. In his late fifties, Zack had been in practice for nearly thirty years. He'd moved here all the way from North Dakota, and I'd found him by chance when I'd needed an emergency vet for Radar when he'd swallowed a chicken bone.

It also said something about him that he didn't just come barging into my territory. Radar and Kosher, although somewhat occupied with Hemi, were not totally ignorant to what was going on, and Zack knew that.

"Zack, come in please. Viddy, this is Zack, the horde's vet. Zack, this is Viddy. Viddy's dog, Hemi, is the one I called you about earlier." I said, leading him over to the couch.

Viddy's hand was still in mine, holding on incredibly tight as Zack cooed and cawed at Hemi.

"Oh, Hemi. You're a strong one, aren't you? Are you ready to go home, good ol' boy?" Zack asked as he started to set up his things.

Zack had enquired with Hemi's vet to be sure, and he'd concurred with Hemi's prognosis. Hemi only had another couple of days, at most, to live and after today, he didn't have much of an outlook, and would probably be in severe pain if precautions weren't taken.

"Now, do you know what euthanasia is, my dear girl?" Zack asked in his grizzled, no nonsense voice.

Viddy was shaking her head before he'd even finished with the question. "No, sir. I don't have the first clue. It's not going to hurt, is it?" She choked.

Zack patted Viddy's hand and led her to sit on the couch next to Hemi's head. "No dear, it won't hurt. Now you just sit here and talk to him, okay? He won't feel a single thing, I promise."

Zack spoke throughout, explaining exactly what he was doing, and why, all the while Hemi laid still, taking in the scene around him, but not putting up one ounce of fight.

"Now that I have the IV in, I'll put the solution in. It'll be exactly like he is going to sleep. One minute he will breathe, and the very next he will not. Do you want to say anything to him before we do it, baby girl?" Zach asked her softly.

"I promise to never use your dishes on another puppy. I will forever keep your name sacred, and I will forever remember you. When I go to work and find some of your hair on my shirt, I'll remember that you used to roll in my clean laundry, and smile. I love you so much, and I'll miss you like crazy, Hem." She said quietly into Hemi's fur.

As she spoke, I watched as Zack depressed the plunger on the large syringe in his hand, and counted down from twenty.

At seventeen seconds, Hemi's eyes closed.

At eleven seconds, he inhaled deeply.

At seven, Hemi took his final breath.